GET ON TOP

Also by David Homel

Sonya & Jack
Rat Palms
Electrical *orm*

David Homel

GET ON TOP

A NOVEL

Stoddart

Published in 1999 by Stoddart Publishing Co. Limited
34 Lesmill Road, Toronto, Canada M3B 2T6

Distributed by General Distribution Services Limited
325 Humber College Blvd., Toronto, Ontario M9W 7C3
Tel. (416) 213-1919   Fax (416) 213-1917
Email Customer.Service@ccmailgw.genpub.com

03 02 01 00 99 1 2 3 4 5

Cataloguing in Publication Data

Homel, David, 1952–
Get on top: a novel

ISBN 0-7737-6048-2

I. Title.

PS8565.06505G47 1999   C813'.54   C98-933088-5
PR9199.3.H65G47 1999

Cover design: Bill Douglas @ The Bang
Design and typesetting: Kinetics Design & Illustration

Printed and bound in Canada

Thanks to the Conseil des arts et des lettres du Québec for their faith and support. To Harry Crews for the writerly advice. And to Louis Schmier of Valdosta State University for the look back.
                                                                    – David Homel

Stoddart Publishing gratefully acknowledges the Canada Council for the Arts and the Ontario Arts Council for its support of its publishing program.

In memoriam,
the peddler uncles,
Eddie, Rudy, Sam and Abe

How shall we sing

the Lord's song

in a strange land?

PSALM 137

I

Her Uncle Tommy

SABBITHA HUNTER stood in the raw light of noon on the loose gravel apron of the Continental Trailways bus terminal. The early spring wind had scoured the sky down to a glinting, inhospitable mineral blue, and now it was working on her jacket and the scarf she had tied around her blond hair. Both pieces were flat black. Mourning black.

Not that Sabbitha Hunter was in mourning for anyone. But she calculated rightly that the only way a woman could travel unimpeded through this country was to dress in the color of death. Black clothes have always had a way of putting a woman temporarily off-limits, and making men behave all delicately around her. Temporarily was long enough for Sabbitha.

She wasn't in mourning for anyone, though according to her home town of Ebenezer, which she was about to leave, she should have been. Everyone knew in Ebenezer that her mother had followed her father down to the churchyard six months to the day after the latter's departure. That was sure proof of the Hunter ménage's love for one another, or so town wisdom ran. Some of that love, according to the town's men, bachelors or otherwise — including Simon Chandler of Chandler's Confectionery and Sundries — must have rubbed off on Sabbitha's golden skin.

At least they hoped so. But they never speculated out loud for fear of awakening the lust of their neighbors. It was better for a man not to advertise his strivings. But they all made it their secret business to find out whether Sabbitha really did have that gift for love that so few women, tragically enough, seemed to possess.

She didn't see her parents' marriage that way. Both her folks had gnawed themselves to death with cancer, and she had absorbed enough contemporary folk literature to understand that the disease was the body's mortal attack upon itself, the literal outcome of a person not being able to stand himself. As far as Sabbitha was concerned, that process didn't have anything to do with love, unless love was some cruel and cannibalistic practice.

Inside Chandler's shop that overlooked the parking lot where she waited, the limp, sun-yellowed curtain waved open, then snaked shut. Simon Chandler rubbed his sand-colored arms and let loose with an all-purpose curse. He wouldn't curse Sabbitha. A tick of fear accompanied her name and kept him respectful. He watched her prepare to get on that Trailways bus with a mixture of spite and relief.

Relief, because her simple presence was proof of the tired old traditional sin of adultery that he'd committed with her. The thing was as common as dirt, she reminded him at the time, and that had hurt his sense of pride and propriety. "Only adultery" she'd called what they'd done the first time they'd lain on the rag rug in front of the couch in the big gloomy house she'd inherited from the late loving couple her parents had constituted. She and Chandler ended up on the rug because, several days earlier, she had wrapped all the furniture in shrouds of transparent plastic in preparation for her departure. The slipcovers would not have their bodies; bare moist skin and slick plastic sheeting turned out to be a terrible match.

Just as well, Chandler made the mistake of musing out loud. The neighbors won't see us this way.

Sabbitha responded by strolling naked up to the window. Simon Chandler's bowels went squirty, which spoiled his appreciation of her body. That was her vocation, it seemed: terrorizing law-abiding men like Chandler.

The fault lay in her good looks, he had concluded that night. Not that she was directly responsible for them. But she was responsible for how she used them — that careless way. Chandler distrusted beauty, and in that way he was no different from every other man around Ebenezer. What good was it? Most men couldn't even bring themselves to pronounce the word. "She's a beaut," they'd say instead, and when they did, it was usually while slapping the front fender of a new automobile or kicking a tractor tire. When it came to women, beauty was a hindrance. It got in the way of the day-to-day business of raising a family, frying supper and keeping society from pushing out in all directions at once.

A beautiful woman was to be avoided. Beauty gave women power. Give a woman power, Ebenezer wisdom ran, and she's likely to do anything.

Which is exactly what Sabbitha Hunter intended to do, though she didn't know what form that "anything" might take.

The Trailways bus raised a cloud of bone-white gravel dust as it rattled into the lot in front of Chandler's Sundries. The door sighed open. A pair of middle-aged maidens stepped down, smelling of camphor. Holding a wicker picnic basket, Sabbitha Hunter climbed on board. The basket held a change of black clothes and the deed to the house she was deserting. The deed could always come in handy in case anyone doubted that she truly was a woman of property.

The door eased shut and the bus pulled out in a second cloud of wind-whipped dust. From inside his shop, Chandler stared through the patterns in his almost-lace curtain. She just didn't know how to care, he told himself. Caring is a basic life skill, but some people never learn it, the way some never learn how to read and write. Both kinds of ignorance made you a cripple in society. In his store once, he'd had a robber armed with a little fishing knife laugh at him when he pointed his chrome-plated pistol at the man's gut. The robber got away with the contents of the till, of course. But he had never known of a woman who had that particular devil in her.

Depart, scandal, he wished her as she rode off. The towns-people's happiness was nothing compared to her own.

But she would return in good time, in her own way, out for vengeance, and then some.

The road out of Ebenezer was a straight, eastbound asphalt ribbon. Sabbitha's basket traveled above her head in the mesh compartment. She wouldn't have the driver stow it in the luggage hold below. She didn't know where she was going to get off, and she wanted to be ready for her destination, just as soon as it came into sight.

She reached into the pocket of her jacket, took out a photograph and began using it to clean the remains of her last Ebenezer lunch from the narrow slots between her teeth. For a woman of property, she had a lot of careless gestures. On the color snapshot, the whole Hunter family complex was present and accounted for. The family complex as it stood on her seventeenth birthday, three years back.

Her mother stared with reproachful intensity at the lens, already unhappy with the results. Her left hand, the hand for secrets, had fanned downward to cover her stomach. By the way her fingers pointed south, Sabbitha knew now that her mother was already dying from the cancer gnawing at her lady's parts. *Guess what this thing is that I can't talk about,* her fingers said.

Sabbitha knew that now, now that it was too late, and her mother gone. One night her mother had come into her room in a long nightgown as gray and shapeless as a potato sack. "Your daddy's cancer has got a twin," Mrs. Hunter told her, and her fingers spread out then as they had in the photo. "But I don't intend to die piece by piece, the way he did." Sabbitha looked at her mother's fingers, and smelled the smell of decay and premature age on her skin, and did not react. She didn't want to understand. She had been with Uncle Tommy that afternoon, and there was the smell of youth and power and sex on her skin, and those good smells shut the door on anything that might have passed for compassion in a teenage girl's heart.

In the photograph, Sabbitha's uncle Tommy was sitting on one of those flimsy aluminum and woven-plastic lawnchairs that filled the summers of an entire nation. A grown man clinging to a little boy's name, nearly a whole generation younger than his older brother, Sabbitha's father. Uncle Tommy had an easy-fitting, I-can't-help-it look in his eyes as his arm snaked around Sabbitha's middle.

His arm showed no sign of the blotches that his older brother had let develop into cancer. Skin cancer or carelessness did not necessarily run in the family. Sabbitha's father liked to claim that the sun's wounds were the natural revenge of the climate against the ruddy-faced, white-skinned folks who had taken over the land. He never did more than observe the course his blotches took with bemusement and even pride, adopting an attitude of non-interference, as if he were Christian Science.

For all his tendency to raise hell, Tommy was more careful. He kept his hat on and his sleeves rolled down, when he wasn't naked.

Sabbitha was balancing easily on his knee. Even in the color-worn snapshot, her eyes were endlessly blue, as empty and curious as a cat's. The sun that punished everyone else's skin loved Sabbitha's. It didn't burn her or mask her face with freckles. It penetrated her and made her glow from inside. Her fine blond hair hung long and disorderly despite the heat, halfway pinned up with a white crepe rose in the same design as her earrings. Tommy had given her both for her birthday. Ingeniously, she had undone the bottom buttons of her shirt and tied the tails into a bow just beneath her breasts. Her navel was deeply indented, and the baby fat on her stomach made you want to open wide and take a great big bite out of her.

Sabbitha had her tongue stuck out delicately. The shutter had snapped just as she was licking a bead of perspiration off her upper lip.

Her father wasn't in the picture. He preferred the safe side of the camera, where he stood, concentrating on taking a snapshot of his little bother, who was regularly making love to his daughter on the edges of the fields, on the banks of the Sandspur River, on the canopy bed in her upstairs room and in every other conceivable place that he and his baby could think of.

In the background, azalea bushes stood by a fence, drunk with blossoms and slightly out of focus. A small flock of beer cans lay on their sides on a metal table that was visibly rusting away in the summer humidity.

Later on, people would claim that Sabbitha Hunter had no past, no family. That she'd created herself out of nothing.

Nothing could be further from the truth. This picture proved it.

After a while, she left off cleaning her teeth with the photograph. The color emulsion had leaked onto her tongue and left a bitter taste there. She let the picture fall onto the floor of the coach, and spat between her knees. When it came to spitting, she was a good shot.

The blacktop of the two-lane road dipped down towards the bridge over the Sandspur River. The bus slowed to negotiate the grade, and Sabbitha had ample time to gaze at the river's banks one last time. She followed its wide, lazy course until it took a wrong-headed turn and got lost in the woods and scrub. Down below, along its banks, contrary to the river's name and invisible to anyone passing on the bridge above, there were stretches of ocher sand as fine and sifted as talc. The Lord Himself had set out this welcome mat in the midst of His tangle, on the shores of a river the color of black cherry wine. At least that's how her uncle Tommy put it to her the first time they lay in the shade of the trees down below, and who was she to disbelieve him and his fine words? That was the day he told her she was going to be his. She liked the idea — that she was going to be somebody's.

"I better be yours," she told him, "because I certainly ain't myself's."

Her words alarmed Uncle Tommy at first. That wasn't the kind of thing he expected from a young girl. But he went back to the business of loving her. Those crazy things she liked to say just added spice.

On one of those stretches of private paradise, which didn't turn out to be so private after all, happiness first visited Sabbitha Hunter. It hadn't been like anything she'd been expecting. She was lying under the green-black canopy of trees, on the shady sand, watching her sundress dance back and forth on the tree branch where Tommy had tied it so it would stay unwrinkled and immaculate. That's how Tommy was; she would have left it on the ground, wherever it fell. She watched that dress sweep right and left in the soft wind, graceful in a way no human body could ever be, and she imagined herself that way, outside herself, as much at ease in the world as the wind was in the air. She put her arms around Tommy's back and squeezed him as tight as she knew how. He was delighted. He imagined it had something to do with him.

I am a dancing spirit, she told herself. My tired old self has passed away. I stepped out of it when I stepped out of that dress. It's that simple to get out of yourself, which is where I like to be. All that stuff about happiness is as easy as getting naked. Who knows what that dress will do now that I'm outside of it? It might just fly away with all my troubles and pettiness and weight inside it, the way those brooms in that television cartoon started in sweeping all by themselves, free of human hands.

And who knows where I'll fly to, now that I'm outside myself?

That, Sabbitha Hunter concluded from her seat in a Trailways bus, was my golden age. The prospect made her laugh out loud, more bark than laughter. A few men in the coach slid their eyes in her direction. They saw black clothes, and decided that mourning must have driven her squirrelly. So pretty, and so crazy. A shame, they thought, a downright shame.

The so-called golden age of love will do that to you. It'll make you bark with bitter laughter in a milk-run bus, and drive your thoughts to vengeance.

It had been in the natural order of things for Sabbitha to become Uncle Tommy's lover. On the radio plays that ran on "Crime Theater," which formed the soundtrack for her evenings when Tommy was not around, the detectives were always going on about motive and opportunity. That's what you needed for a crime to occur, and she knew the rest of the world would have judged her love affair as a crime, had they known about it. The detectives seemed to be talking to her through the small round speaker covered in beige cloth, her and her alone, challenging her sense of the rightness of what she and Tommy were doing together.

Uncle Tommy had both motive and opportunity. The same motive all men had, Sabbitha supposed, when they cast their eyes on a girl like her. But he had something no other man had. Opportunity. No end of it. He was family, and family is always around. They're allowed every access. They watch you grow up, they know you best, they follow every step you take as you move towards womanhood — if they're attentive enough. Tommy certainly was that. He had the gift of attentiveness to women. He was always present, always her confidant. She couldn't remember a time when they weren't together.

Sabbitha didn't feel any of the physical pleasure she thought she should, the kind she'd heard about through the overheard hints of other women. Most of those women were black, and she wondered whether white ones like herself could even qualify for those sensations. Being Uncle Tommy's lover was forbidden — that was why she'd started up with him, and why she kept on. And there was the prestige of the affair, too, even if she couldn't tell anyone about it. *She* knew; that's what mattered. Here was this great big capable man so eager to crowd into her, full of all kinds of outlandish compliments and promises, and so dependent on her, because what if she just said *no* one day — what would he do with that terrible drive?

Breaking a taboo gives a person power. That was an irresistible discovery for a girl like Sabbitha.

She and Uncle Tommy turned the earth into one great big bedroom. Under the oak and bay and hickory, by the river before the mosquitoes got too fierce, or after the first freeze had put them down for a while. In the fields in the evening, with the mist rising out of the warm ground to conceal them. Upstairs in her room, under the ruffled sky of her girlish canopy bed, when the rest of the family was away on a picnic, and she feigning a periodic malaise. Being naked in the great outdoors is a thrill, she told him, but nothing beats a bed for comfort. Tommy protested: it was wrong here, under her father's roof. It's wrong everywhere, so what's the difference? she answered airily. Her simple logic, which he thought of as a lack of propriety, shocked him, and to get her way, she had to be awful forward with a certain part of his body.

"If I can't sleep with you in my bed all night," she told him sweetly once she'd turned down the bedclothes, "at least I want to smell you on my sheets."

He shook his head in admiration.

"Where did you learn to talk like that?"

Like what? she wondered, then answered, "It's not the talking, it's the thinking. I just naturally think that way."

"You do have a gift. Nature has favored you something fierce."

Tommy cared for her. He did. He seemed to know his way around a woman's body, though when they were together he swore he was completely hers. He was ingenious. He taught her how to calculate the time between her periods so she could tell him when it was safe to let go inside her. When it wasn't, he pulled out just in time, or so she presumed.

"You're mine," he would swear.

Then he'd collapse upon her and sleep deeply for a minute or two as she held him close and gazed at the world around her.

Those were her favorite times. It was like with the sundress on the tree branch. She was with a man, but temporarily free of him, free to think her own thoughts that no man would have wanted to hear about. She considered her next move, because already she knew this thing could not last forever. The frenzied way he took his pleasure, the sheets of compliments he had to lay down first, the way he got back into his trousers as soon as they were through — all those things were symptoms of the discomfort he felt at taking what he wanted. Or what he thought he wanted. That discomfort was foreign to her.

If I'm willing to do it, she reasoned, then it can't be wrong.

When he began telling her that what they were doing was wrong, at first she didn't think twice about his objections. Gently, automatically, to soothe what she figured must be his conscience, Sabbitha contradicted him.

"You're doing this thing," she reminded him. "It can't be wrong."

That kind of reasoning upset him even more. Tommy started in talking about a busy, scratchy little voice in his head that he called his conscience. He declared that their love affair was *introverted*. He used the word more than once, as part of his increasingly elaborate arguments. She was acquainted with the word. It meant shy. But there was nothing shy about their love, except when other people were around.

Sabbitha went to the red-coated dictionary her parents kept in the parlor, and rarely consulted. "Inward-turning," the entry read. She was furious.

"We're not inward-turning," she told him.

It was the perfect woman's ambush. First she got him inside her, helpless and sweating and making promises he could never keep. Then she slammed the brakes on love and made him listen to things she could not have said otherwise, and that he wouldn't have listened to either.

How about that? she realized. A woman can get a man to listen to her, if she really wants to.

"What are you talking about, baby?"

Tommy was vexed and breathing hard.

"'Introverted,'" she reminded him, and bit his shoulder hard enough to leave the signature of her slight overbite on his skin. "It means inward-turning. I looked it up in the Webster's New Collegiate Dictionary. And you're wrong. We're not turning towards ourselves. We're turning towards each other — at least I am, mister."

"It means we're part of the same being," Tommy protested. "It means we're family."

"I know that, Bozo. How else would I have met you?"

"That's what it means. Family."

"Then how come it doesn't say 'family'? Dictionaries say what they mean. Unlike some people I know."

"Shit, Sabbitha, it's an expression. A way of speaking. It means we've turned to each other instead of turning outwards, towards other people."

She narrrowed her eyes to a squint.

"You want somebody else? Is that what you're trying to tell me?"

She used her two strong knees to push him off her. He found himself out in the cold, cruel world again.

She stood up, naked, put her hands on her hips and gave her long hair a shake. An intimate storm of petals and leaves fell from it.

"You want somebody else? How can you want somebody else when you can have this? Isn't this good enough for you?"

He kneeled down in the pine needles before her, kissed her blond belly and begged her to take him back. She made him promise never to say "introverted" again. He promised. But she knew his promises meant nothing.

Poor Uncle Tommy suffered from a form of cancer called conscience. It was gnawing him away from inside with its own virulent logic. He stopped saying "introverted," and he didn't say "unnatural" either, though that's what he secretly felt. According to everything he understood, a love affair was supposed to get you away from your family, out of the house and into the world, free from mama and papa and all the relations.

That's what his conscience told him, and he believed it — theoretically, at least. In the meantime, he kept on seeing Sabbitha every free moment he had. She watched him twist and turn with the dilemma. Sometimes she was amused, other times exasperated, but his sense of wrongness never touched her. Sure, she knew it was forbidden; the fact that she couldn't tell anyone about it proved that much. But forbidden doesn't mean wrong. She was part of this so-called wrongness, she helped plan and premeditate their every meeting, it wasn't like someone was forcing it on her. She was enjoying the exercise of her free will, or so it seemed to her. No one in Ebenezer ever told her she was the victim of some age-old family perversion, so it never occurred to her to feel like one.

On the contrary: she was dangerously proud. Coming up through the fields, back from the clearing where they had lain together during one of her safe periods, which were nearly all the time according to Tommy, so frequent she wondered how women ever got pregnant, her hair wet with the evening dew and the rest of her from Tommy, Sabbitha Hunter felt as big as the universe. Where the fields met the yard, in the shadow of the Hunter house, Tommy tucked their blanket under his shirt and put a firm hand on her shoulder.

She didn't like the way that hand felt. It wasn't a lover's hand, it was a father's.

She shrugged it off.

"You've got to bathe as soon as you go in," he told her.

"And why is that, Mr. Know-It-All?"

"Your mother. She'll smell it."

Sabbitha laughed like crystal. She tossed her pretty hair where columbine petals and straw clung.

"She will not. She couldn't smell the smoke if the house was burning down around her. I don't believe she knows what *it* smells like."

"Well, she made you."

"Don't be so sure!" Sabbitha gave her right shoulder a quick, appreciative sniff. "Mmm, that's better than French perfume. Where there's smoke, there's fire, lover-boy!"

She waltzed away from him, towards the front porch with its wan yellow mosquito light. In the darkness behind her, Tommy was one very worried man. *My goddamned playhouse,* he realized, *could come crashing down on me any moment now.*

He got into his car, pushed the lighter and let it pop out without lighting his cigarette. Waiting for the blade to fall was making him sick with worry. He set the blanket on the seat next to him. The leaves and grass and flower petals on the cotton read like a signed confession.

"I'm just too damned dick-wild," he said to himself under the gloomy dome-light of the automobile.

He made an effort to see the affair the way the authorities would. She was his niece, a blood relation, and even if she wasn't, what was she? Seventeen, eighteen years old? Jailbait, in any case. Too young, but wilder than he'd ever be, he realized with some humility. It's like the girl's got absolutely nothing to lose.

But he did, even if he couldn't quite name what. His reputation? His freedom? His carefreeness? His usual sense of detachment from the object of his pleasure?

Here's dick-wild, standing proud and feeling big. Then along comes trouble, and guess what? Up pops shit-scared like a jack-in-the-box. When shit-scared meets dick-wild, guess which one's going to come out on top?

He was scared of her. But he couldn't let her go. Not just yet, he told himself. Next week. Next week, maybe.

When it finally did happen, Sabbitha was not particularly surprised. He'd certainly given her ample warning. A week went by without him coming around, then a note showed up addressed to her in his scraggly hand. No one in the Hunter house showed any surprise over the letter. They all studiously ignored it.

He had written "The Road" in the space reserved for the return address. How pretentious, Sabbitha thought, then opened the envelope.

He was leaving, he wrote, for her own good. Somehow she'd been expecting that kind of ass-backwards reasoning from him. He couldn't tell her all the reasons why just yet, but he begged her to believe that the important ones were truly out of his control. Some day he'd tell her everything, and she would understand, and that was a promise.

In the meantime, he advised stupidly, she should go out on dates, meet fellows, be careful about where she went and who she went with, and how she disposed of the gift Nature had given her. That was the last piece of advice he ever offered her. Considering that he was her elder, and so much more experienced in the world, it was pretty paltry, disappointing stuff. Not much different from anything else he'd ever told her to do, she realized.

"Poor man," Sabbitha said to herself. "I could have kept on a while more. Quite a while, actually. Okay, not forever, but who's talking forever?"

Of the two of them, she was easily the strongest. At the time, that thought fed her pride and provided some consolation.

II

Retreat

A S THE BUS labored eastward through Bacon County that day, Sabbitha Hunter had plenty of leisure time to revise her personal history and career as a woman. She demoted her uncle, who had once ushered her into a golden age of love, into a mealy-mouthed, cliché-spitting coward who hadn't even provided her with the pleasure that now, it seemed, was every woman's due. She brooded over vengeance, but it proved impossible: she had no idea where the man was, and there was no one around to ask.

That's the problem when your family dies off, she discovered. There's no one left to help you unearth the secrets.

At every stop, in places even more insignificant than Ebenezer, she peered down through the tinted glass at the passengers moving in and out of the oily clouds of diesel smoke. She wouldn't get off in one of these places. She might not ever get off; she had the money to keep on riding until a worthy destination appeared. She watched men in straw hats climb on the coach as their women looked on fearfully, wringing their hands in worry, as if their husbands were going off to war, and not to the next town to look at farm machinery.

Careful men and silent women, all observing a social order that made Sabbitha want to scream. She wondered if there'd ever been a time when she blended in, and like many prideful people, she decided there was not.

I've always been like this, she decreed. I've never been part of this smug race that's taken personal credit for building this land, when all they did was harry out the people who lived here before they showed up, and whose greatest virtue was that there weren't so many of them.

Sabbitha reached up to the mesh compartment and placed her wicker basket on the seat next to her.

She needn't have bothered. A few men did cut their eyes in her direction, and admired her glowing skin and her hips that had escaped the curse of starchiness that ravaged the other women of the land. They wondered what she was doing on this bus, but no one would have sat next to her. She was wrapped in mourning black from head to toe, and everyone knows that death is catching.

Sabbitha Hunter couldn't figure out which noise was to blame for waking her: the tree branches scraping at the bus window or the driver's cursing every time it happened. She'd wanted out of Ebenezer's rich, smug landscape, and it looked as though she'd succeeded.

She yawned, then took her brush from her basket and began to comb out her hair. No one saw those private things that she was doing in public; the coach was practically empty. This was one of the bus company's money-losing routes.

The early twilight landscape appealed to her immediately. Dark, closed ranks of slash and loblolly pine stood knee-deep in still water that flashed dull silver in the lowering light. A surfeit of green so intense it veered off into black. There wasn't a single fertile field anywhere. In this place, she sensed, no one could make a virtue out of the stubborn, straight-and-narrow mindset it took to live off the land. What land? If you went to walk on it, your boots would fill up with water.

After a day's traveling, Sabbitha Hunter had reached what Ebenezer people and their landlocked kind called the Salvation Coast. They'd meant the name as a derogatory joke. On the Coast, they would chuckle, what with the heat, the waterlogged, acidic land and the fevers that sapped you as if you were living in Africa, there wasn't much else for a man to do but pray to be saved, and the sooner, the better.

Like plenty of insults nowadays, this one got recycled by the very people who were supposed to be the butt of the joke. The Salvation Coast population turned the insult into a point of pride, and proceeded to do their best to live up to it. They began by studying their past and, unsurprisingly, discovered a long line of utopians, church-builders and escapers from responsibility among their ancestors. Those historical discoveries made them feel a lot better about being who they were. We were destined to be this way — it's an honor, they all agreed.

Among the heroes from their past was a British colony-builder who refused to kill Indians, would not allow slavery, forbade the drinking of alcoholic spirits and let everyone worship the god of their choice — Christ-killers included. What kind of frontiersman was he?

He was the first great utopian to hit the Coast, and naturally, his colony failed. But his failure deterred no one. On the contrary: people were attracted to it, his failure was a morbid challenge of a kind, and before long, ex-nobles came washing ashore from the European capitals, fleeing one or another of their cyclical revolutions. They ended up on the Coast and tried to live like mincing barons and coy countesses among the snakes and fevers and swamp spirits. It took them just a few years to see the light. They soon married with the purple-skinned blacks and the silent, mirage-like Indians and left nothing but their names. These days, the descendants of the counts and baronets are cooking up she-crab soup and making lye soap.

On the Salvation Coast, you never had to worry about anyone suppressing you if you wanted to conduct an experiment in some new and private social order. And if your utopia got shredded by reality, you could always blame the heat, the bitter soil, the relentless insects and the various spells and spirits that lived in the woods and wetlands. All of them were close at hand, and all were willing to serve any master. Service was in their nature.

Sabbitha Hunter sat on the edge of her seat, gripping her Little Black Riding Hood wicker basket, alert to the landscape. "Retreat Community," a road sign read. She reached up and jerked the stop-request cord.

The driver slowed but did not stop. Sabbitha had to get up, move down the aisle and stand close behind him, making sure that a few stray blond hairs grazed the raw nape of his neck.

"You sure you want to get off here, Ma'am?"

"Retreat," she said, confirming her stop.

"I don't know why you'd want to do a thing like that. There ain't nothing here."

The driver laughed at his joke.

"That's why they call it Retreat," she told him. "It's a retreat from your kind."

The man was trifling with her. And she would not have bus drivers mocking her wishes. Despite her fake funereal get-up and lack of destination, Sabbitha Hunter could still be an Ebenezer lady if forced to.

"I see the stop up there," she told the driver, as if she was a frequent visitor to Retreat.

The driver pulled off reluctantly at a wider place in the road. Sabbitha Hunter descended from the vehicle, grasping her basket by the handle.

"I just want you to know I told you," the driver called after her. "This is no place for a lady to be getting off at. I mean, even I wouldn't get off here."

"You're not — I am. I'll remember what you said," Sabbitha assured him. "Now drive on, mister, your conscience is assuaged."

The bus pulled off, leaving Sabbitha standing in diesel-scented silence.

In the quiet that gathered after the bus's departure, she considered her surroundings. Retreat. It wasn't a town. It wasn't a hamlet. It wasn't even a crossroads; there weren't two roads to cross. The sign that called the place a community had been overly optimistic. The only sense of community was provided by the squirrels and the cardinals that worked the broad branches of the oak trees.

Retreat was a utopia that was temporarily out of service. A multipurpose facility for periodic Salvation Coast experiments in communal living. A spot out on the highway where you could go and have an in-body or an out-of-body worship experience in whatever way best fit the current apocalypse, without having to suffer an audience of gawkers, skeptics, doubters and other moral authorities. It was the spiritual equivalent of a roadhouse. But right now, the place was as dead as a juke joint on a Sunday morning. And Sabbitha Hunter was standing in the center of it, unwilling as yet to admit that getting off at this place was a mistake.

A decaying semicircle of cabins stood around a wide charred spot on the ground like spectators at an accident. Open-mouthed, shocked spectators: all the cabins had had their doors staved in.

A diamond-back rattler eased out from under a pile of stones and splintered two-by-fours. The snake could have been a runaway from somebody's primitive Christian rite. Maybe it had gotten fed up with being handled by humans and bent out of shape in the name of the Lord. Nobody ever considers what the props in the ritual might feel.

Sabbitha watched the snake twist over the blackened flagstones of the fire pit and cross her path. The rattler hesitated, thrust out its tongue, bobbed its head and sniffed for her scent.

"I know you're poisonous, Mr. Snake," she told it. "And I know you didn't choose to be that way, any more than I chose to be this way. Everybody in the whole world knows your nature. But you and I don't have any hostile business together, do we?"

The diamond-back found her scent to its liking and her voice melodious. You could almost say it was charmed.

"Tell me, Mr. Snake, what's this place all about?"

The snake was familiar with *place*, but not with the concept of *all about*. It slid past her and across the clearing in search of a field mouse to ingest.

Sabbitha called all animals Mister, with a charming mix of exaggerated respect and girlish flirtation. That was her way of keeping large and potentially dangerous things at a distance from which they could not harm her. Once with Uncle Tommy on the riverbank, as he slept in brief, perfect male repose on her breast, she opened her eyes and found herself staring into the face of an enormous buck, not ten paces away. The animal's size terrified her, and so did its smell. Flirtation was her first line of defence. "I suppose you think I'm beautiful, too, Mr. Buck?" she asked the deer in a voice soft enough not to stir Tommy. She didn't want him to catch her talking to anybody or anything else in that irresistible tone. "This fellow does, and he wants me for it. Do you want me, too, Mr. Buck?" The animal dipped its heavy antlers. Sabbitha took that for a yes. "Well, that's sweet of you, Mr. Buck, but I'm taken right now. I think even you can see that. But I'll write your name down in my little black book. You never know. Things can always change."

A minute later, the buck faded into the woods. Her method had worked once again.

Sabbitha peered into one of the cabins. It made no sense to have kicked in the plywood door. There was no lock on it, just a flimsy latch that a child could have flipped open with a finger. But when given a choice between opening a door with their hand or staving it in with their boot-heel, most men choose the latter.

The inside of the cabin was a jumble of tipped-over chairs and shattered tables with a leg or two sheered off. Jutting out of the wall was a bare wooden platform made of crisscrossed laths. A person could sleep on it, Sabbitha supposed, if he was dead drunk or had no nerves left in his body. Mouse droppings were scattered across the floor like tiny marbles. A trail of red-brown stains ran from the sleeping platform to the door. Blood, she surmised. Human blood. You get off the bus in utopia and end up at a crime scene.

Whoever last used this retreat must have brought all their baggage from their former life. Being out in nature didn't soothe people. It only freed them to be more savage than ever. Which is why, in this country, people kept heading for the great frontier.

Sabbitha Hunter reknotted her black scarf and began to walk away from the cabins. The bus driver had been right: getting off at Retreat was not a good idea. Maybe none of this was a good idea. But going back to Ebenezer was a worse one. She discovered a road that formed beyond the last wrecked cabin. A rough track made of water-filled ruts and tufts of bitter grass that even winter couldn't kill. Sabbitha began to sweat under her black cloak as she labored along, and the north wind that rose up with twilight chilled her. She felt the boot-heel that had staved in those plywood doors as if it had caught her full in the stomach.

When she saw the truck bouncing over the ruts in her direction, she automatically figured the worst was at hand. A variety of things could happen to a woman in the wilderness, even one dressed in protective black, and none of them was any good.

She veered off the road. There was no other alternative but the ditch.

When Nathan Gazarra saw the figure of a young woman angle off the road and take to the ditch, he was not overly surprised. He had come across a lot of things in ditches along the roads and tracks of the Coast in his decades of working it, and a woman, even a young, handsome one, was not that unusual. In fact, it was as common as trouble.

The road occasionally made him gifts of that kind. It ought to, he figured. After all, he'd given it nearly his whole adult life.

Sitting behind the wheel of his pick-up, negotiating the rutted road in agonizingly slow second gear, he didn't rule out the possibility that there had been no woman at all. Among the road's gifts was that of delusion. It kept a man going.

Gazarra brought the truck alongside of where he figured the woman should be. She wouldn't have cut across the fields, not here. There weren't any fields — just wetlands. A woman might be crazy enough to jump in a ditch, Gazarra reasoned, but no one is so nutty that she'd take on that snake-filled blackwater just to escape a kindly old man like himself.

He stopped the pick-up. There was the usual gentle music from the pots and pans lashed to the outside frame of the truckbed. Gazarra peered out the window into the ditch below, and squinted whoever was down there into focus.

The woman did look like someone who would jump into a muddy culvert. She was carrying a silly-looking wicker picnic basket, and her head scarf was knotted so tight under her chin he wondered whether she'd choke to death before he could rescue her. A heavy black cape sat like a tent on her shoulders. But that great mass of blond hair changed everything. It made her silliness into something intriguing. He would have sworn that color didn't exist outside his dreams.

"What's happened to you, lady?" he called down.

He creaked open the truck door and stepped onto the wind-crusted mud.

"I have fallen among thieves," came the voice from below.

"I see," Gazarra said. He pulled at his gray beard, streaking it with orange clay. "I hope it wasn't too irreplaceable what they took from you."

He squatted down by the edge of the road, his knee joints cracking, and wondered idly whether he'd be able to achieve the standing position again. But this woman is worth it, he gauged. She could cure a man's knees. She was quite the find.

"It's time to get out of that ditch," he told Sabbitha. "You made your point, whatever it is."

He held out his hand. She refused it and scrambled up the bank by herself. Generous whorls and rooster-tails of greasy orange clay mocked her black mourning outfit.

"What are you doing on this road?" he asked her.

"Going where it goes."

"Sorry, lady. It doesn't go anywhere."

"That's impossible," Sabbitha countered. "It has to go some-where. They all do."

"I suppose you know about roads?"

"Theoretically," she admitted.

He turned and lent an ear to the nervous hissing of the radiator.

"Get in, we have to drive. If the truck doesn't move, the radiator overheats. It's nervous, it likes to go places."

"That's the weakest line I've ever heard in my life!"

"Whatever was afflicting you," Gazarra pointed out, "it has disappeared. You're acting like a normal woman now. I'm happy to see that."

Then he climbed into his truck and goosed the accelerator to rescue the sputtering engine.

"I'll ride in back," Sabbitha told him. "You never know with men."

Sabbitha was halfway into the truckbed when Gazarra threw it into gear and lurched off down the track. His response to her crack about men. She tipped forward into something that looked like a den of thieves who all suffered from an obsession with order.

The back of Nathan Gazarra's truck was an illustration of how deprivation sharpens some people's ingenuity — if it doesn't deaden them completely. There were baskets and neatly knotted sacks and bags swinging from the crosspieces of the canvas roof. There were metal tackle boxes and tool cabinets welded to the floor and sides of the truckbed. There were clean surfaces for food and fabric and a greasy one for merchandise that didn't care about cleanliness, like roofing nails and spools of fence wire. There was a perfect demarcation between clean and unclean. A board that acted as a bookshelf was pushed up against the rear of the cab, behind a wide bunk bed, with the books tightly packed to keep them in place.

Sabbitha pulled one down. *A Thousand Dreams Explained*, she read. She opened the book to a page that explained the significance of dreaming about hats. That's ridiculous, she argued with the book. No one would dream about hats. Hats don't mean anything. The next thing she knew, the truck bottomed out on the muddy track and all the books slid onto the floor.

The truckbed was wider and longer than anything Sabbitha had ever seen in Ebenezer, where with the prosperity, men's trucks tended to be factory produced and store maintained. "Beauts," all of them. She bent to gather up the books of divination and saw that the rear section of Gazarra's truck was composed of two smaller beds welded together. The edge where the metal had been joined looked like a wandering scar a drunk doctor would leave. The whole construction looked like a Wild West covered wagon on wheels.

The joyful music of pots and pans announced that Gazarra was slowing to a stop. Sabbitha Hunter looked out the back of the truck. She was not particularly happy to see the cabins of Retreat again.

He came and stood on the ground below her, a bag in his hand. He put his hands on his hips and looked up. She stared back. His cheeks and chin were covered by an overgrowth of gray beard, and what wasn't covered with hair had been burned brick-red by years of Salvation Coast sun. But his eyes were blue, she noticed, blue-green, the color of a glacial lake.

"What are you looking at, mister? Wondering how much I'd fetch per pound?"

"I am wondering what a woman like you was doing out on the road."

"Is doing."

"Yes, is doing. I stand corrected. And dressed in black, on top of it. Very sad looking."

"It could be I'm in mourning," she said.

"For your life, maybe?" he queried. Before Sabbitha could retort, he offered, "Come down from there. I have someplace more comfortable where you can mourn."

Sabbitha tried to force open the tailgate but it would not go. It was welded to the body. From below, Gazarra offered his hand.

"No, thanks," she told him.

Before he could avert his eyes, she raised the hem of her dress and vaulted over the tailgate in a scissors move, ambushing him with a view of her thighs. Of all the possible ways she could retaliate, that was the most eloquent.

One cabin in Retreat, it turned out, hadn't been brutalized. Gazarra used it as his quarters whenever he was in the area. He unlatched the door, lit a lantern and started pulling provisions out of his kit bag and putting them on the table. He held up a half-loaf of bread and a split smoked mullet.

"Don't make me eat by myself," he appealed as she stood on the threshold. "I do that too often as it is."

"I suppose I have no choice," Sabbitha said, stepping inside. "I can't very well spurn my rescuer."

Gazarra watched in awe as she untied her black scarf and shook out her blond hair. Then she lifted it and twisted it into a temporary chignon, letting him see the nape of her neck.

"You're not from around here, I can see that," he said.

"Why? Don't I have the right accent?"

"That I can't tell." He brushed the lobe of his ear to show he was deaf to those distinctions. "But you're not from the Coast, that's clear."

"Who says?"

"There are no women like you here. It's a sad fact. An unfortunate tradition."

Sabbitha Hunter laughed. She listened to her laughter and wondered when the last time was that she laughed with a man, instead of at one.

"I took you for a woman running away from her husband."

"And I took you for the devil himself."

"The devil drives a pick-up truck? You know something I don't?"

"They say evil takes on all disguises. Who knows what you might have been hiding in the back of that truck."

"People are always saying that about us. You rode back there. What did you see?"

"A lot of stuff I wouldn't know what to do with. I'm not much for housekeeping. What do you do with all that?"

"I sell it. What else would I do with that stuff, keep it? I'm not a hoarder, I'm a peddler, and the last of my kind."

Gazarra sounded proud, but Sabbitha saw no motive for pride. To be the last of anything could not have been a very happy situation.

"We call it selling on the road," he explained. "You must live in a town. A big town. Otherwise you'd know about me."

When he came upon someone who needed instructing, Gazarra never missed the opportunity. He might have been just a peddler in everyone's eyes, but pedagogy was his true calling. In another, fairer world, he would have been given the chance to do just that. The world was a harsh, raggedy place, but even at this late point in its sad story, it could still be improved upon through his teaching, and other people's learning.

"The storekeeper wants you to come to him. I go to you. The storekeeper wants you to buy from his stock. I get what you want and bring it right to your door. Maybe you want to know what's going on in the big, wide world, or in the next town, and there are no newspapers, or what you want to know isn't in the newspapers. I tell you the news. Maybe you've gotten a letter and you can't read it, and you're too ashamed to ask someone you know for help. I read it for you, then I keep two secrets — what the letter said, and that you couldn't read it. Maybe your man of God is indisposed, or maybe he has a crisis of faith. I'll lead your church, no matter the denomination, because they're all the same to me, and all religions come from the same place anyway. Pretty good, wouldn't you say?"

Gazarra was positively beaming with his own tenacity. The tendons rippled beneath the brick-red reptile skin of his leathery neck. But Sabbitha shook her head.

"Too good. It sounds too good to be true. If you're so many things to so many people, how come you're the last of your kind?"

Gazarra nodded sadly. "That's a good question: why am I not necessary any more? It's because of change. People are settling down now, they're becoming modern. They have actually learned to like the stores better. They like the bright colors of the packages. They want the goods. They don't want to have to talk to the person who sells them."

"So that's the end of the peddlers," she concluded.

"The end of the others, yes. It's already come. But there are more than enough routes for me. I have no intention of giving up."

"You're what we call a stubborn mule," Sabbitha told him.

"I had mules, too, before I had horses, before I had trucks. Yes, definitely," he agreed. "I refuse to die."

Sabbitha spotted a book lying on the lath sleeping platform. It was bound in luxurious buttery calfskin, gloriously out of place in the cabin.

"Is that yours?" she asked.

He nodded.

"You leave things like that lying around here?"

"I use this place sometimes."

"And no one takes it?"

"People know me," he told her. "And they know my things. There are . . . superstitions attached to my things. At least, that's how they see it. So they don't steal."

Sabbitha reached for the book. Gazarra grabbed her wrist. His grip was like a vise. For a first touch between them, it was not particularly promising.

"Your hands," he told her.

"What's wrong with my hands that you letting go of them won't cure?"

She looked at her fingers in his knobby, tenacious, arthritic grasp. They were slick with mullet oil.

He released her, then reached into his bag that sat on the table beside them. He drew out a wooden pointer in the shape of a human finger.

Gazarra opened the book with it. The first page swam with crooked, twisted, backwards-leaning letters.

"'Darkness was on the face of the deep,'" he began.

"I know," she told him. "I've been there."

And that was how Sabbitha Hunter met her first Jew.

As the luminous blue evening turned to black night, painful with stars, she and the peddler filled the cabin with their talk. He told her about the first round he ever rode, only weeks after he'd arrived in America, how he'd been schooled to fear bears and wild Indians, though he never saw either kind of beast. Instead, true terror resided at the doors of strangers, and every man and woman in this country was a stranger. He understood he was to knock at an unknown person's door and offer his stock for sale. He was completely unprepared. As a boy, in his village, he'd never been called upon to speak to someone he didn't already know. In this place, whether he survived depended on that ability, and on his skill in selling goods whose uses he scarcely understood to people who spoke a language he did not know. Every call at every house and shack was an act of extreme self-sacrifice. He threw himself on the mercy of strangers. The first time he tried it, he opened his mouth and found he could not speak. He had gone mute with fear and embarrassment at being who he was. He wrote figures in the dust with a stick and pointed at them, smiling stupidly, full of hope, an educated young man rendered illiterate by immigration, reduced to the competency of a preschooler. "It good," he finally learned to say. "You buy?"

Most astonishing of all, more incredible than the absence of bears and wild Indians, were his customers' many kindnesses. They greeted him with the delicate courtesy reserved for strangers on the Salvation Coast. They knew he was a Jew, but it hadn't occurred to them — not yet, in any case — to hate him for that. When his would-be customers saw that he hadn't learned to speak their language, they gave him their children's old primers and taught him how to pronounce the strange words on the pages, and once he had done that, they taught him how to string those words together into something that approximated sentences. He learned the language laboriously, slowly, formally and comically from those old battered books where little American children romped in perfect union with Mother and Father and Doggie. He recited his lessons aloud to the trees and fenceposts and telegraph poles as he traveled from house to house, settlement to settlement. The language held secrets from him even where there were none, and he wasted hours and days trying to puzzle out the hidden meaning behind places called Black Ankle and Red Level and Low Bottom.

It was years before Gazarra was willing to accept that particular phenomenon found along the Salvation Coast. It was so strange and against all nature that he was tempted to consider it a perversion, or a scandalous secret only he was aware of. Yet it was true: people here did not hate him because he was a Jew. In fact, they wanted him to be a Jew. The more Jewish, the better. In proper houses and in shacks alike, blacks and whites both would beg him to speak Hebrew.

"What?" he would ask them. He feared a trap. "What do you want me to say?"

"Say God's name," they urged him. "Say God's name in God's own language."

"We can't do that," Gazarra told them.

"How come you can't?"

Their question was asked with blunt, honest curiosity.

"I cannot oblige you," he said, sounding very much like a book. "God's name is unnameable."

His answer delighted the inhabitants of this strangest of countries. They love riddles, these people, Gazarra thought. Maybe that's their religion. Then, since he could not say God's name, he recited all the prayers for all the different occasions. And since the customers wanted more, always more, he was forced to invent new ones that suited his predicament. *Help me to understand these people*, he implored the Salvation Coast sky in Hebrew. *Help me sell the stuff on this cart. Help me find a shield against loneliness, as you made a shield for David.*

Once the sale was made, Gazarra would hurriedly pack up his wares from the farmers' porch railings and chair backs and grassy spots where they'd been exhibited. But even then there was no escape. The women would ask him inside for something to eat, with broad hints that, no, of course, there would be no meat from pigs. Once he had taken a seat at the table, still uneasy, wondering when the blade would fall or the chair be pulled away from under his rear end, the farming families would quiz him about the real meaning of the Bible stories.

"Honestly, this was not how I'd pictured the American home," he admitted to Sabbitha. "The strange things they would ask of me! You speak His language, they would tell me. We have to read the Word translated out of many tongues, but you, you're closer! Then they would have me stay the night without asking for money, or if they did ask, it was only a quarter. Once I heard one of them boast to another, I gave shelter to the Jew last week! Can you imagine such a thing? I was wanted — not for what I did but for what I was! As if it was my fault!"

He laughed uproariously, and Sabbitha laughed with him for his triumph.

"The mistakes I made at first," he confessed to her. "I was such a greener. I let a black man try on a hat that later I sold to a white man. If the white man found out, I would have lost all my business! Then I went and spent the night in the black man's cabin!"

He clapped both hands to his head, marveling at his own innocence. The next moment he cackled mischievously.

"What they don't know can't hurt them!"

He told her about the mules and horses he had outlived, and how he'd had to shoot every one of them before he finally converted to the internal combustion engine.

"I saw the last mule. I saw the last horse. I have the last pick-up truck of its kind. And I am the last peddler!"

Then he leaned very close to Sabbitha. She thought he was going to kiss her, but he only had a secret to confide.

"There used to be a lot of us on the road, you know. There used to be a camaraderie, like with soldiers — we *were* soldiers. Once a month we would meet someplace hidden. In a hollow, by a spring, on a stretch of sand beach far away in the marsh that no one knew about. We knew this country better than the people it belonged to — that was our revenge. Some revenge! In those places when we met, we would tell our troubles and exhibit our wounds and talk about the ladies, and there would be drinking and dancing and music. We would dance in the sand to the fiddle music, men dancing together because that's all there was. At the end we would be so drunk from liquor and homesickness that we would fall in a heap and sleep, one on top of the other like dead soldiers in a trench. When we awoke with the dew on our shoulders, we'd be new again and ready for the pain of the road. That's what the Sabbath was invented for — to make the rest of the week tolerable!"

He leaned very close to Sabbitha again. His unkempt, wiry beard brushed her cheek.

"Not such a kosher idea, I think!" He laughed. "Of course, all this celebrating had to happen out of sight of our customers. We couldn't show them we could be hurt or happy like normal people. That's not what the peddler is."

"What is he, then, if he can't have his feelings?"

"He's everywhere, he knows everything, he helps everyone when he can. But no one knows anything about him. Most of the time they don't even know his name. Usually he has three names: the Jew. The Peddler. The Jew Peddler."

That was how Sabbitha Hunter and Nathan Gazarra came to give their real names to each other. With mock formality, they shook hands, though they were long past the stage of introductions. His hand was as tough as an animal's horn.

"Sabbitha?" he repeated.

"My parents' idea. It's not my fault if I was born on a Saturday."

"It's an honor," he told her.

"An accident."

"I don't believe in accidents," Gazarra stated. "Chance is just what it says it is: an accidental happening that means nothing."

"So that means you were supposed to meet me?"

Gazarra shrugged. "Maybe, maybe not . . . I took you for a woman escaping from her husband."

"You said that once already. No, Mr. Peddler, where I come from, women don't escape. They just stand there and take it."

Then she narrowed her eyes.

"But I'm not innocent, if that's what you want to know!"

Gazarra blushed under his beard. He may feel tough on the outside, Sabbitha thought, but he doesn't know a thing about women. In the quiet that followed, she listened to the field mice rustling under the floorboards.

Suddenly the peddler was on his feet.

"I'm going to sleep," he announced, as if he could will the

thing to happen. "I'll take the truck. You stay here, it's more comfortable."

She looked dubiously at the wooden sleeping platform.

"You might not think so, but it's true. Trust me, I know. So, it's good night now!"

He swept out of the cabin, leaving Sabbitha the lantern with its meager ration of fuel. What was the hurry? Why was he leaving now, after all that fine talk?

It was unreasonable, but she wanted the man. Not necessarily the man who told the stories — the man *in* the stories.

III

Choosing a Miracle

*G*AZARRA didn't realize he'd forgotten his calfskin-bound Testament in the cabin until he was outside. He hesitated between the cabin's plywood door and the tailgate of his truck. The thought of that strange, forward woman smearing the pages of his precious book with mullet grease pained him. But it was too late to turn around and barge back into the lady's improvised boudoir. Too late, or too soon. He headed for his truck.

Nathan Gazarra was a careful man of meticulous habits. If you came across him in his clay-colored clothes and tangled beard, at the wheel of his gypsy pick-up truck, you wouldn't have thought that he enveloped every action with ritual.

Take the simple matter of drinking a consoling shot of whisky — America's national pastime. Gazarra wouldn't use just any old glass, despite the apparent disorder of his life. In the back of his truck, behind his bunk where he hung his lantern and above the bookshelf where Sabbitha had rewedged the manuals of divination into place, he kept his cache of things that were not for sale. The determiners of who he was. Among them was his ceremonial drinking glass.

The glass had been presented to him upon his accession to manhood in a village of bogs and birches and human slaughter. The occasion was his bar mitzvah, the rite of passage according to which a boy becomes a man at the unlikely age of thirteen. Thirteen? How optimistic of his religion to imagine that childhood could go on that long! Under the pressures of Europe's precarious years between her two great wars, and all the local ones that hardly bore mentioning, children were propelled into adulthood by the age of eight. In the village Gazarra came from, most of them skipped childhood altogether. They often went from a state of helplessness to having to fend for themselves in one violent night.

His drinking glass had been blown in Bohemia, and was destined to hold the sweet Tokay wine of celebration. But its destiny had veered off track. It had traveled to America, wrapped in a handerchief and newsprint, and ended up being a vessel for the anesthetizing corn liquor of the great American road.

Why would anyone bother carrying a glass all the way across the Atlantic Ocean? The glass really wasn't worth anything, and considering the age at which he'd made the trip, Gazarra was too young to have owned any objects that might have accumulated sentimental value.

For the peddler, the glass's value wasn't sentimental. It was philosophical.

The glass was blown to resemble a heavy crown, with hollowed-out indentations in its sides for the jewels that would come to ornament it. That was its philosophical point. What kind of jewels could someone like Gazarra, from a village like his, ever hope to possess? None, it seemed. Not in that desperately, eternally poor place. But that was the riddle of the gift, he was given to understand by his elders who had instructed him. He was meant to discover or devise the jewels that would grace his time on earth. They would be his personal, though imaginary, crown. Which was the only kind allowed a boy born into poverty.

Gazarra received a sense of mission very early in life. But there was only one problem. He was the product of a time and place that allowed no missions to be fulfilled, other than the most threadbare kind of survival. Gazarra's world did things that way. It told you that being a man meant having a mission, a vocation — then it turned around and withdrew all the tools you needed to get the job done.

But Gazarra didn't see things that way. At the age of thirteen, he displayed all the earnest romanticism of an underclass boy trying to pull himself up into a state he thought of as worthiness. Worthy of what, he didn't think to ask. I must search and excel: that is what is expected of me, he resolved. The jewels might be the real stones of wealth. They might be the imaginary ones of study. But the riddle is real — that's all that matters.

Now, years later on the Salvation Coast, it looked as though Gazarra would find no jewels of any kind. Lately, as he drove the roads between the farms and settlements, he would glance into his rear-view mirror, and through the fine orange dust that coated it, looming out of the ocher clouds of sand, he'd see the ghost of himself, the young man he'd been when he'd come to America. Calmly, with grim satisfaction, he recognized the shimmering image as that of his death. A reminder, a faithful camp follower, tireless and patient and impassive. More boy than man, sitting high on the bench of a splay-wheeled cart, pulled by a pair of mismatched, split-eared mules, his merchandise barely protected from the weather by a creased, cracked oilcloth lashed down by lengths of fraying rope. His former self. Gazarra the earnest, the romantic, the foolishly hopeful. The young man with the glass where the jewels were supposed to go.

That disappointed ghost gained a little more ground on him every day.

When it catches me, he said to himself, it'll be the end of my road.

So what? he retorted a moment later. I won't be the first man who ever died. There's absolutely nothing original about dying.

But Nathan Gazarra had made a secret decision concerning the matter of his death. He had resolved not to die like everyone else had on the face of this earth, unredeemed, in an impassive age, uselessly, unchanged in an unchanged world.

It was a big resolution for a little man. But that's what happens when you drop an earnest, romantic boy into the wilderness and make him ride a lifetime of empty roads. He gets lonely. He gets foolish. He starts getting ideas.

During his truncated career as a student, he'd learned about the great miracles. The bush that burned yet was not consumed. The parting of the Red Sea. The quails that rained down from heaven and nourished the children in the desert. The first time he was told about these great and righteous works, a question immediately came to his lips.

Could these things happen to us, here, where we live, in our time?

Immediately, he sensed the answer was no.

But why not? Who says?

It was the most natural of questions. He never dared ask it. He was just a boy. He was to listen to his elders, not pester them with fantastic speculation. A shame, he thought, I should have asked. I should have risked the disapproval, or the slap in the face. Now it's too late. My elders are dead. I'm practically an elder myself now, but no one wants to know anything from me.

In the back of his truck, he took another sip of the liquor he'd bartered for the previous week. The jewels might have been missing from that crown-shaped glass, but at least the whisky wasn't. Things could be worse.

He lifted his glass.

"I refuse to live in an age of no miracles," he told his lantern.

The lantern didn't answer. Neither did the rest of the world, starting with the moths that circled around the light. So far, the world had flatly refused to cooperate with the peddler.

But what if he made it cooperate?

Some time later, Gazarra took a blanket off his bunk and folded it neatly under his arm. He swung himself down stiffly from the truckbed and onto the ground. His recalcitrant knees had begun to imitate his arthritic fingers. They froze up on him without warning. Every movement became an adventure. When he berated them, they answered back with rusty creaks and unpredictable pops.

"Move," he told them. "There's urgent business at hand. We have to go warm up the lady."

He eased open the latch of the one good cabin and stood just inside the door. Sabbitha Hunter slept uncovered in the blaze of her lantern, her cape spread under her body to soften the wooden slats, her hair streaming out behind her like a comet's tail.

Gazarra unfolded his blanket and spread it over her. She did not stir, which he found unusual, since a sleeping person always reacts to being tampered with. Then he realized she wasn't sleeping, but only pretending to, and he pretended not to know this. He turned to the table to pick up his book. It was unsmudged. His hand was trembling.

The beginnings of Parkinson's, he thought. Or maybe it's love.

He went to her side again. She awaited him, hands balled into fists under the blanket.

Okay, Mr. Good Samaritan, she asked him silently, are you here to do what I think you're here to do?

But that wasn't the kind of man she'd fallen in with. Rape was much too ordinary for him.

Gazarra stood above her. He felt her body tense under the blanket. Heat poured off her like an asphalt road in July. He bent and kissed her pale forehead. The hairs of his beard, then his dry, cracked lips brushed her hairline. She smelled dust and whisky on him and fought the impulse to open her eyes.

A moment later he was gone, out the cabin door with his book under his arm in place of the blanket.

Sabbitha awoke to chilly, brilliant sunlight on the cabin floor. She remembered the peddler's sandpaper kiss and put her hands to her face. No damage done, at least not as far as she could feel.

She stepped out of the cabin and onto the scrubby grass. So this is running away, she thought. So far, it's not very distinguished. The morning was raucous with cardinals quarreling among themselves over some matter, maybe whether it was the right time to migrate north again. The pick-up truck's hood was open, and Gazarra's head and shoulders were deep in its engine compartment.

"There you are, Mr. Good Samaritan," she said softly. "How much do I owe you for not forcing me last night?"

Gazarra pulled his body out of the truck's cavity.

"I am tending to the old mule," he said by way of greeting.

He looked half-prophet, half-frontiersman, with a greasy squirrel-fur cap on his head.

"People are wrong to think these machines have no souls. They're not as dumb as we think they are."

He stepped away from the truck and used a handful of young leaves to wipe engine oil off his hands. He seemed immensely satisfied with the day, and it had only just begun.

"Did you sleep well?" he asked.

"No."

"That's normal. It was your first night."

"My first night doing what?"

"Your first night on the road. You get used to it."

"I suppose you have?" she queried.

He slammed the hood shut.

"I've thought it over," he announced. "I need an assistant. I'm getting too old to be climbing in and out of this truck all day long to show merchandise to ladies who don't know what they want, and couldn't pay for it even if they did know. My knees are frozen like an old clutch. My fingers are as crooked as the roads I drive on. You don't seem to be very occupied by anything just now. You're free. You could be my assistant."

"How do you know how free I am?"

"I don't know, I was just hoping," he admitted. "I'm sorry, I know my offer doesn't sound very . . ." He grasped for the word, which successfully eluded him. "Appetizing," he tried.

"Appealing," she corrected him.

"Yes. That, too. Not very appealing. Excuse me, I've gotten out of the habit of conversation."

"You talk just fine, mister."

Gazarra smiled thinly. "Only after I've rehearsed."

"How much are you offering the assistant?"

"I'll give you half of everything I earn — probably more than half, considering that my needs are so . . . stingy, or however you say that. Excellent, no? What businessman ever split fifty-fifty with his employee? I'm no capitalist. I don't believe in piling up the filthy lucre like an old man licking honey off his dry, dusty fingers. And if ever I should retire, or die, which is the same thing as far as I'm concerned, you get everything. Everything! The stock, the transportation, the deals with the suppliers, the route and all its years of good will."

Sabbitha Hunter laughed out loud, startling the cardinals in the oaks.

"You're offended?" Gazarra asked anxiously.

She shook her head. "That's the second time I've laughed in less than a day. Pretty soon I won't recognize myself."

"That's the idea."

"And it is laughable," Sabbitha said, "the whole prospect of it. Your offer. Here I am, a proper young small town creation, plenty marriageable, with a big house I could be filling up with children and conjugal discontent, and never working a day in my life. And now I'm supposed to go on the road with some grizzled old peddler who can't even say what he means, and sell sundries and notions and powders and fabric and coffee and roofing nails, all sorts of stuff I've never had to bother with in my proper, normal small town life — now, that's cause for laughter."

The peddler shrugged. "Maybe. If so, so much the better. Laughter can be hard to come by sometimes."

"Especially where I come from."

Gazarra was working his old peddler magic. He was a master at it. The best on the Coast, despite his trouble with words. Or because of it. Words didn't matter. The warmth of his persuasion did. And the merchandise, too. He was selling something to Sabbitha that she'd never heard of, that she didn't need, that she didn't even want, that she hadn't known she needed and wanted, and that all of a sudden she couldn't live without.

That something was Sabbitha Hunter herself. A brand-new version of the woman to replace the one she was wanting to leave behind. And with it a chance to get out in the world and do some damage.

She ran her fingertips over her forehead.

"I wouldn't mind freshening up first," she said. "That is, if there's any running water in this place."

That was how Sabbitha Hunter took to selling on the road. The most momentous decisions are made that way. Don't bother looking for hidden motivations. There aren't any. It's a clear, brisk morning, the cardinals are in the trees, there's the sudden discovery of laughter that stands for freedom. So you go.

The pump handle in Retreat was rusty, and it squeaked and scared the birds again. The water tasted vaguely salty and definitely sulphurous, and it wasn't cold at all. The wells are shallow on the Coast. You didn't need to dig far to hit water.

Gazarra worked the handle for Sabbitha. She cupped her hands and splashed her face, then rinsed out her mouth and spat. The moment was painfully intimate for Gazarra. A woman washing herself in the morning. Closing her eyes to let the water run over her fine skin, reaching out blindly and trustingly for the towel he offered. He couldn't remember the last time. There had been no other time like this.

He handed her a block of lye soap, the kind some families along the Coast still insisted on making, even though they could have bought a bar of Dove from the store. Sabbitha looked at the black hunk of soap dubiously.

"You swear you can get clean with this stuff? How does it work?"

Gazarra showed her. He rubbed it against his wet palm until it raised a meager lather. Sabbitha scooped it from his hand and applied it to her face.

"It doesn't make many bubbles," he admitted. "But it'll take the road off your skin."

The truck engine fired up on the first try and Sabbitha climbed in front. Gazarra eased the pick-up over Retreat's soft ground, among the stumps of trees that had been felled to make the cabins that had been vandalized by the very people who'd built them. Sabbitha put her head out the open window, into the cool, moving air, and tasted the pleasure of not knowing where she was going.

Then something happened.

The truck's racket flushed out the diamond-backed rattlesnake, which slithered blindly into their path.

"Stop!" Sabbitha ordered the peddler.

He did. With the front wheels resting firmly on the snake's head.

"You ran over Mr. Snake!"

Gazarra put the truck in neutral and they both climbed down to have a look. The animal's head was embedded in the spongy ground under the tires, and its rattle was pointed towards the sky at a 45-degree angle.

"He's dead!"

"You knew this one? Personally?"

"I met him yesterday."

Gazarra grasped for some appropriate words.

"May you suffer no further loss," he told her.

He got back into the truck and moved it forward a foot or two. Then he stepped out of the cab again, carrying a rag. He examined the rattler with a connoisseur's eye.

"Mr. Snake is dead," he admitted, "but we'll bring him back to life for you. He'll be resurrected, as you say. You'll see."

He grabbed the snake's crushed head behind where its ears would be, carefully, in case it was only playing dead and had intentions of turning on him. Gazarra went to the back of the truck and hoisted himself up awkwardly, holding the snake away from his body in one hand. Once inside, he stuffed the dead animal into a jute sack kept for just that purpose.

"He had beautiful skin," Sabbitha said when he returned. "Covered with diamonds all moving in the same direction."

"All creatures, no matter how low, have something to recommend them. And that includes us. Why would the Lord put something on this earth just to spurn it?"

With that elegy, and the snake riding safely in the jute sack in back, they pulled onto the Coastal Highway. The engine heat pouring into the cab made her sleepy. Sabbitha took off her black jacket and folded it into a pillow. That was a much better use for her mourning clothes.

IV

We Buy Snakes!

THE SOUND GAZARRA MADE as he rummaged around in the truckbed behind her head woke up Sabbitha Hunter. They were parked on a wide strip of gravel in front of a long, low building, a shed or a warehouse of some kind. She squinted against the noon light and read a sign roughly jigsawed from sheets of plywood and propped up on the building's roof: WE BUY SNAKES! The letters were cut in the shape of snakes, so you got the message even if you didn't know how to read, which was considerate of Mr. Grady Rainbow, the owner of the business.

Sabbitha stepped out of the cab just in time to see the peddler striding by, holding his road-kill jute sack. Mr. Snake had had time to dehydrate in the back. He made an arrow-straight rigor-mortis line in the bag. She fell in behind Gazarra and the snake.

A woman the likes of Sabbitha Hunter had never been seen in the Doctortown tannery. That much was clear by the way Grady Rainbow, the snake-tanner, looked at her. He was a barrel-chested, ruddy man of forty, with sandy hair and fragile pink skin. Unlike Sabbitha's father, Grady knew enough to stay out of the sun. The lines around his eyes let you know he considered the world an endless source of amusement, and that he didn't mind the occasional joke, even at his own expense. His gut was still solid and kept well in check. He had a healthy measure of pride in his person, a feature that tended to fade fast in the Salvation Coast population when it hit middle age. When it came to talking, Grady loved inquiry and the inconvenient question, but his native good manners kept that quality under control.

A ceiling fan turned to disperse the odor of the tannery. Its breeze toyed with Sabbitha's hair, which she brushed out of her face with loving impatience. Gazarra opened the bag and pulled out the snake, but Mr. Rainbow didn't have eyes for snakes.

Gazarra moved the dead rattler into his field of vision. Even that didn't break the spell.

"Now where'd you make a find like that?" Rainbow asked in a state of wonderment.

In Doctortown, practicing the trade he did, Grady didn't encounter many occasions to have an emotion. Besides, emotions weren't part of the landscape for a man; silence was. Now suddenly he had one, and he didn't know how to hide it.

"I ran over it in Retreat. Got it by the head. Look, the hide's in perfect shape."

"I'm not talking snakes, you fool," the snake-tanner stated the obvious.

"Oh, her! Her I found by the side of the road."

"Jesus! I've got to get out more often."

"When you've been on the road as long as I have, you have a right to hope for this kind of miracle."

"No one has the right to miracles," Mr. Rainbow disputed. "But she does look like an angel!"

He raised his fingertips to his nostrils and sniffed the tannery smell. It was a nervous tic, designed to bring him despair. The smell of snake-leather, he feared, would never attract angels.

"Well, she must be trouble," he concluded darkly, trying to console himself.

"A deep, troubled soul," Gazarra agreed.

"You and your souls!"

Rainbow laughed easily and shook his head. A man laughing trouble away.

"A transparent soul," Gazarra pursued.

"I'm not sure that's such a good thing to have. You can't live in society if you don't cover up some. I'm proof of that. I'm so covered up I've just about lost myself. I don't even know if there's any way out any more."

Sabbitha looked at him with a level gaze.

"There must be," she told him. "You dug yourself in. You must be able to dig yourself out. It makes sense, doesn't it?"

"I never considered it. But I do appreciate your confidence. What I don't know is how you can encourage a man you've only just met."

"See," Gazarra cut in on them, "I told you she has a great soul. She has prescience."

"I suppose if you have to judge someone without the benefit of any experience of them, you might as well judge for the good. Maybe that'll make the world a better place."

"But you can't say you have no experience of me, can you?" Sabbitha asked.

"No," Grady told her. "You're right. I can't say that any more."

She pointed to the rattler in Gazarra's hands. "That's Mr. Snake."

"Indeed, it is."

"She knew this snake," Gazarra let on. "Personally."

"Personally?" Rainbow echoed. "In that case, my sincerest condolences. Tell you what. I'm going to make you something out of his skin, anything leather that your little soul desires. That way your friend will travel with you wherever you may wander."

There was a silence. No one could think of an appropriate snake-leather item for Sabbitha Hunter.

"That's the problem with the woman who has everything," Grady Rainbow said. "Sometimes you don't know what to get her."

"I know what she needs," Gazarra announced suddenly. "A ribbon for her hair."

"A rattlesnake hair ribbon?" Rainbow looked dubious.

"Okay, so 'ribbon' isn't the right word . . . I don't know what you call it. What do I know about women's things?"

"Don't be selling yourself short there, Mr. Gazarra. You consort with women every day, you sly dog."

"A hairband — that's what it is! A hairband to keep her hair from falling in her face."

"I've never made one of those," Rainbow admitted, "and I've made everything out of snakes, from hatbands to condom purses." He turned to Sabbitha. "Begging your pardon, of course, ma'am."

She smiled indulgently.

"You can do it," Gazarra insisted. "You can make anything. You're the best there is."

"I'm the only one there is," Rainbow pointed out. "The last craftsman. Like you."

Gazarra hurried out the door to the truck and jumped into the back. Suddenly he'd become an athlete.

"The gentleman certainly knows what he wants," Rainbow remarked.

Sabbitha had no time to answer. Gazarra was coming back across the gravel parking lot, holding a stack of trays piled high with all the equipment needed for feminine beauty on the Salvation Coast. Hairbands, ribbons, barrettes, all kinds of baubles for keeping your hair in place. Gazarra picked up a wide piece of elastic.

"Here, take this and make one exactly like it. You use the elastic, only you cover it with the snake, understand? The rest of the hide you keep for yourself."

"I've never seen you so enthusiastic, Mr. Gazarra."

"You can't refuse me. You and I have done business for a long time."

"And you knew my father before I did," Rainbow cut in. "I'll say it before you can."

The two men laughed together and put aside the unorthodox nature of Gazarra's request. They bantered about their differences for a time, one being a snake-tanning son of the soil, and the other a wandering Jew, then about how similar they were under the skin, about the stink of the tannery and the loneliness of the road, and how a man was supposed to remain human in those conditions.

Then Mr. Rainbow turned and spoke to Sabbitha in his sweetest voice.

"You're going to be something special with snakeskin running in that pretty yellow hair of yours."

"Why, thank you."

Sabbitha gave him a smile full of promise.

"You're in love, Mr. Rainbow," Gazarra accused him.

"Maybe I am, maybe I'm not. I couldn't rightly say. I've never known anything of the sort, let alone admitted it out loud. But I do know one thing. I'm going to make her the prettiest thing a woman ever put in her hair."

"Don't make it too pretty," Sabbitha advised him, "or you'll just be advertising me to other men."

Mr. Rainbow and Mr. Gazarra laughed uneasily. They weren't used to that kind of wisdom coming from a woman.

But that's exactly what Gazarra intended to do, with all the risks involved. Advertise Sabbitha Hunter. That shouldn't be too difficult, by the looks of things.

Lunch, that day, came courtesy of Mr. Rainbow: a long packet wrapped in wax paper, blooming with grease stains on both sides. Between the tannery and Doctortown proper, Gazarra pulled off the road alongside a creek. By the bridge over the creek, under the willow branches, immobile one-hundred-year-old ladies were busy yanking catfish out of the murky, still water.

He separated the long filets of deep brown meat. They were tangy with hickory smoke.

"Smoked things keep forever," he told Sabbitha. "It's convenient that I like the taste, isn't it, considering I don't have a fridge on board."

He offered her a piece. She gave the meat a long look.

"Go ahead, I know you're hungry. It's not *your* Mr. Snake."

"Snake? You're going to eat snake?"

"Yes," he snapped, "I'm going to eat snake. Just watch."

Gazarra unhinged his jaw as wide as an alligator's and dropped a length of meat onto his tongue.

"There, I've broken a law."

He looked up towards the sky, though he couldn't see past the ceiling of the cab.

"So strike me down," he dared the sky.

The sky declined to do so. Gazarra chewed and swallowed with great satisfaction, having beaten heaven once again.

"One more law defiled. So what? I was born into so many laws I couldn't get up in the morning without first thinking which side of the bed would please the Almighty, and which side would step on His toes. And His toes were everywhere. Like a centipede, He was. A millipede. Everything was a choice. But of course you had no choice — it was all was written down for you ahead of time."

"All that sounds like an old family argument," Sabbitha observed, "that I'm not a part of."

"It is a feud," Gazarra agreed. "Like the Hatfields and the McCoys." He laughed at the comparison. "I remember when I first came to the Coast. I was as green as marsh grass in the spring. I watched people eating pork meat, and I must have had awe in my eyes. Of course I wouldn't do it — my customers didn't want me to. They wanted me to obey all the old laws."

"That was considerate of them."

"You would think so, but they did it for themselves, not for me. They liked thinking they were dealing with someone straight out of the Book."

He patted his jacket pockets.

"I did my routes with nothing but boiled eggs in my pockets — I must have smelled real good! Egg-eater, people called me, because I wouldn't eat anything else. It wasn't an insult — at least I don't think so. It was a description. Then one time I got stuck at a farmer's house. That's all there was for dinner. Pork meat. Maybe they weren't knowledgeable about a Jew, what he was and wasn't supposed to eat, otherwise they wouldn't have let me. They thought a Jew that obeyed all the laws was more biblical or something. And they wanted me to be as biblical as possible."

Gazarra slumped back on the seat with a voluptuous sigh.

"I had some. It was wonderful. So sweet, so fat . . ."

"So forbidden," Sabbitha put in.

"Yes, that, too. After the meal I excused myself and stepped out into the yard. Maybe by then they realized I'd snapped one or another of the many threads of the Covenant. They feared the worst for me, and for themselves, too, because it had happened under their roof. But no, I didn't throw up in the yard or get down on my knees to bawl for forgiveness, the way every other Jew peddler who ever ate pork meat in this country did. No, I stood on my two feet, and I told the Lord in no uncertain terms that if He'd wanted me to obey the spirit *and* the letter of every one of His laws, then He shouldn't have cast me into this strange land in the first place. Because once you break the first law, all the rest are free to come tumbling down like cards. And there are so many. It's a life's work."

"And when they all fall down," Sabbitha asked, "when they're all lying flat? Then what?"

"That never happens," the peddler grumbled. "There are too many of them. And we're not that strong."

Sabbitha laughed. "I am. I bet I'm a better law-breaker than you are. It comes natural to me. You have to think about 'why' all the time. I don't."

It was a cosmic kind of dare. Neither knew exactly what they were getting into. Meanwhile, the Lord of peddlers rode above them in His own battered pick-up truck, laughing under His breath, rubbing His hands in anticipation of the fun. He liked a challenge, too.

The snake meat went back into its packet strapped to the backside of the sun visor. It hadn't tasted as good as Gazarra had hoped. He'd made the mistake of remembering why the law against eating scavengers had been devised in the first place. It was because of what they ate: anything and everything. Rats, field mice, gophers, shrews. He sucked his teeth and argued with the meat stuck between his incisors all the way towards Doctortown.

No wonder the peddler loved selling. It got his mind off all the old family feuds.

With his elbow leaning on the horn, Gazarra pulled up in front of a wood-frame house on a clay road on the outskirts of Doctortown.

"Now, finally, we can work," he grumbled.

Then he turned and surprised Sabbitha with a predatory wink.

All feuds came to an abrupt halt when the peddler went into

action. He achieved transcendance through the grace of his shtick. "Hello, ladies!" he would call out the open window of the truck, since he knew that the chances of a man being in any of the houses were almost nil. "Peddlerman again! Peddlerman always comes back!" Then he would kill the engine in anticipation of a lengthy stay on the front porch or in the kitchen.

Every sinew and wire in his body was tuned to the campaign. The pain drained out of his knees and his fingers straightened. Selling was a state of grace for him. A performance. He was every-where at once; best of all, he was outside himself. Demonstrating, proving, lowering prices to cost, below cost, just for the pleasure of a sale. Money was truly no object. Victory over rejection was what was at stake.

When he called for the ladies with his horn and his nasal, accented English, they ambled out of their houses and onto their porches, arms crossed over their breasts against the biting north-west wind of early spring. Some had run to fat: they could scarcely transport the massive mounds of their own flesh from place to place. Others were bitten down to the quick, all skin and bones and resentment, scarecrows escaped from a field of stubble. Some were young and some were old, though not many years separated the two. Young could turn into old overnight. Whatever their age, they all looked abused by fate. Drawn, worried, lined, born with suspicious hearts. As girls, they'd been taught to get ready for the worst, and their expectations had been more than met.

But they were always happy to see the peddler. Not that they'd ever show it, for fear his prices would rise, which they never did. He asked each of them about her troubles, and they obliged by telling Gazarra every last one of them. There were lumps in their breasts, kicks in their wombs, dark circles from insomnia and over-work and black eyes from when they'd walked into a door getting up in the middle of the night to spend a penny, even if they never slept a wink because of worry. They told Gazarra things they couldn't have told their own mothers, and certainly not their husbands.

To Gazarra a woman could tell her troubles. No one ever asked after his own. What he'd told Sabbitha was true: he didn't exist. He was the Peddler. He kept his troubles to himself. That was part of the bargain.

After confession came business. Softened with trust, the women wanted a memento to preserve the moment, and besides, everything Gazarra had to sell was so wonderfully useful.

Handkerchiefs draped over the backs of chairs. Bolts of fabrics displayed over porch rails. Ribbons streaming between his fingers in the wind like flags. Hats with flowers on top that were better than anything nature could have grown. If a woman hesitated over a hat, Gazarra would model it himself, and she would laugh with delight, then snap it up.

He would do the tailor's job, taking women's measurements to sell them cloth for a dress. Left sleeve, right sleeve, bodice. Once more just to be sure. Hips and waist. He would treat himself to a quick helping of their smells. Sometimes he'd recognize a perfume he'd sold them the previous month: cheap, cutting and floral. Other times the smell of cooking would make his stomach growl. Real food on a real stove, not smoked mullet or snake wrapped in wax paper and stored above the visor. More often than not, though, the women's odor was astringent. Scrubbed and chlorinated. To smell clean, or to smell of nothing at all, was a distinction on the Coast. It raised a person out of the muck.

He finished the measurements and wrapped the tape around his wrist.

"Assistant!" he cried.

No one understood. Since when did the peddler need an assistant? Since when could he afford one?

Then from inside the truckbed, Sabbitha Hunter drew back the canvas flap and appeared like a mechanical god, holding a bolt of cloth.

"And with that, a Number 2 awl!"

Sabbitha disappeared into the truck to do his bidding.

Up and down the road that afternoon, the women were astonished by the peddler's good fortune.

"Now that's a pretty little thing," they said slyly. "Where in creation did you find her?"

"She found me," Gazarra replied. "She was sent to me."

The women laughed to hear this wiry old man sounding like a moonstruck boy. It did their hearts good.

Those kind of women were the more generous sort. There were a few of them along the road that day. But most of Gazarra's customers narrowed their eyes when Sabbitha Hunter appeared.

"Admit it, it don't make no sense," they challenged the peddler.

Gazarra had to agree. But sense or not, it was true, and that's what mattered.

He told them so.

"I found her. Finders keepers," he said with crude gallantry.

"The world's not going to let you keep her," they warned him.

"The world?" he wondered out loud. "The world doesn't know I exist. If it does, it had better send word quick."

That stymied the doubting women for a second or two.

"She's not going to stay with you very long," they declared.

"She'll stay as long as she needs to," Gazarra said with supreme indifference, all of which was feigned. "Every minute she's with me is a blessing."

He displayed his stiff, knobby fingers. The women giggled maliciously.

"I bet that ain't the only thing that's stiff about the old man!"

They fell to elbowing each other viciously in the ribs.

"You're just jealous," Gazarra told them, to more peals of salty laughter.

Sabbitha listened to the conversations from inside the truck as she searched for a Number 2 awl. She wondered about this tendency people had to talk about her as if she wasn't there. Grady Rainbow and the peddler had done it. They'd discussed her nature as if she were an exotic butterfly pinned to a piece of miserable corkboard. The Doctortown women predicted happiness or heartbreak for the peddler because of her, as if she were snake eyes on a pair of dice or the jack of diamonds in a deck of cards, and not a woman like they were. Not one of them was interested in why she was riding around in the back of this truck.

What did it take, she wondered, to get a person to address you directly, and care a little bit in the process? Maybe you had to slap them real hard in the face to get their attention.

Meanwhile, she couldn't find the Number 2 awl. She didn't know what an awl was. An owl? An all? The way the peddler talked, you couldn't tell what he meant. Sabbitha hadn't even heard of the country he claimed he was born in.

Gazarra's voice came through the canvas flap. "At the back, to the right. The bottom drawer in the metal chest!"

Sure enough, there were things in a drawer that could have been awls. A kind of puncturing tool, it turned out, and fairly dangerous looking. The Number 2s, conveniently enough, all had the number 2 carved into their wooden handles.

"And with it the candies!" the peddler ordered from outside.

Sabbitha rounded up a scoopful of hard fruit candies, Gazarra's present to the children who hung around the truck, whether or not their mothers bought anything. The candies didn't look half bad in their dusting of confectioner's sugar. She fit as many as she could into her mouth and sucked off the sugar.

The routine was the same all through Doctortown that day.

Gazarra listening, sympathizing, offering advice for problems that rightly needed a social worker or the sheriff and his deputies to solve. Gazarra cajoling and coaxing the women, and the women putting off the moment of surrender. There was so little sweetness in their lives, and they wanted to draw out the moment for as long as possible. So did he, for that matter.

Then came the surprise.

Sabbitha Hunter would appear from behind the canvas flap of the truckbed, all clad in black, her skin pale and glowing, her blond hair uselessly and beautifully long, her eyes hooded under their heavy lids, two pools of blue secrets, with the natural distinction a proper Ebenezer lady could display when the occasion demanded it. Or even when it didn't.

In those poor settlements, Sabbitha played up her appearance for all it was worth. It was like some new race of human being had arrived on the Coast. She was discovering a talent for drama she never knew she had.

What are you doing, out on the road like that?

Funny how no one thought to ask her.

Fooling the Creator

GAZARRA WAS FEELING as hollow as an old gourd by the time he finished his rounds. Charming and cajoling the ladies for a profit measured in small change had exhausted him. Constant performance has a way of breeding self-contempt in the performer. He sat slumped over the steering wheel like a murder victim, the nose of the old truck pointed away from town and towards the coast, on a track out of sight of the last Doctortown house. Far enough down the road so the villagers couldn't see that he bled like any other man.

"Every word I spoke was a lie," Gazarra said. "I feel like a whore at sun-up on a Sunday. But with words instead."

"Whores get paid better, I suspect," Sabbitha observed.

"I wouldn't know . . . And it's not over yet. That's the worst part. I have another duty. A pastoral duty."

"Peddling and preaching?" Sabbitha inquired. "Not a very original combination."

Gazarra glared at her. He was too fatigued to reply.

There was a church of no particular denomination in a community on the other side of Doctortown, he told her, where people loved hearing the old stories, the way they do everywhere. Unfortunately, these people didn't know how to read. They knew how to worship, but not read. Worship was in the blood. Reading had to be learned.

Illiteracy had become a tradition among the congregation. Normally, the ignorant are ashamed of not knowing how to read. The man who can't make out the menu at a roadside restaurant will claim it's because he forgot his glasses. Not these people. They cultivated their ignorance as a new and advanced form of spiritual purity. Not reading put them at a noble remove from the world. Instead of wasting their days paging through the sports section or reading up on some foreign act of butchery, their thoughts were free to wander into higher realms.

That was your typical Salvation Coast strategy. You took the raw deal life had given you and transformed it into dogma.

The members of the congregation did all right in the world. They weren't cast-offs or dregs, or useless people. The church deacon was the postmaster of the community, and he delivered the mail decently enough. He could read numbers and addresses and he knew his people. He knew who was likely to get a letter, and from where. But Scripture was over his head.

"They made it difficult on purpose," the deacon liked to say. "It's too rich for my blood."

Gazarra raised his head from the steering wheel and propped his chin on the back of his hands. He looked a thousand years old, as old as hope and just as futile. Sabbitha sat at his right hand. The hamper of food he'd bartered for during the day rode between them.

"You helped me today," he told her.

"I didn't do anything. I just appeared. Like a ghost in a ghost story. I appeared and let people talk about me."

"My knees tell me you helped."

They sat in silence for a while. Gazarra opened the hamper but did not eat. Sabbitha spotted the top of a whisky bottle standing straight and true.

"The church," he explained. "Advance payment for my sermon this evening."

He pulled the cork, sniffed and tasted it.

"It had better be a good sermon, too."

"They pay their men of God in hooch?"

Gazarra smiled sadly. "They know I won't overindulge and miss the service. Not like some would."

He took a second careful pull from the bottle and jammed the cork back into the neck. Then thought twice about it. Was it or was it not the gentlemanly thing to do to offer Sabbitha Hunter a drink of whisky, and from the same bottle he'd just placed his lips on? He fidgeted with the bottle neck. The left side of his mouth said yes, the right no. He ended up doing nothing.

"About this church," Sabbitha said. "It wouldn't be a Jewish one, would it?"

"Does it matter?"

"I thought you people don't believe in what they say about Jesus."

"We don't. But I'm willing to help out those who do."

"And that's not against your principles?"

Gazarra laughed. "I suppose it's a little unusual, if you think about it, a Jew preaching to Christians. But I don't think about it. It doesn't matter to them any more than it does to me. It all comes from the same place."

"You look too tired to preach," Sabbitha observed. "You look too tired to attend, let alone lead."

"You don't know me. I'm like this old truck. Once I get going, I pick up speed and forget what tired means. Anyway, I do the old stories. Those I can do in my sleep."

"You *do* them?"

"Interpret them," he corrected himself wearily. "I don't preach. I interpret."

"That's what all preaching is. I mean, except for the kind where you've got a guy up on the hood of a car, telling people how they're going to go to hell. Those people are scolders. I don't listen to scolding. I've heard enough of it to last me the rest of my life."

"If you don't want to hear the buzzing of the scolders in your ears," Gazarra told her, "you have to get high enough so their voices won't reach you."

"I see," Sabbitha said. "Have you reached that lofty position by being a peddler?"

"Of course not! Being a peddler is a disguise."

She reached across the seat and untenderly fingered his clay-colored jacket, held together by road grit and habit.

"Well, it's the perfect disguise. You could have fooled me."

Gazarra muttered something to himself. A foreign curse, maybe. Sabbitha didn't catch the words. Now I've gone and bruised the old man's pride, she thought, falsely contrite. She attempted an attitude of penance and looked away, out the window, at the Salvation Coast landscape. The scrub was busy strangling itself. Under the metallic blue sky that had lost most of its light, the dull orange road really did seem to lead nowhere.

"When you look at it," Gazarra told her a minute later, "you just see wilderness."

"That sounds like an accusation. What am I supposed to see? Castles in Spain?"

"It does look empty, I admit. It is, for the time being. The wilderness is in waiting."

"Really, Mr. Peddler, is that so? What's it waiting for?"

He didn't answer. It was too soon. There was a rhythm to this kind of thing. All selling has rhythm.

He reached across and brushed a few unruly strands of hair out of her face, as gently as he knew how. His smile was boyish and eager.

He began to sing tunelessly:

"It ain't no sin
To take off your skin
And dance around in your bones."

That was exactly what he felt like doing. Things were going according to plan.

"Mr. Gazarra, our well known Hebrew peddler, is going to speak to us tonight in the language God Himself speaks. He will answer all questions you might wish to put to him about God's holy word in the original tongue. He will do his best to settle all disputes, keeping in mind the impenetrable mystery of it all."

For a man who could barely read, the deacon of the Doctortown congregation of illuminated illiterates could sure talk. One quality generally complemented the other.

The congregation broke off discussing bad soil and worse worms and whatever else was afflicting them. Silence filled the building, which was round so as to give the Devil no corners to hide in. Fluorescent tubes buzzed and rattled profanely from the ceiling fixtures. The only decoration was the paint on the walls and the strip of chest-high wainscoting.

Gazarra obliged the deacon, a tall man whose narrow body floated inside a pair of wide overalls handed down by an obese father.

"*Baruck atoh adonoi eloheinu melech,*" Gazarra told the hall, "*ho'olom shehecheyonu vekiyimonu vehigionu lizman hazeh.*"

If absolutely necessary, you could sing the Lord's praises in a strange land, the peddler had discovered over the years. But when you did, you sounded terribly out of place.

The congregation didn't mind. They had fallen into a rapid state of rapture. By the peddler's side, the deacon closed his eyes and smiled. No one in the building needed to know what Gazarra's prayer meant. He could have been calling upon the encouragement of all the hairy devils in hell, and that would have been fine by them.

Just to be able to say "Have a nice day" in God's tongue was a miracle. The sound was pure music, unfettered by words. It reached all the way to heaven. Nathan Gazarra was a character out of the Book, and the Book itself. He had the dead language of the Lord in his mouth, and no one else on the Coast could boast of that. It gave him all kinds of authority.

Gazarra gazed down from the raised platform. He rocked slowly back and forth, as if he were standing on the edge of an abyss. The front rows of the congregation, he saw, were peopled by ghosts. That didn't surprise him. They sat on the rock-hard wooden pews but did not complain. He recognized the elders from his Belorussian village that had since been planed to the ground, the ones to whom a wondering boy would not have dared address any impertinent questions. He saw the members of the old army of peddlers who'd let on, by a bass stream one day, that there was no sense worrying his mind about unanswerable questions as long as the fish were biting.

Sabbitha Hunter sat in their midst. He knew the ghosts would disapprove of what he was about to say, but that didn't matter. It only mattered what she thought. His ghosts were too careful and conservative anyway; they'd been happy just to survive. They didn't have his need, his impatience at the world's slowness, and they'd never had the luck of meeting Sabbitha.

"There was a man born to serve his brother," Gazarra said in Hebrew, "but who believed that the older should serve the younger, not the other way around. These two were two manner of people, two nations."

He said the same thing to the congregation in their language. Compared to the Hebrew that sprung intact from his memory, English was a rusty tool in his hands.

"This man wanted to be on top. He was meant to be on top, that's what he thought. But the traditions of the family and the old ways stood between him and his goal."

The congregation nodded. This was going to be a tale of family envy and jealousy, maybe even incest. Everybody had some experience with that.

"What this man didn't know was that he was God's experiment. It was a test. The kind of test the Lord will send you if He thinks you're worthy."

The audience knew that tradition, too. It was the ancient argument their own church used to get them to accept their suffering, so much of it useless and random, and often self-inflicted.

"To get on top, this man set out to gather up all the blessings. He started with his father. That was the first approval he wanted because his father preferred his older brother to him, for no other reason than he was older. It so happened that his father was blind. This man knew exactly what to do. He fashioned a disguise and tricked his father into believing he was the older brother. It worked! But he had cheated his father, and aren't we supposed to honor our parents?"

The congregation didn't commit itself. They weren't taking sides yet. It was too early in the story to get to the moral. Besides, everyone on the Coast knew that the peddler's stories could wind around themselves like a cottonmouth on a tree branch.

"This man went out into the fields. Was he ashamed, or was he proud of himself? We don't know. We don't know what he felt — we only know what he did. He went out into the wilderness, just like the one on the other side of these walls. There the Lord threw him on the ground and made the stones of the field soft as feather pillows for him. The Lord does that when He wants you to have a dream. It's a sign He loves you when He burdens you with His dreams. It's not a happy situation to be loved that way. It's like a doctor putting you to sleep to cut something out of you. A sick piece of your body that wants to kill you. Only it's the other way around. The Almighty does that to put something of Himself into you."

A few women in the congregation lifted their shoulders ever so slightly, then let them slowly relax. It was such a subtle movement that even their sisters who were doing the exact same thing next to them couldn't have felt it. Wouldn't that be the perfect excuse for having strayed? *I was thrown to the ground and inhabited.* Some of the women made a mental note to try it, then changed their minds. It would never work down here, in this world.

"This man woke up to see an angel at his feet," Gazarra went on. "He grabbed on to that angel and demanded, Give me your blessings! The angel didn't have the authority to hand out blessings. He was only the messenger, but this man wouldn't let go. The two fell to fighting. They fought all night long like two rabid dogs with their tails tied together. All the angel wanted was to get free and go back up to paradise where this kind of thing never happened. No other man could have wrestled a spirit to the ground. His hand would have passed right through it, like he was wrestling the wind. But by the time morning came, that's exactly what this man had done. The angel of light had to give him his blessing and hurry back up before it was too late, before he got trapped down on this earth.

"This man had gotten the blessing of his earthly father and of the Lord's representative. Was it through good works and repentance?"

The congregation couldn't believe the peddler was heading in that direction. They hoped a parable or a paradox or something complicated like that would save the day.

"He did it through trickery and combat!" Gazarra shouted at them, spittle bursting from his mouth. "Strange works and rule-breaking and transgression. And we're still talking about this man and his victory today!"

The good people of Doctortown turned and twisted on the edge of their pews. Sabbitha Hunter looked across the hall, into Gazarra's face.

You're out of your mind, she said to him silently. I know that story, and you sure as hell bent it out of shape. That's not interpreting, that's hijacking. You just committed grand theft.

"I didn't know that kind of stuff was in the Good Book," the deacon admitted.

He shifted his body around inside his baggy coveralls, as if he were trying to get comfortable with his skin. Then he took a sagging paper plate of chicken and gravy from his wife and handed it to Gazarra. The peddler passed it on to Sabbitha.

"It's an interpretation," he told the deacon.

"Sure it is," said the deacon's wife, who had authored the chicken. Lines of work and worry that ran from the top of her nose to her hairline gave her a severe look, but her voice was soft and playful. "But it seems to me your ways of interpreting have changed lately. Am I right? Do I detect a note of desperation?"

"That man talking up there on the platform, just a minute ago, he wasn't the meek and selfless peddler we know," the deacon added.

"Now we're wondering just how well we do know you!" a woman from the congregation spoke up.

Sabbitha recognized her from their rounds this morning. All the women Gazarra had sold to had come to the hall with their men. Sabbitha wondered which one had cracked whose ribs. Who'd chipped whose teeth, and who'd planted which wayward seed in whose womb. They all looked like they could have done it, given the opportunity.

"I myself wonder," said the deacon, "what would happen if people around here were to take your story to heart. I mean, if they actually took to living that way."

"It would be a different world," Gazarra admitted.

"I like it. That's the kind of world I could pray for!" one of the Doctortown men piped up.

"You don't know how to pray," his wife told him. She was the one who'd walked into the door on her way to the bathroom in the dark of night. "So don't start getting excited. You'd pray for any world as long as there was something in it for men."

"I don't know why it'd be just for men. I mean, who says?" another of Gazarra's lady customers wondered out loud. She'd bought the hat this morning, and her flanks had smelled like bread.

"Don't go getting naive on me!" the black-eyed woman told her neighbor. "Don't you know anything about history?"

"History?"

"The history of men and women!" she practically shouted.

Her husband put his hands in the air to indicate innocence. He wasn't convincing, not with his weak mouth, unlaced shoes and the slippery look in his eyes.

"Hey, I didn't invent the system," he claimed.

"Discussing your personal problems in congregation is unseemly," the deacon reminded them, putting a temporary stop to the marital recrimination. "I'm interested in Mr. Gazarra telling us what the world would be like if blessings flowed from law-breaking."

"So am I," the delinquent husband chimed in.

The congregation's eyes told him to quiet down.

"The prospect," said Sabbitha, "is enticing. Please elaborate, Pastor."

Her voice was slow, cool, poised and elegant, and it cut right through the banter. Everyone turned to look at her.

"It would be a terrible challenge," Gazarra warned those who were still paying attention to him.

But no one was. They were all bewitched by Sabbitha. It turned out that this mechanical god who rode around in the peddler's truck could speak with the intensity of an oracle. And like an oracle, no one could quite be sure what she meant. That's where her power lay.

There was a gravy spot on her upper lip. Gazarra dabbed it off with his handkerchief. It was a caress, not a correction.

"But what would it mean concretely?" the deacon insisted, twisting his hands in his pockets. "That's what I want to know. It's easy to preach something if you know it's never going to come to pass in your lifetime. The end-of-the-world people are always doing that. The world ain't ended yet."

"I'm not talking just to hear the sound of my voice," Gazarra told him.

An uncompanionable silence followed that promise. The deacon's wife broke it by excusing herself for having run out of chicken and gravy. The paper plates wouldn't have handled any more abuse anyway. As the delinquent husbands and plaintive wives of the congregation drifted away and headed home for their nightly battles, the deacon and his wife and Gazarra and Sabbitha Hunter stepped out onto the concrete-block steps in front of the hall.

"It would be an honor for us if you spent the night here," the deacon told Gazarra.

"You know me," the peddler answered. "I cover tomorrow's

distance tonight. But I'll be back. We have all the time in the world to solve the unsolvable."

They shook hands by the pick-up truck. The engine fired up right away, but the headlights didn't come on until Gazarra and Sabbitha had been rolling down the dark road for an anxious half-minute.

The deacon stood on the sidewalk in front of his building in a state of spiritual confusion, watching the truck lights grow fainter.

"I only wish I could read that story for myself," he told his wife. "Then I'd know for sure if what he says is true."

She slipped her arm into his, then lifted his hand out of his overall pocket and took it in hers.

"I like you the way you are," she told him. "Don't ever change."

The road went from tar to hard-packed sand without warning. Gazarra took his foot off the gas. His lights caught a deer nibbling a mushroom at the edge of the trees. The animal looked up, froze, then peeled away into the woods at the last second. The hollows filled with cold, saline mist straggling along the damp ditches that bordered the road, water calling to other water.

Gazarra stopped the truck and rolled down his window at a spot that looked no different from anywhere else. Cool, salty air flooded into the cab.

"There's a nice grove of trees here, if I remember right. They make a windbreak. That keeps the canvas from flapping in the wind all night."

"There's nothing out there," Sabbitha said. "What are we doing here?"

Gazarra cut the lights. Night rose up, opaque at eye-level where the mist blew in, glittering and transparent straight above their heads, where stars glowed in the clear air.

"Welcome to the bluff."

"Blindman's bluff?"

It turned out Gazarra didn't know the game.

"There's no town here," she deduced. "Not even a wrecked cabin. This is worse than last night. I didn't know I was signing up for this kind of madness."

"You'll see, it'll be better than last night. There are no signs of man and his need to ruin things."

Sabbitha got out of the truck and wandered along a high rump of land anchored in place by the roots of oak and pine trees. She rubbed her shoulders against the chill. A wide, currentless river flowed ten or twenty feet below in the darkness. A river with no other side: it merged into the marshland where tall grasses waved and chattered in the wind.

She turned to Gazarra.

"You sure know how to pick your spots. This is the weirdest place I've ever been. Especially in the middle of the night."

"It is the Lord's creation," he assured her.

"That's what everyone says when they've messed up, like you have here — they blame the Lord. He's the all-purpose excuse, and if you ask me, it's the tiredest one going. So now what? Is God going to jump out from behind a tree and throw me on the ground, and inflict me with a vision like in one of your stories?"

"I'm sure you're worthy," he told her.

"I don't know if I'd like it. It sounds like rape to me. Out here in the wilds, it must hurt worse."

Gazarra didn't care for the word. The Lord was no rapist, and neither was he. Last night in the cabin in Retreat should have proved that much. But if you looked at life the way some women did, and considered that any of the million things you have to do every day against your will is the equivalent of rape, yes, then that's what a dream or a vision was: rape. That's what life was. One long, endless rape.

"But really it has nothing to do with being worthy," Gazarra pursued. "You become worthy when it happens to you. Not before. Before, you don't even know who you are."

"It? What's *it*? There are too many 'its' in your conversation for my taste, Mr. Peddler."

"It's my English," he said weakly.

Sabbitha stopped pacing.

"Don't blame your English," she told him. "That excuse won't work with me. Your English has nothing to do with this."

She went to the edge of the bluff. The wind rose and fell and rocked the branches above her head. From below, along the river, the marsh grass whispered to her in the malicious voice of Ebenezer, with a sound like knives being sharpened. She pictured her home town again, her street, her house among the other houses with drawn blinds, the pairs of eyes behind each blind, watching her, judging her for her incapacity to feel what she ought to have felt, the conventional emotions. When people judge you for being a monster, there's only one thing to do: exceed their expectations.

Gazarra touched her on the shoulder. She jumped. Then she let him lead her to the truck.

He threw open the back flap.

"This is our cabin for the night. As you saw, there are two pallets. Two sets of blankets. Two everything. So we will have . . ."

Gazarra couldn't locate the word. It wasn't "privacy," because there was certainly none of that on the road. "Intimacy" seemed to suggest something else. He settled for "decency," even if it sounded ugly.

"Propriety," Sabbitha told him. "That's what you want to say."

"Maybe I do," he admitted.

She climbed into the truck and he lashed the canvas shut behind them.

"What's it like having so many things to say, and not being able to say them?"

He smiled "You're the only person who ever cared to ask that question. Now you know why I do the pastor's job. These interpretations. They're my way of speaking. Thanks to them, I can live in a foreign language."

"A lot of people have your problem, even people born here. The secret is to stay away from the big words, and not try to say too much."

"Yes. Of course. I considered that. But sometimes you can't help it."

A blanket made of animal skins lay across both pallets. Squirrel, Sabbitha judged, by how many had been sewn together to make the cover. In the light of the lantern, she sat on the edge of the bunk, took off her jacket and unbound her hair. Then she stopped.

"Is this within the bounds of propriety?" she wondered.

"It is within the bounds of intimacy."

She laughed. "Your English is a lot better than you like to let on, you dog. You just enjoy tricking people. Well, why not if you can get away with it?"

Outside, the nocturnals called from tree to tree. The canvas roof pulled as taut as a sail in the gusts of wind. The pots and pans sang together like chimes from their ropes on the frame outside.

Gazarra came and lay down near her, on his pallet.

"And there really are two bunks," Sabbitha said.

"I don't trick women. If I was going to do that, I would have last night."

"Am I supposed to thank you for that?"

"No."

She patted her bunk. "Were there a lot of assistants before me?"

Gazarra laughed. "Do you see a woman living this life?"

"What am I, then?"

"Different."

"Different? Is that a polite way of saying something else?"

"If you weren't different, you would have stayed in your home town, wherever that is."

"It isn't anywhere. So don't ask."

"I promise I won't."

The lantern burned low and yellow. Outside, the pine trees whistled and moaned. Gazarra had spent a thousand nights like this one, on his own, listening to the wind blowing up and lying down again. He never thought it would be possible to share something so monstrously lonely.

Sabbitha raised herself on one elbow.

"Well, peddler priest, don't you think it's time for you to tell me about my soul? You've told everybody else. All those perfect strangers. I feel downright naked. So don't I have a right to hear about it, too? Everybody likes to hear about themselves. It's a natural form of vanity."

"I refuse to live in an age of no miracles," he announced.

"That's splendid. That's very nice. Poetic and all. But I don't know what that has to do with me. Everyone who believes in miracles knows they come down from above. Are you going to take over from the Man Upstairs?"

"We can bring about a time when miracles will happen."

"Oh, I get it," Sabbitha teased him. "'Repent, repent, for your time is at hand!' Frankly, Mr. Gazarra, I'm a little surprised at you. I'd never have taken you for one of those scolders, especially not after what I heard tonight. You had those people scared!"

"I'm not a scolder. And I'm not asking you to repent."

"Then what are you asking from me — I mean, besides the usual?"

"You're my miracle, Sabbitha."

"I was somebody's miracle before," she said somberly. "It didn't work out."

"You were?"

"Mind you, I haven't been anybody's since then."

"What happened? Whose were you?"

"Uncle Tommy wanted me to go walking with him to the edge of the field, where the land dips down towards the river, and where you can't see any houses, and where no houses can see you. I didn't say yes, but I didn't say no. I went with him — I guess that's what counts. Just when we got to where the land slopes out of sight, he took my hand and raised it as far as it would go, towards the sky, further than it should have gone, because he hurt my shoulder. Then he hollered, 'Sabbitha, you're my miracle!'"

She stared glumly at the lantern for a minute.

"Everybody wants to be somebody's miracle. But somehow I don't think that's what you have in mind."

"No," he admitted.

"Well, in my home town, they said I was a self-indulgent monster, uncapable of daughterly feeling. They said I was a prisoner of my moods. All right, I had moods, I confess. Still have them, too, as a matter of fact. Proud of them, even. But I never had illusions about the outside world. You've been selling on the road too long, Mr. Peddler. You know those puddles of water you see on the blacktop on a hot summer's day? You're actually starting to believe they're the ocean."

Gazarra let her talk. Of course she'd resist. Who wouldn't? He would have, too.

"Anyway," she reasoned, "why me?"

That was Sabbitha Hunter's fatal mistake. With that one question, she was all but begging to be convinced. She was like everybody else. She wanted to see the impossible become plausible, then downright necessary, and she wanted to be there when it happened.

"It has to be a woman this time. Every other time it was a man. All those men failed."

"Hold on," she said with a laugh. "You mean this happened before? And here I thought I was so original! Where did it happen? How many times? How come I didn't hear anything about it?"

Gazarra motioned off into the distance. "It was a long time ago, in other places. It wasn't a miracle. It was a fraud."

"Don't keep me in the dark."

"I won't tell you. Why should we be weighed down by other people's failures?"

"If nobody else could do it — whatever *it* is — what makes you think I'll be able to?"

"Because it's so completely unlikely!"

"I see," she said. "I guess it's pretty hard to argue against that logic."

Gazarra didn't hear the disappointment in her voice. She'd had her heart set on some more tangible, personal proof.

"I want to kiss the new Messiah," he told her.

"You already have, remember?"

"I want to kiss her on the mouth this time."

He smelled of cinnamon and nutmeg, Sabbitha discovered, underneath the layer of road dust.

"You want the Messiah, if I understand what you're getting at. You and everybody else. Well, you should be it. You believe harder than anyone I've ever met."

"It can't be me, because it's you. There's only room for one. I don't have the vocation for it. You do. I'm just a luster after the event."

"You've got a lot of company," she told him.

"No," Gazarra said forcefully. "There is no Messiah like this one. This one is . . . outside tradition."

"Well, I am outside tradition, you got that much right." Sabbitha considered the proposition and laughed. "So I'm the new Messiah. Your own personal miracle. The Messiah of Doctortown — what a distinction!"

"We have to start where we are. Where else?"

"I suppose so . . . But let me get this straight: what do I get to *do?*"

"What is necessary."

"There's a whole hell of a lot of that!"

"So you understand," he said.

"I get to rule, I get to trample out the vintage where the grapes of wrath are stored."

"Not just that."

"I get to be your miracle — a peddler's miracle."

"A peddler is only a disguise."

"Yes, you did mention that. Well, Mr. Peddler, if you believe in me, then you're crazy. And I'm crazy to let you do it."

"Crazy, yes. That argument has always been made. By small minds, in order to refute."

The whole thing is crazy, Sabbitha thought. But irresistible. At least for the time being. And so what if it's play-acting? I've been acting all my life. The first time I was someone's miracle, I got tricked. Say it: *screwed.* That's because I depended on someone. And not just *someone*: a man. This time, miracle number two, I'm going to do it on my own. I'm going to have a little fun.

"What exactly does this job entail?"

"No one's ever been this thing before," he said.

"You're not being very fair. Here I am, ready and willing to play the game, and you're not helping one bit. You told me there were plenty of people who tried it."

Gazarra turned to her. He began easing her black dress off her shoulder and kissing the little hollow that her collarbone made. He was like a thirsty man drinking from a spring, but a careful thirsty man, which is a rarity. He wasn't careless, he didn't spill a drop.

"They were all failures," he said into her hair. "But no one has ever succeeded."

"What if I turn out to be a fraud, too? What if I'm a failure? What's to keep me from turning out like the rest of them?"

"Your works."

"My works? What works? You mean I have to do something?"

He rolled the rounded edges of her collarbone between his lips. No one had ever done that to her, not even Uncle Tommy, who claimed he'd done everything there was to do. There must have been a secret passageway between that part of her body and the other part men usually went for, because by the time Gazarra moved on to her other collarbone, she'd made up her mind to be his miracle, at least for tonight.

"Your strange works," he told her. "Your strange works will set you apart."

"Well, so far, so good."

And Sabbitha threw back her head and laughed.

VI

The Enemy from Within

*T*HAT NIGHT, Gazarra the peddler devoured Sabbitha Hunter wholly and completely, without spilling a drop or wasting a crumb. He did it in orderly fashion. Sabbitha couldn't have said, "He neglected the crook of my left knee. The third toe of my right foot was not attended to." Gazarra's age gave him an unhurried kind of method.

Before long, she forgot his age, and so did he. His fingers straightened as the night went on. His knees didn't protest when he got down to kneel. "The miracle of love," he explained when she asked him how his infirmities could have disappeared so quickly.

The peddler had nature on his side, too. Through the night, the wind rose and fell, carrying the smell of salt and tidal mud and the chatter and gossip of the marsh grass. The wind rocked the slash pines and howled in their branches like prayers in an asylum. Wildcats fought over their prey so close to the truck Sabbitha would have sworn they were right underneath it. But it was warm under the truckbed's canvas top, and secure, too, with Gazarra's peace-making shotgun loaded and in easy reach on hooks behind the bunk.

As the lantern burned to a dim glow, the peddler's merchandise faded into the background. He wasn't a peddler any more at all. He became the man who wanted the Messiah so badly he went and invented her.

Take that, world, the peddler was saying. If you don't co-operate, I'll remake you!

Had he persuaded Sabbitha Hunter to be his Messiah? No. She didn't believe. But more important, she didn't disbelieve either.

Through the night, she would open her eyes, awakened by the strangeness of the place and the sounds of the wind and the peddler's weight on top of her, then next to her. She discovered that somehow he was still inside her. How could that be? She'd never spent a whole night with a man before. Maybe they all did it this way. If a man had no reason to draw out and leave her, why would he? Why had Uncle Tommy always come out of her as soon as he could, and gotten back into his trousers?

Then the rocking of the sea and the hissing of the marsh grass lulled her, and the wind in the pines hooted at her, and she wondered whether she wasn't making this whole thing up. How could she be lying naked under a squirrel-fur cover in the back of a gypsy pick-up truck with a man who could have been three times her age, and a foreigner, too?

Then he began to make love to her again, slowly and hypnotically like the tide, like the wind, and at first she did not understand what was happening to her. She had no words for it, so no defence against it. It was the discovery of her body's own pleasure.

When it happened, she didn't feel sentimental or consumed, the way she had the first times she'd been with Uncle Tommy. My body's doing this, it has nothing to do with him, or even me, she thought. Funny how having pleasure with a man takes you away from him. Is it right to feel that way?

When the sun came pooling up over the marsh, it occurred to her that he might never come out of her. For a moment she was alarmed. What if he'd changed her somehow during the night, while she slept with him inside her? How could she tell if he had? How could she even ask the question? You couldn't expect a straight answer from a Bible-twisting man like Gazarra. "It is the way of a man with a maid," he'd probably tell her, or some other phrase he'd stolen out of the Good Book and warped all out of shape.

So what if I am changed? she decided. Was that thing I was before, back in Ebenezer, so precious? Of course not! Otherwise I wouldn't be here in the first place.

When the sun hit the canvas roof of the truckbed, Gazarra stepped out to take a piss. She watched him return to the truck, naked, his skin like old parchment, his chest hair gray and tangled with sweat and his schmuck still standing up, leading the way.

"What's it like to go to bed with the Messiah?" she asked.

"There are no words for it."

"Come on, you're the word-man. Tell me."

"I have been waiting for a long, long time."

"You certainly had been storing it up."

He left the canvas flap open. The sky was pale blue and the wind had fallen during the night. The leaves in the oaks had unrolled an inch. A new season had definitely come to the Salvation Coast.

In the fishing port of Shellman, Gazarra did some business involving line and sinkers and bobbers and hooks while Sabbitha waited in the cab and watched the proceedings. It was bad luck for a woman to set foot on the dock, let alone on any of the boats. They all bore women's names, but that's as close as any woman could get to them.

Right then, Sabbitha didn't feel very changed. A little damp, a little funky, but not changed. That came as a disappointment. Is this what it means to be a miracle, and the light of the world, and all those other things he'd called her the night before: to sit in the cab of a battered pick-up truck and watch weather-beaten men spit on an oily wooden pier? Then again, if no one had ever been this thing before, the way Gazarra claimed, maybe this was the way it was supposed to be. Maybe she was destined to be sitting in the cab of this truck, waiting for her prophet and lover to trade fishing line for a brace of smoked mullet.

That was the damned riddle of the whole thing. What was she supposed to do next? Sabbitha Hunter was an impatient Messiah. She couldn't wait to see action, whatever that would turn out to be.

The town of Eulonia was a proper village with its own general store, and not a place where a peddler would normally be needed. But Gazarra had business there, the nature of which he kept from Sabbitha. It was a bit odd, holding back on the Messiah. That's the problem with a human Messiah: she's bound to find herself in any number of all-too-human situations.

Gazarra's business in Eulonia had to do with the general store, which was owned by a former peddler, a man named Sam Brenner. Years ago, before pick-up trucks, Brenner had sold off his horses, knocked the wheels off his cart, built a kind of shack around it and called it a store. That was a generation ago, when horse carts still ruled the roads. Brenner was a kind of pioneer: the first to go off the road. His decision had caused rancor among the brotherhood of peddlers. They knew they were practicing a doomed trade, and they hated to lose anybody.

Brenner set about establishing his store and transforming himself into an honest merchant and a respectable citizen. But he had neglected two important facts. First, Eulonia didn't feature much in the way of respectable citizens and had no use for them. And whatever he did, no matter how respectable and generous he was to that crossroads town, despite the uniforms he donated to the Little League team and the credit he bestowed, he would always be as much the outsider as Gazarra was. A Jew, in other words. An outsider who lived there, as opposed to one who had the excuse of just passing through.

Gazarra steered his truck up to the gas pump in front of Brenner's store on the Coastal Highway. He didn't particularly need gas, but it was always better to buy something, if only to show Brenner that he had the means. As usual, there was a battalion of gentlemen of leisure on folding chairs on the porch outside Brenner's store, keeping watch over the road so it wouldn't get up and sneak away into the woods.

Gazarra got out and fiddled with the gas pump.

"I hear you made yourself a find, Mr. Gazarra," one of the watching gentlemen called to him.

"Good news travels fast," Gazarra answered.

"We got to keep informed. Anything could happen out there."

"It will," the peddler promised him.

"I hear you got yourself an assistant," a second gentleman of leisure took up the refrain.

"At my age," Gazarra said, unhooking the hose from the pump, "a man begins to need help for the little things."

"Nonsense, Mr. Peddler!" one of the gentlemen retorted. "You ain't but half my age. You always were an exaggerator!"

Gazarra smiled sheepishly. "You're right. It comes with the trade."

The assistant, the find, Sabbitha Hunter decided to make herself manifest. If I'm the Messiah all of the sudden, she reasoned, then I'm not going to be anybody's find. I won't have people talking about me like I was a mute slab of female ribs. If I'm the Messiah, then I can sure as hell speak for myself.

She stepped out of the pick-up, slipped her hands onto the nape of her neck and shook out her hair. The way she chose to speak was outside tradition, like the rest of her. She produced her pearl-handled brush from her basket and began combing out her hair. The public performance of something usually reserved for the happy few was electrifying.

The gentlemen of leisure ceased their commentary and watched as she worked the wind-driven snarls from her long hair. One of the buttons of her blouse winked open, transforming it into negligee. The men craned their necks for a fuller glimpse of that young, white, uninjured skin. Sure, the audience was an easy one to win over; those gentlemen didn't have a whole lot else to look at. So what, Sabbitha thought. I'm just practicing.

As Sabbitha advertised herself, Gazarra went into the store to pay Brenner for the gas.

"Just topped up," the peddler told the storekeeper and put a couple of singles on the counter.

Brenner pushed the cash aside. "You know I can't take money from a landsman."

"Crap," Gazarra said, and pushed it back. "You have before."

Brenner considered the charge, wondered if it was true, decided it was, then slipped the money into the till.

"How goes the wandering Jew?" he asked Gazarra.

"Behold, I bring glad tidings."

"No shit?"

Brenner put his elbows on his desk and his chin on his palm, as if his head were a burden too heavy to bear. The sedentary life had doubled, then trebled, that chin.

"Yeah," Gazarra told him. "I bring you news of the Messiah."

"The Messiah of the House of Gazarra, maybe?"

"Infidels, prepare to know fear the likes of which you can only dream of! Infidels, prepare to believe!"

Brenner gave a low whistle of appreciation. "You're good at that stuff. You should have gone into another line of work. Ever consider being the Messiah yourself?"

"I am unworthy," Gazarra said glumly.

"Don't take it personally. We all are. That's the point, peckerhead."

Brenner figured that the more he swore, the more American he'd be. That was another of his miscalculations.

Gazarra made a grand gesture towards the plate-glass window, a little cracked here and there, but still Brenner's pride and joy. In the sunshine, competing with the sun, Sabbitha Hunter was finishing up her public grooming. She held up her brush and squinted as the pearl handle winked in the light. She didn't just shake loose the blond hairs trapped there. She let the breeze play them from her fingers, and it was all the gentlemen of leisure could do not to chase after those golden strands across the gas station lot.

"But *she's* not."

"Not what?" Brenner wanted to know.

"Not unworthy. She's not unworthy."

Brenner was overwhelmed by a storm of objections so fierce he actually forgot to swear for a second.

"Look, Gazarra," he finally managed to say, "I'm going to do you the favor of taking you seriously, which is probably a mistake in your case. I'm going to tell you why your new assistant can't be the Messiah in a reasonable tone of voice. I know we've had our differences over the years. You've never forgiven me for coming off the road instead of living like a tramp in the back of a truck. But I'm going to answer you like a man of intelligence, a philosopher, even. First of all, you schmuck, she's a woman — "

"Any fool can see that."

"And a woman cannot be the one. Period. Second of all, she's not a Jew, unless my eyes deceive me."

"We don't know what she is. Either does she, probably. That's one of the prerequisites. These days, there are too many people making claims. Who can believe in a Messiah who's self-proclaimed?"

"Look, we're not talking Dr. Frankenstein's monster here. This is serious business. You know very well that this waiting for the Messiah business has ruined our people's lives and made us the laughingstock of the Gentiles. You can't go around making public jokes about things like that. Messiah and pogrom — they go together like peaches and cream, remember?"

"I'm not joking."

It did not look like he was. Gazarra might have been a fanatic, but he was no joker. His face glowed as if it had been burned by the sun, but that wasn't possible. His skin was too brown to burn any more. Brenner found him painful to look at.

"Listen here, you peckerwood, it's just impossible. You know it can't happen here. This isn't the place, nothing's been predicted or mentioned about this place. Eulonia! Doctortown! Shellman! Listen to those names — do they have any echoes? Not a one! Have they ever been mentioned? Never! The idea is ridiculous. This isn't sacred ground — on the contrary. It's savage ground! Obscure ground! You should know that by now, you of all people."

"That's what I thought, too, when I first came here, a long time ago."

"I know how long ago it was," Brenner interrupted. "So don't remind me."

"When I left the old country, they told me like they told every-body else: we were going into a wilderness, a strange land, but it was the only way to escape death, or worse. I was a scared little immigrant who thought that nothing good could ever come of this place where I had to go, except that maybe I wouldn't be killed. Some consolation! I believed in all that. I believed this was an empty, barbarous place, full of barbarous people, bears and Indians, a place of no blessings, no miracles, no happiness. Just survival and work, and I should be satisfied with that. Well, I'm not."

"I never knew you had so many words in you, brother. You must have rehearsed that speech for a long time. Your dashboard must get tired of hearing the same old complaints."

Gazarra ignored the insult. Poor Brenner, he thought, that's the only way he knows how to talk. That, and profanity he doesn't even understand.

"I'm not going to settle for this way of living any more. It's not living at all," the peddler went on. "All right, I understand why they beat that idea into our heads. They didn't want us to hope. They didn't want us to really live here. Somehow it was a virtue not to be where you were — that meant you were on a higher plane. Like you were superior. What crap!"

"Maybe it was," Brenner admitted, "but that's what we lived by. It's too late now. We thought we had to protect ourselves from America, and that made sense, admit it. It was the only way to stay being Jews. That's how we did it. We were apart and aloof. Maybe it was a mistake. If it was, it was the mistake of our lives. But what does that have to do with your . . . your assistant?"

"It has everything to do. It has to do with who she is. Why can't this place be a place of miracles? Who says no? Why not here?"

Brenner kept quiet. "Because of tradition" was the only answer he could muster. But he couldn't use it. Gazarra would scoff at him, and he'd be right. Already they were both living far outside tradition.

"Okay, let's say it is a wilderness," Gazarra argued against

Brenner's silence. "We're in a wilderness surrounded by wild races. Strange people. Strange women. That makes it all the more the place."

Outside, by the gas pump, Sabbitha Hunter was theatrically lounging on the front fender of Gazarra's truck, with the careless wind in her hair. Inside, Brenner watched the performance and laughed bitterly.

"You're probably just in love with the broad," he told Gazarra. "That's fine, go ahead and pork her. Have your fun. Even a peddler needs love, and sometimes he gets it, the lucky stiff. But don't confuse your schmuck with the business of the Almighty, or He'll burn it off you with a bolt of lightning like in the good old days."

"Of course I love her," Gazarra said coolly. "You'll come to love her, too."

The word *love* pushed Brenner past his limit. Suddenly he realized how much he hated the peddler. What gave him the right to come in here and fill his quiet store with these noisy questions? He didn't need to be told that their lives in America were based on an enormous mistake — he knew that perfectly well.

"How dare you even consider such things?" he exploded. "What gives you the right? If there were a Messiah, who says he would be for you?"

"*She,*" Gazarra corrected him.

Brenner pounded his scarred counter, vilifying Gazarra in Hebrew, a language that sounded decidedly out of place in this crossroads store in Eulonia.

"You madman, do you think you can make the Messiah come just by talking about him? By hoping? Your words are hollow, your hopes are asinine, and all you have to offer are the most outlandish fantasies! That's the worst blasphemy, the most outrageous pride a man can be guilty of! What makes you so confident all of the sudden, you two-bit peddler? Were the Messiah to come, what makes you think he wouldn't wipe you and your name and your pick-up truck and that whore of yours off the face of the earth? Love! I will come to love her, will I? You'd better give up that illusion while you still can. If you don't, I swear, I'll expose you and torment you till you fall down upon your knees!"

Brenner was standing now, punishing the counter with a fist almost as crooked as Gazarra's. Two old men in the wilderness, trying to settle the fate of the world that refused to be settled.

Gazarra considered the spittle that hung from Brenner's lip. He shrugged.

"If not now, then when? If not here, then where? If not us, who should it be?"

That kind of logic drove Brenner mad, and Gazarra knew it. It would drive anyone mad. To argue against it was to argue against your own life.

He strolled out of the store and stood on the verandah. The cola-drinkers looked up at him.

"Now what was that all about?" one of them inquired. "I thought you Jew fellas were a peace-loving bunch."

"Not among ourselves, we're not," Gazarra explained. "Only with you. With each other, we're savages."

He moved slowly across the concrete apron towards his truck. Sabbitha was sitting on the running board with her knees bent under her chin. A girlish pose for a grown woman, Gazarra thought. She was holding a bottle of Coca-Cola in her hand.

"One of those gentlemen bought me this," she reported. "Being the Messiah has no end of rewards."

He opened the door for her and she sat down.

"Don't you think we should leave the man something for the bottle deposit?"

"No need to. I'm sure we'll see him again."

Gazarra glanced back at the store and its drawn blinds. You

tired old onanist, he addressed Brenner, you're probably in there slamming your ham already, and to thoughts of the Messiah on top of it.

"We've just made our first enemy," he told Sabbitha.

"Really?"

She looked alarmed.

"Yes. And I am taking it as a good sign."

VII

Miracles and Proof

WHEN NATHAN GAZARRA got in behind the wheel, his hands were shaking from the heat of the argument. And an old argument it was, as old as the world itself. Can we change our lives? Can we change the world by the way we live?

No, Brenner would say.

Yes, Gazarra countered. And I'll show you how.

Public opinion and the world's own way of behaving, Gazarra had to admit, were stacked on Brenner's side. That didn't deter him. On the contrary. Someone had to do the noble and necessary job of running against the tide. Someone had to sacrifice. Gazarra longed for sacrifice.

He threw the truck into gear. Sabbitha watched his trembling hands as she drained her Coca-Cola, then let the bottle slip to the floor. They picked up speed as they drove out of Eulonia and past the settlements where Gazarra's services were needed. But with Brenner's curses ringing in his ears, he didn't feel much like doing business.

He wondered what practical harm Brenner could do him. The Salvation Coast was a violent place, he knew that much. Once at a fair outside the town of Coffee, he'd watched, unwillingly because he had no idea what was going to happen and neither did anyone else apparently, as a man who'd been roasting a marshmallow over a bonfire calmly finished eating his confection off the end of his sharp, red-hot stick. Once he'd taken the last sugary bite, he straightened himself, strode over to his neighbor and jabbed the stick as far as he could into the man's right eye. "That'll teach you not to look at my wife that way," he chuckled, then fitted another marshmallow onto the pointy end still running with his victim's seared eye-jelly.

That kind of thing happened all the time. But not to him. People were kind to strangers on the Salvation Coast, and Gazarra the peddler was nothing if not a stranger.

After all these years, he'd been shot at only once. And even that had almost been accidental, and the shot had been aimed over his head. On the Coast, you were never assaulted by someone you didn't know. Your murderer was always a friend, a family member, your husband or wife. You found out too late that you'd been sleeping with the enemy.

Gazarra had no family and he had no friends. He was safe.

Until now, that is.

Now he'd stepped out of his anonymity. People knew about the Messiah, even if they still called her his assistant, or called her nothing at all, and thought of her as an ordinary woman. That would change. And there was Brenner, too. He qualified as family, and he had an age-old family quarrel with Gazarra.

Brenner? he asked himself. That old man? What would he do, take out his limp gelding cock and club him with it?

Gazarra laughed out loud and slapped the steering wheel.

"What's the joke?" Sabbitha asked.

"Nothing. I was just thinking about an old man's dick."

"You know what? So was I."

Gazarra shook his head in wonderment. "You'll say anything, won't you?"

"You started it," she accused. "Anyway, don't I have to?"

"Yes, you do. You have to say things no one has ever said before."

"Then what's the problem?"

"I'm just not used to it, you know . . . "

"No, I don't know."

"I'm not used to it from women."

Sabbitha smiled sweetly.

"Get used to it," she advised. "It's the new age. You said so yourself."

He nodded. She was right. It was one thing to discover the Messiah in a ditch by the side of the road and urge her into strange works. It was another thing to live with those works. It would be strenuous labor, Gazarra sensed. It would leave them neither peace nor privacy. His thirst for sacrifice would be quenched many times over.

This was their idyllic time, when only the two of them knew the secret. If only this time could last! the lover in Gazarra pined. But the lover was not the strongest of the men inside him.

It couldn't last. The truth had to be told. Otherwise, it wouldn't be the truth. Sabbitha Hunter had to be advertised.

It was a cruel and inhuman mission. His lover, his miracle, would have to become everybody else's miracle, too. A man would have to be unnatural to willingly surrender Sabbitha Hunter to the crowd. Unnatural, or a believer of the rarest commitment.

But on this fine afternoon with the beginnings of summer in the air, the world didn't know about Sabbitha Hunter yet. There was time for one last moment of sweetness before the outbreak.

At the bridge where the Coastal Highway crosses the Altamaha, he turned onto a sandy track that only a peddler with decades of experience could have known about. He followed the river, easing the truck over the massive tree roots and through the deep sand. The track was overgrown with flowering weeds. No vehicle had been down it since the last freeze.

He stepped out of the cab. Sabbitha did the same. They came together in front of the truck, by the hissing radiator. He took her hand to lead her towards the bunk inside the truckbed. They never made it. The ground was soft, and sweet herbs grew in the sand, dappled with shade. The spot was a thousand times better than the way he remembered it, back when the old army of peddlers met there. Now he and Sabbitha were turning it into a lovers' lane for two of the unlikeliest lovers who had ever embraced.

The old peddlers — may they sleep easy in foreign ground — might not have appreciated Gazarra's scheme to remake the world, but they gladly gave their blessing to this mismatched couple. After all, Sabbitha was the kind of woman they'd always told stories about, the kind they dreamed of meeting one day in a brilliant, blind stroke of luck.

She raised her arms high and Gazarra carefully pulled her black dress over her head. Her body glowed with premature summer heat. Beads of sweat moistened the blond nests of her underarms. He threw his trousers over the fender, and she didn't look away when he exposed his sunburnt, gnarled hide to her.

What can she possible see in this old skin? he wondered. For sure, I don't deserve her.

Then he caught himself.

I don't? Why not? *Why not me?*

Mr. Rainbow the snake-tanner was occupied around the back, in the tanning shed, Gazarra and Sabbitha were told. He'd be out shortly to attend to them.

His apprentice, who had delivered the news, eyed the couple. Then he pointed a stubby finger at Sabbitha.

"I hear she's the hope of the world."

Sabbitha said nothing. A smile played at her lips and an unfocused look rode in her eye. Her lips were dark and bruised looking from the peddler's kisses.

"I know that," Gazarra said to the boy, "and you might, too. But the rest of the world doesn't."

"I heard something about her soul."

"It is a great soul."

"Yeah, something like that. Am I supposed to believe it?"

"You will," the peddler predicted.

The apprentice screwed up his near-sighted eyes.

"I got nothing against believing stuff like that, at least not on principle. You won't find nobody around here who'll admit to not believing in miracles. But doesn't she have to prove something first? You know, something everybody can see? That's the way it usually works, don't it? Otherwise, she's just a big talker."

That was Salvation Coast tradition. The crowd had its demands. If you wanted to make the grade, you had to cure what nature or an accident had done to some poor curse. You had to deliver a miracle from a tightly circumscribed, acceptable catalogue. Make a blind man see or a lame man walk. That would do. And don't get caught engaging in sleight of hand.

Gazarra knew they'd have to face that obstacle sooner or later. It would be sooner by the looks of it. He would have preferred later. But the Salvation Coast people were an eager, impatient lot when it came to spiritual matters.

"She'll do works," Gazarra promised the boy, though the peddler had no idea what works she would do, or how she would do them.

"If she's going to do works and all, maybe she could start by talking."

"When the time comes for speaking, I'll speak," she told the boy. "You'll hear me loud and clear. Though I might not use words, not with you."

Sabbitha's voice was cool, deep and formal. To prove her point, she reached out her hand and touched the apprentice on the side of his neck, just below his jawbone, where his skin was bare and raw from the tannery chemicals, and the carotid artery pounded, carting blood up to his tradition-bound mind. On her fingers rode the womanly smell of what she'd been up to with the peddler for the last couple of days.

The boy had always dreamed of being touched by a woman like Sabbitha, and who smelled like Sabbitha did. But it didn't look as though it had ever happened to him outside of his dreams.

He felt something stirring in his trousers and he blushed. A big pecker-shaped lump that this woman would be sure to see. He half-turned and started backing away, but he kept his eyes on Sabbitha.

"Mr. Rainbow," he stammered. "Mr. Rainbow will be along shortly."

The boy walked awkwardly towards the tanning shed, his legs bowed like a cowboy's.

A minute later, Grady Rainbow came strolling across the lime-rock parking lot in their direction. His boyish cowlick stuck straight up into the air, and sandy hair popped out of the top of his open shirt. He was in an expansive good mood, and happy to see Sabbitha.

"You're right on time! I was just wrapping up the presents, like Santa Claus."

He was holding a little package in his big, ruddy hand.

"We shouldn't be standing out here in the yard, that's not neighborly. Come on into the office."

He took Sabbitha's elbow and steered her towards the building.

"What did you do to my boy, Miss Hunter? He was all turned inside out."

He gave her what he hoped was a penetrating look. "Tell me the truth, now. Did you give him a kiss, by any chance?"

"Not exactly. I was just exercising my new powers. I gave him an emotion instead."

"Him, too?"

"It was easy," she told Grady. "All you have to do is do the unexpected."

"Your boy had a revelation," Gazarra explained.

"I wouldn't expect any less from Miss Hunter!"

Grady Rainbow's office smelled just as strong as the tannery out back, and the fans just served to blow the odor around. He presented her with the package. It was wrapped in pale blue silky paper, the finest packaging that a snake ever enjoyed.

"From me to you, Sabbitha."

Grady Rainbow put his right hand over his gallant heart.

"Is it Mr. Snake?"

"A piece of him. Or one just like him. Tanning doesn't happen overnight, you know."

"Wear it in good health," Gazarra wished.

Sabbitha parted the paper. There, as ordered, was the snakeskin hairband made from a diamond-backed rattler. She slipped it on. It fit perfectly, as if she'd been born to wear it. Gazarra's grade-A elastic did the practical work, and Mr. Snake added the charm.

"Now," said Gazarra, "you look like a queen!"

"The queen of snakes," Mr. Rainbow added.

"What's it look like?" Sabbitha asked flirtatiously.

"I can't tell you. I've never seen anything like it before," Grady admitted. "That snake died and went to heaven. A lot of snakes are going to envy this one, even if he is dead. You know, getting to be that close to you and all."

"You can be, too. Anyone can."

"Wait a minute, Miss Hunter. Me and anyone aren't exactly the same thing. If I'm going to start having emotions all of a sudden, at my age, and because of you, I don't want them being as common as jealousy."

Gazarra had hurried out to the truck, and he came back with the hand mirror he kept for his rare coquettish female customers. He held up the mirror so she could admire her reflection.

The Messiah had never looked like this before, that much was obvious. Her pale skin was burned by the road and her forehead was dusted with ocher sand. Her black mourning clothes wore all the colors of the countryside. Dirt was encrusted in the corners of her mouth, and a mullet bone that she hadn't bothered to extract was embedded between her perfect front teeth. There were hollows under her fine cheekbones. Her blue eyes had darkened, and turned huge and devouring.

She shook her head. Her hair stayed in place.

"You'll be able to see where you're going," Grady told her, "now that your crowning glory is out of your face."

"My veil," she corrected him.

"If that's what you want to call it." He turned to Gazarra. "Well, now, Mr. Gazarra, you've got this beauty on your hands, and she's wearing the strangest damned hairband on the Salvation Coast. What are you going to do with her? It's a sin to hide your candle under a bushel basket, that's what I've always heard."

"She has to be revealed," the peddler said grandly.

"Sure, she does. But how are you going to do that?"

Gazarra slipped the hand mirror into his loose back pocket.

"I don't know," he said gloomily.

"Well, I'm pulling for you. I wish I could do more. But you know me, Mr. Gazarra: I'm an expert in skins, not souls. That's my particular cross to bear. Though I admit that's changed since you brought her in here."

The two men stood at an impasse. The doubt in the air was as palpable as the smell of tanning snakes. Gazarra consulted the stubble on his chin and visited a mosquito bite behind his ear. Nothing inspirational in either location. Then he examined the plank floor. From out back in the tanning shed, men's voices rose. The tannery workers were singing sweet and high and mournful, making art out of what was on hand, with no need to improve upon the world. Briefly, Gazarra envied them.

"There's no shortage of stages around here if you want to put on a show," Mr. Rainbow went on. "You've got juke joints and roadhouses, but the revelations don't last too long in those places, and that's not your style anyway. You've got a church on nearly every corner in town, but they've already got their God, and I don't know as they'd be willing to replace Him."

"Miracles," Gazarra said. "That's what people want. Miracles and proof."

"Funny how those two words don't sound right together."

"They go hand in hand around here."

"I suppose you're right," Rainbow conceded. "But miracles and proof — they're two different domains, I'm telling you. They ask two different things from us."

"We know that. But who else does?"

The two men stood in silence for another while. They didn't know it, but they were waiting for Sabbitha to get them out of the impasse. She obliged.

"I heard someone say 'proof,'" she told the two men. "Well, I'm not in the habit of proving anything to anybody. Whatever people want, they'll just have to prove it to themselves. And they will."

"You'll just *be*, if I understand correctly?" Grady asked.

"Whatever that means."

"I don't know myself, Miss Hunter. But once I heard something about men having to *do* all the time, and women just having to *be*."

"I suppose you read that on the back of some Hallmark card from the last century?"

They walked across the parking lot of WE BUY SNAKES! Grady Rainbow was smiling all the way. He didn't mind losing a point, as long as it was to Sabbitha Hunter.

"I'm wishing you the best of luck with not having to prove anything to anybody," Rainbow said into the open truck window as Sabbitha and the peddler prepared to get back on the road. The hairband was back in its pretty paper, temporarily in Gazarra's possession. "I must say, it's worked on me already. But then again, I'm in love — or so says Mr. Peddler here."

Then he patted the front fender tenderly, as if it were her derriere.

"I'll be following your career all the way."

Grady watched the lime-rock dust disperse as Gazarra eased the truck out of the parking lot and onto the Coastal Highway, taking his source of emotion with him. That old peddler has a way of getting in between us, doesn't he, that jealous old fart, he said to Sabbitha as she disappeared from view. But that's all right. I'm a patient man. We'll have our time together before this is all over.

Sabbitha had given the snake-tanner the gift of waiting, which some call hope. And she hadn't had to lift a finger. All she did was be herself.

What do you do in the meantime as you wait for the world to change? You fill in time. That filling-in is the sum of most people's lives.

Gazarra and Sabbitha did what came naturally: they got back into their truck and drove. They returned to the business of selling, with a little pastoral service thrown in.

Making a few bucks off the commerce of the soul is an honorable tradition in this country. But Gazarra's designs on the world were too vast and outrageous to make any cash off them. He didn't want more money. He wanted a time to come when people would hold money in their hands and not remember what it was for, or why anyone would have killed and maimed for it.

He turned onto Alma Road with its wooden cottages and bare-bones plots of land that the stubborn occupants had almost coaxed into being farms. As he drove along slowly, a tire in each rut, he puzzled over how people believed what they did. How did belief work? What were the mechanisms, what was the exact chemistry of the thing?

Most people, he knew, believed out of tradition. They were born into their churches, and as long as nothing traumatic happened in their lives, like immigration or some other crisis of faith, they stayed in the building they'd been christened in. But he and Sabbitha didn't have the benefit of tradition.

Or did they? There wasn't a race, tribe, band or individual on this earth who didn't long to be free. And there was no shortage of things to be freed from. Gazarra counted them on the fingers of his steering hand. Ordinary, daily life, the burden of working for a living, your neighbor's mediocrity, your own sorry self, the original sin you catch from your parents' anxieties — that was a start, wasn't it? Everyone suffered from at least one of those afflictions. Everyone was vulnerable.

In the old times, Brenner would have reminded him, miracles forced people to believe. Miracles were the proof they demanded. That was just as true now as it had been in the days of the Holy Land. But Gazarra was just an obscure peddler. He had no miracles at his disposal.

His truck disturbed a flock of turkey vultures performing a public service by cleaning the bones of some road-killed animal. As he drew closer, the bald-necked, perpetually hungry birds protested in their irritable voices, then attempted to rise up from their work.

But they couldn't. They'd eaten too much. Practical birds that they were, they vomited up enough of their take to get airborne again.

The crowd would demand miracles, and Gazarra knew it. In her cool, detached way, Sabbitha claimed she had nothing to prove to anyone. That was wishful thinking of the most outrageous sort, a luxury he never knew anyone to possess. Like Grady Rainbow's apprentice, the people of the Salvation Coast would call for their entertainment. Public miracles. Then what would he and Sabbitha do?

Just for the sake of argument, let's say she's right, Gazarra debated with himself, watching in his side-view mirror as the vultures touched down again at the greasy spot in the road. Let's say the need for proof just disappears. Let's say the people take me at my word when I tell them the story of Jacob, and what the moral of that story is, and how Sabbitha has appeared to lead us into a new and changed world. Let's just say I tell them to believe, pure and simple, with no proof. People believe in Jesus with no proof — why can't they extend the same courtesy to me?

The idea was so unlikely it might just catch on in this place. The pure-hearted, plain, Puritan folks around here might be attracted to it. There was something showy and gaudy and downright Catholic about miracles, and long ago Gazarra learned that though Jews were all right on the Coast, Catholics were on par with the devil.

Just believe, he'd tell his next congregation. Forget about miracles. They're for the papists. Like Santa Claus and the Easter Bunny, they're for children, or the spiritually impaired and immature.

Half the time miracles didn't work — not any more, anyway. People were immune nowadays. They'd seen it all before, and better, on TV and in the movies. Real life wasn't up to scratch. Show people a miracle and they'd demand more and better, then reserve judgment and wait for you to bump up the special effects.

The moralists blamed modern life, but they were mistaken.

Miracles had never worked. The crowd had always been grasping and skeptical, even in the days of the great miracles. Back in Egypt, the Almighty had to practically beg His people to pay attention to His miracles and not turn up their noses at His divine proof. One single burning bush hadn't done Moses that much good. One plague hadn't persuaded the Pharaoh to turn virtuous. It had taken a whole brace of them and a parting sea on top of it.

Once you got into the miracles game, you were caught, it was an addiction, you needed more and more. Miracles created a tyranny that would drive any mortal man mad. Could a Salvation Coast peddler like Nathan Gazarra expect to do better than the greats of history?

People would have to believe in his Messiah without the smoke and mirrors of miracles. The snake-tanner's boy wanted tangible proof, did he? He'd have to do without, he and all the other snake-tanners' boys around here!

By the time he reached Thelma Cruice's place on Alma Road, Gazarra's hands were trembling the way they had after his argument with Brenner. Like a prophet of old, on the battleground of his mind he had dismissed, harried out and crushed the childish and vulgar population who insisted on those gaudy baubles called miracles.

The Maccabees had kicked the Greek idols out of the Temple. Jesus chased away the money-changers. That afternoon, Gazarra the peddler resolved to banish miracles and proof from the Salvation Coast. A small accomplishment compared to his predecessors', perhaps, but along similar lines.

Somewhere in his struggling mind, he must have realized his scheme would never work. He had Sabbitha. She was his miracle. Why shouldn't everyone else have theirs?

He pulled up in front of the Cruice house before that thought could disturb him further.

❦

The only time Gazarra had been shot at, Mrs. Cruice of Alma Road had done the shooting. The excuse was that he had strayed too close to her personal distillery, and that she hadn't realized it was him. It was a lying excuse, and both of them knew it.

The Cruice woman's house was the first one on Alma Road, and despite the misunderstanding involving her shotgun, Gazarra wouldn't have considered not stopping there. He owed her that courtesy, as he did everyone else. But he never enjoyed the stop. Misery hung over the place like a fog. Manmade misery, Mrs. Cruice never failed to point out.

When she did, Gazarra displayed his usual compassion. He would nod understandingly as she accused his gender of constant and wholesale betrayal, right down to her own male children. But the peddler wondered silently how she could vilify men when she acted just like one herself.

In the glory days, when the peddlers gathered on the riverbanks and bluffs for their sabbath, the veterans of the trade liked to boast of their adventures with the women on the farms and in the settlements. The women were voracious and lawless, they let on. They were like a loaded rifle in the arms of a blind man: you never knew when they would go off, and in what direction. They liked everything that came from far away, the ribbons and bolts of cloth and spices and scents that only the peddlers could bring them. And among the things from far away that they liked were the peddlers themselves. Sometimes. You never knew when. And who. And, especially, you never knew why.

Gazarra's modesty kept him from believing the stories. Modesty and incredulity, because it had never happened to him.

When it did, it was exactly how the older men said it would be. One evening, Gazarra finished his rounds at the Cruice woman's house, having started at the far end of Alma Road. The sun set over his truck that refused to fire up. The starter ground away in vain, but the engine would not catch, as if it was starved for fuel. He and the truck were new to each other back then. He didn't have the experience and the tool kit he had now. It was too far to the next town's filling station, which was closed at that hour anyway. He was stuck there for the night.

Mrs. Cruice stood in front of her door with crossed arms and refused to let him into the house to sleep.

"What will the neighbors say?" she asked, though there was not another building or human being in sight, outside of her own children.

Gazarra was just as happy that way. He had glimpsed the inside of the shotgun cottage and knew it contained a wormy swarm of kids who had only the occasional passing male hand to slap them into temporary submission. When darkness fell, Gazarra ate his provisions, then settled onto the couch to sleep on the gently sagging porch.

When the night was at its rawest point, with the cold dew glinting on the weeds and the peddler sleeping away comfortably, fully dressed, Mrs. Cruice materialized at his side, a scrawny, emaciated Florence Nightingale with a ragged sheet around her for a nightgown, bearing a kerosene lantern with the chimney smudged black. She offered no explanations. She was a woman, he was a man, for a brief moment no one was watching — what else should he expect? She climbed underneath his blanket and her sheet fell away. He felt her fleshless hips and chapped skin against him in the darkness as she worked on his belt buckle.

For once a little luck, he told himself, if that's what you call this. But why me?

Then he remembered the loaded rifle in the blind man's arms.

The next morning, at first light, he awoke alone on the couch. So it was true what the peddlers said about the women in this place. They were lawless and irrational and they hated you if you cooperated with them, but they'd accuse you of rape if you didn't. Before he could get to his feet, Mrs. Cruice emerged from her house, dressed in her overalls, which he remembered selling to her some years earlier. She was wearing a furious look on her face. She marched out to the truck and scraped the sand and grit out of the carburetor and adjusted the choke for good measure. The engine responded immediately. Her free repair job was his invitation to leave, and the buckshot that had whizzed over his head out by her property line was her suggestion that he forget her brief midnight visit.

Today, in the raw light of noon, Mrs. Cruice waited for the dust cloud to settle before she stepped out onto her porch. Same porch, same sagging boards. The couch, however, was gone. Maybe she'd burned it. She strode across her bare yard and peered into the passenger window.

"I want to see if what they say is true," she announced.

"What can they say?"

"That you've got yourself an assistant. A woman assistant who's too good for you."

"All women are too good for all men."

"Don't try making fun of me," she warned him.

"I'm sorry if I don't deserve her. It's not my fault."

"Deserve? I don't know anything about deserve. I got nothing I deserved, and a lot of things I didn't."

The Cruice woman thrust her arm through the open window and grabbed Sabbitha's hand. She stood flush against the truck door, keeping Sabbitha inside.

"I'm pleased to meet you. He treating you all right? Don't you be afraid to tell me."

"He says I'm the light of his world," Sabbitha reported.

Mrs. Cruice narrowed her eyes. "The light of his world? Men

are always telling women stuff like that. Usually a few minutes before they hit them."

"Hit them? Really? Why, that's terrible! I've never heard of such things."

"You have so. Men are always trying that kind of stuff. Trying to dominate us."

"No one's ever dominated me," Sabbitha boasted to Mrs. Cruice, "not since I was a little child. I wouldn't have allowed it."

"Oh, yeah? I suppose you've got the tools for the job?"

"A cat will dominate a mouse, but that's in the natural world. We don't live in the natural world, and I'm no mouse."

"You try that out on a man," the Cruice woman said with some relish, "and see what he does to you."

Sabbitha cocked her head to one side.

"I don't see what's so special about a man. Sure, they're bigger than we are most times, but like I said, we don't live according to the laws of nature. I never understood this business about being afraid of them, as if they were witch doctors or wild animals. They don't have anything that scares me. They're just as weak as we are, or worse. And you can take that to the bank."

The Cruice woman took a step back from the truck, as if she were afraid of catching something.

"You must not be from around here," she deduced. "Too free-sounding, and too naive in the bargain. Where are your people from?"

"My people?" Sabbitha paused to lick the dust off her lips. "Why, they haven't shown up yet."

Gazarra looked on with transcendent pleasure. When it came to frustrating people's expectations and confusing them with riddles, Sabbitha had no rival. It was like she'd been born into the tradition.

The Cruice woman pointed to her house that stood in the

center of a sandy plot of land where some dispirited grass and goat-eaten bushes grew.

"I don't know what you're talking about," she admitted, "and I doubt if you do either. But when you get in trouble, you can always come here. Don't you forget it."

"Why, thank you." Sabbitha smiled sweetly. "But can I come if I'm not in trouble? I don't care much for suffering, the way some do."

Gazarra stepped out of the truck and slipped between the two women with a bolt of denim in his hand. Peddler's instinct. A frustrated customer is no customer at all, and he didn't want to lose a sale. Mrs. Cruice looked like she was about to explode with outrage. A black eye, a pair of cracked ribs, deep and desperate trouble — now that she could understand. But not a woman who claimed to be unabused, and who made fun of other women's suffering.

As a few yards of cloth and a small sum of money were changing hands, Sabbitha reached out the window and put her hand on Mrs. Cruice's arm.

"We'll meet again, you'll see," she told the older woman.

Mrs. Cruice shivered under the touch of Sabbitha's fingers.

"I'll help you. We'll be like sisters."

Mrs. Cruice inched away from her. "Women doing that isn't allowed around here."

"Why not? Everything's allowed nowadays — or almost."

The thought filled the Cruice woman with terror. The prospect was worse than a big, drunken, murderous man with his fly unbuttoned — much worse. She backed away from Sabbitha, trailing her excuses and a few yards of denim.

"I've got to be going. The kids'll be burning down the house, most likely."

The report of the screen door on an overwound spring ended their interview.

As Sabbitha worked the peddler's circuit from the back of the truck that day, and the days following, next to a brooding Gazarra, she discovered just how many victims there were along the Salvation Coast. Nearly everybody, it seemed. Men and women both, though she was inclined to think the women had the worst lot, if only because they complained more stridently. But that was just appearances, and she saw right through them. Men had to cling to their code of silence. It was indecent for a man to claim victim status. Instead, he did the manly thing by destroying himself, and a few others along the way, in a brilliant flash of violence.

Surrounded by so many Thelma Cruices, Sabbitha Hunter couldn't help but wonder whether she, too, might not be a victim. But whose victim? After all, if you're a victim, don't you have to be a victim of somebody?

A victim of a man, that was the obvious answer. Or of all men, the Cruice woman would have told her. At first, Sabbitha didn't think she had anything in common with the sorrowful sorority of Alma Road, or the women around Doctortown. Their bodies were stripped of all flesh, their teeth were boulders in their mouths, their hair hung lank and colorless, their skin was the texture of dust, their eyes were empty horizons, their shoulders were bent, waiting for the next blow — she wasn't like them at all.

But maybe I am a victim like they are, (and I just don't know it. Maybe it's been growing inside me all this time, like a cancer, and I'm unawares. What kind of woman does that make me?

She considered the meager list of men she had known. None of them ever made me his victim, she decided proudly. Uncle Tommy had adored her in his exaggerated, showy, childish way. He left her because he was afraid of her, as most people were. Simon Chandler? Chandler was a fool, and if she'd spread her legs for him a few times, it was only to make him see that fact, and pass the long winter before she could desert Ebenezer. Her father? How could that jovial blotch of pink, metastasizing flesh make anyone afraid? Gazarra the peddler? He didn't even understand the concept of hurting a woman — that's how foreign he was.

She quickly disposed of that modest list of men and half-men. But it wasn't as easy to dismiss the feeling that an injustice had been done to her that somehow went beyond any one man. A persistent, nameless sense of trauma. After all, why else would she be riding around in the back of a pick-up truck, her and this kindly old madman, play-acting a role he demanded she play? Isn't that kind of conduct a pretty eloquent symptom?

If you're a victim, then you definitely need the Messiah. But if the Messiah is a victim, too, whom does she need?

It was a riddle worthy of Gazarra at his best.

VIII

Olive Oil

A S SABBITHA AND GAZARRA sat dining on fried chicken that evening on the bench in front of the Alma take-out stand, strange works were being prepared. It looked as though the circus had come to town. The organization had been Gazarra's doing. He'd issued invitations, casual but full of promise. He'd raised expectations. He'd dropped a word here, a word there. Naturally, his word spread. He had credibility.

Every time he thought Sabbitha was out of earshot, he nudged his customers and pointed in her direction.

"She will transform us," he assured them. "Just you wait."

Normally, no one would have bought a line like that. But they didn't have to. Gazarra's show had no admission charge, so who could afford to refuse? If something happened, that was fine. If it didn't, it was no skin off their noses. What else was there to do on a Friday evening in a place like downtown Alma but run the risk of being transformed?

Sabbitha patted the grease off her lips with a folded paper napkin and went to wash her hands at the pump around the back of the stand. A stake truck blew by, trailing reddish-orange dust, filled with farm workers in their Sunday best, even if it was only Friday. She squinted through the airborne grit and sand and wondered whether the agitation in town might have something to do with the outrageous claims the peddler had been making about her whenever he thought she couldn't hear.

"Transformed, my ass," she said out loud by the pump. "People don't mind being transformed, just as long as everything stays the same."

Gazarra materialized beside her. After he'd meticulously soaped and rinsed his hands two or three times in the cold, sulphurous well water, he fiddled in his jacket pocket. Out came the hairband in its pretty blue paper.

He pushed back her fine blond hair and slipped the snakeskin band over her forehead, at her hairline. His rough hands weren't very skillful. Sabbitha had to see to the final fit.

"With this hairband, I thee wed," Gazarra said with a self-satisfied smile.

"You're not marrying me for yourself," Sabbitha pointed out.

"I've done that already," he boasted.

She ignored his smug claim.

"You're marrying me to the crowd," she told him. "I don't see why you want to do that. I don't see why you don't want me all to yourself. Everybody else does. You must not be a natural man."

"We're all very moved to have the famous Hebrew peddler with us once again tonight."

The people of Alma met in a plain hall, a carbon copy of the Doctortown facility. Their deacon, on the other hand, was built like a football player, compared to the reed who led the other congregation.

He slowly turned his belly and his beefy neck in Gazarra's direction.

"I understand the sermon you preached the other night in Doctortown caused the deacon there to have to delve into his conscience. He was relating some of his confusion to me."

Gazarra nodded proudly. Fortunately, his beard hid his flush of pleasure. That kind of pride would have been unseemly in a church.

"Now, I'm willing to venture that's why so many people have come here this evening. Spiritual matters are important in these parts. And everybody knows, with you being an expert in tongues and all, that you have a special, authoritative way of interpreting things. I'm sure there'll be no end of people wanting to ask you questions."

And with that, the deacon lumbered off the platform as quickly as he could, as if he were afraid of getting hit with rotten vegetables.

"Friends," Gazarra began optimistically.

In the first row, a man popped off his pew as if the Devil himself had slipped a thumbtack onto it. He pulled on the edge of his T-shirt, which advertised the joys of fishing, in hopes of covering his starchy gut. Knots of muscle moved uneasily under the skin of his arms.

"Now, Pastor, I want to discuss this Jacob, who was in the lion's den."

"Jacob had the ladder, there, brother Raymund," his neighbor, brother Elden, said. Elden looked like he was home to a foot-long tapeworm. "It was Daniel who was in the lion's den. Which one are you wanting?"

"Thank you, there, brother Elden, I appreciate the correction. It's Jacob I'm after."

Then he pointed a nicotine-yellow index finger in Gazarra's direction. The knuckle-to-fingernail section of it was missing.

"This Jacob, now, he wasn't one of ours, he was one of yours. A Hebrew, I mean, or so I've been given to understand. But we've taken him in and made him one of our own, so I figure we're kind of responsible for him. What I want to know is how you can claim that this great man of the Book got his blessings through trickery and low-down behavior. Explain yourself, Pastor."

"I will," Gazarra told his inquisitor. "You don't mind if I explain it with a story?"

"As long as you don't fancy it up too bad," brother Raymund told the peddler. "I don't like the way some people hide behind parables."

"That's the way they've got to do it," brother Elden assured him in a stage whisper loud enough for all the congregation to hear. "It's the tradition."

Gazarra nodded his thanks to Elden.

"Two nations were conceived inside one woman," he told brother Raymund and the people of Alma with him, "and even before they were born, they began to struggle against one another. When there are two that way, one of them has to come out on top. That's nature."

Brother Raymund slowly returned to his pew. He couldn't find any objections to what the peddler was saying, at least not so far. Gazarra was just describing the kind of thing that went on every day in the fields and on the farm.

"The one born first, according to the laws of man, would lead. But the second one was favored by women, and by no less than the Lord Himself. It was in his blood to be first. So when the first-born found himself in trouble, and was faint with hunger and about to die, he sold off his birthright to Jacob."

Brother Raymund sprung up again, surprisingly spry for a heavy man weary with a lifetime of work.

"Everybody knows that story, Pastor. What's it got to do with low-downness?"

"Just wait," Gazarra told him. "Jacob didn't stop there. He disguised himself as his brother to get his blind father's blessing. He put the skins of the kids of goats upon his hands, and upon the smooth of his neck, and brought the meat his father desired. When his father asked him how he'd found it so quickly, Jacob claimed that the Lord had provided it. But that wasn't true — his mother had done all the work. With subtlety — that means cheating — he carried away the blessings. And what was the reward for his behavior?"

Under their breath, everyone in the hall repeated the formula: the wages of sin are death. But Jacob wasn't dead. He was famous.

"He received even more blessings! He got on top!" Gazarra shouted at the congregation. He had a thin voice, but he made the most of it with timing. "Visions from the Lord! Dreams! The stones under his feet turned as soft as pillows! He was allowed to rename places everybody else knew by the old name. He even got a new name himself. He was given two women to choose from. Two sisters, one tender-eyed, the other well favored. Not a bad choice. But why choose? He had them both at the same time. Then he had his wives' maids. Every woman gave him children. There were so many children by so many women that one of them said, Behold, a troop cometh!"

He waited for the congregation's salty laughter to subside, then told them, "Don't forget, Jacob wasn't just some cold-hearted skirt-chaser. He got his start because of women. They made him who he was. Otherwise we wouldn't even remember his name. His mother held him above his brother, and his brides, even if they were only his brides for a night, gave him more children than any man needs. Even back then, women were changing the course of history."

Brother Raymund went to stand up. All this talk and uproarious laughter weren't going to solve the question that was eating at him. Like the young Gazarra by the bass stream, he would not leave the dispute alone. But his neighbor Elden held him back.

"Don't disturb the story," Elden whispered to him. "Why don't you just enjoy it instead?"

"Everyone knows what happened next," Gazarra pressed on, upping the apocalyptic ante. "He caught an angel at the foot of the ladder and wrestled with that angel till daybreak. And he prevailed, and the angel had to say uncle. As a prince hast thou power with God and with men, the angel had to admit. I have seen the Lord face to face, Jacob claimed. No one has ever been able to make that claim. Imagine it — face to face with the light!"

Gazarra looked out at the congregation. So far, they were with him. Now came the hard part.

"This isn't just a parable," he told the congregation, "though some of your regular preachers might want you to think so because they're too embarrassed to admit that these things went on in the Book. Think about how Jacob got on top. Think what his story tells us. It tells us to search for the sins that'll get us the most blessings."

Gazarra stepped to the edge of the platform.

"Now, do we want to change this tired old world or not?"

The congregation nodded. They all agreed: this world needed changing the way a stinking diaper does. You wouldn't find anyone anywhere who wanted the world the way it was.

"Then we'll change it — right here, and right now. We'll work together and bring down the old world. We'll be like Jacob. When we've made the time ripe with our rule-breaking, when all our transgressions gather together like the clouds of a summer storm, then a new age will come!"

He paused to swallow his spit.

"It won't have any choice," he said softly. "It'll have to."

The congregation shifted uneasily on the edges of their pews.

A new age, they wondered, here in Alma? It seemed like a pretty tall order for such a small place.

This time, brother Elden got to his feet. Gazarra's ravings hadn't shaken his composure.

"Now, if I understand correctly, Pastor, you're ordering us to sin?"

Gazarra nodded, ill at ease. In Elden's plain language, the peddler's plan didn't sound so grand.

"I don't know that any of us need to be told to do that. I think we're all pretty good at it already. I'm afraid it comes naturally to most of us. We're trying to get some virtue instead. That's why we come here."

He sat down to general laughter.

"Generations have tried to purify themselves," Gazarra pointed out. "It hasn't worked. We've gotten nowhere. We have to try the other way."

A scrawny woman was waving her hand anxiously from the back row. Gazarra couldn't see her face through the crowd of men, but when she opened her mouth, he recognized the voice. It belonged to Thelma Cruice.

"What kind of sins are you talking about, Mr. Peddler, and who gets to enjoy them? There'd better be some new ones, because the old ones aren't doing me any good. It sounds like the same old thing, if you ask me!"

"Take my word for it, it's not so easy to transgress," Gazarra told the crowd. "I hear you laughing when I say that word. You're giggling to yourselves. You're saying, Let the fun begin! You think it's second nature. I say you're overestimating yourselves. It takes terrible discipline — yes, discipline. We'll need help. We'll need a guide who's not afraid of the darkness. We're lucky here tonight — we have one. She's here among us. But there's one condition."

"What's that?" a man called from the back, in the general area of Mrs. Cruice. "We got to lay down some of our hard-earned dough?"

The peddler smiled in spite of himself.

"No, brother. No money needed. You just have to believe in her. That's the only condition. Believe, and don't ask her for anything else. There'll be no fancy-Dan miracles. No supernatural proof. No justification from anyone. Belief doesn't need those things any more."

It took the members of the Alma congregation a few moments to figure out what the peddler was asking of them. When they understood, they collectively slumped back in their pews. The excitement went out of them. Their hind ends suddenly began to ache. They fidgeted. What a disappointment! How could there be no miracles?

The deacon lumbered back on stage. It was for the Hebrew's own safety. The poor foreigner was speeding down a blind alley. He should have known better by now, considering how long he'd been on the Coast.

"Now, Pastor, we've all of us seen our fair share of prophets and messiahs and other folks of that ilk," he said, speaking for every member of the congregation. "And every last one of them has been tripped up over the question of miracles. It's the ultimate test, and you're trying to sidestep it. I'm afraid we won't let you. But I must say this much for you: at least you're not resorting to magic tricks. The last one who tried that on us barely made it out of town alive!"

The congregation laughed heartily.

"You want us to give up miracles," brother Elden called out plaintively, digging his fingers in between his ribs as if he were trying to reach in and pull out his tapeworm. "Why would we want to do that? They're part of our daily bread. Or, at least, waiting on them is. I mean, why else would we be here?"

Gazarra railed on against the need for proof in the sacred matter of belief. The congregation was in no mood to listen. They'd stopped paying attention to him.

They were watching Sabbitha Hunter instead.

She was walking down the aisle like a bride. She adjusted the hairband and found it moist, which surprised her. She'd always thought that snakes and their skins were dry and dusty and scaly, but this one wasn't. She winced as she picked up a splinter in her palm from the corner of an unsanded pew. Still human after all.

When people tell of that moment, those who still dare to, they always mention the heat. It was a cool spring evening, the doors to the hall were shut against the chill, but Sabbitha Hunter was on fire. Waves rolled off her, hot with the scent of readiness and release.

That's when the congregation noticed it.

Beads of sweat were making pearls on her forehead beneath that strange hairband. Only these beads weren't behaving normally. They didn't run down her face. They shivered, though they did not flow. They attracted attention to themselves. They weren't clear the way sweat is. They were golden and round and full and plump, like summer fruit.

Brother Raymund the doubter couldn't stand it any more. He jumped up and ran into the aisle, to Sabbitha's side. He plucked up a bead of moisture with his fingertip, studied it, then tasted it.

He had argued with Gazarra. But Gazarra was just words. He couldn't argue with this.

"It's oil!" he declared.

Brother Elden leaped up and did the same. His tapeworm gave him a constant hunger. He sucked the bead greedily off his finger.

"It's olive oil!" he reported. "Olive oil is running down her face! Can you believe it?"

Neither man had ever tasted oil like that. But they both knew immediately what it was.

"She is anointed," brother Raymund declared.

"She went and anointed herself," brother Elden said in wonderment.

"Can a person do that?" asked the man at the back of the hall who'd joked about money. "I mean, is that kind of thing allowed, doing it to yourself?"

No one paid him any mind. There wasn't any room in the congregation hall for doubt any more. Suddenly Alma had something it had always secretly longed for, down through its poor, striving spiritual history. The real thing. The thing no one else had. A miracle. You couldn't argue with a miracle. It was the kind of thing that shut people's mouths for them.

The congregation swarmed around Sabbitha to taste the wondrous oil of her self-anointing. The swell of the crowd terrified her. She stood stock-still, praying for it to subside. It did not. Every sick and lovelorn man and woman in Alma pressed up against her. She had never seen people like this before, not from close up. They seemed to have crawled out of another world to give victimhood a sharp new meaning. One man wore a cyst like a fist pushing up under his cheekbone. A teenage boy went to lunge at her, but his mama slipped a middle finger as thick as a sausage in the rear loop of his jeans and jerked him back. He gave a gasp and grabbed for his crotch. A woman with breath that would fell an ox confided in Sabbitha, "There's this thing inside me that I can't give birth to. Can you birth it for me?" The woman reached for a golden drop of her oil to rub on her stomach, but she was pushed off by a man twice her size. A schoolgirl with Coke-bottle glasses stared dopily at her, her eyes swimming beneath the correction like two sluggish fish. All of them had so many things they wanted to be free of, and here, suddenly, was the chance.

They grasped at Sabbitha and pulled her closer and licked her forehead and temples until they found what they were thirsting for, even if it was only the taste of their neighbor's tongue. Her black blouse got torn off her shoulder, and her cheekbones and neck were burned pink from the frenetic attention of stubble-faced men. She was too afraid to move. The adoration terrified her. It was what idols underwent, but idols were made of stone or gold and had no nerves to feel the disgust of being needed and used this way.

A pew tipped backwards and trapped a few of the more simple-minded members of the congregation underneath it. They fell back, pinned by their legs, and stared uncomprehending at the ceiling, squealing like pigs.

"That's not fair!" one of them called out, "we need her the most. Look at us!"

The deacon grabbed the pew with one meaty hand and lifted it off them.

"Get outside, now!" he ordered Raymund and Elden and the other worshipers. "You're going to get somebody killed."

The congregation streamed out the door, carrying Sabbitha with them. The poor pure-hearted peddler got shunted aside by the very miracle he told people not to hope for.

But the crowd hadn't forgotten the meat of his message.

"What was that about rule-breaking again?" Raymund asked. "I believe this is what the Hebrew meant!"

"Just like the peddler told us, and he ought to know," Elden agreed. "Right out in public, too!"

"I can tell you one thing: this ain't no parable!" Raymund shouted over the din as they piled out the door.

"Parable is a bread-and-water diet compared to this!"

Every phrase that Elden uttered involved food.

"This miracle is a flesh-and-blood one! That's my kind!"

Once they got outside on the stubbly lawn, the congregation milled around without direction under heaven's dark, impassive eye. They didn't know where to start. There were the traditional sins, of course, but who would go first, and how? In their frustration, a few of them fell to their knees and began tearing up the grass around the hall like a football field after a college play-off game.

Someone had to do it. Someone had to pull on the loose thread that would make the whole moral fabric of Alma unravel. Once you found the courage, it was simple. Not exactly natural, but not as hard as the peddler threatened it would be.

Brother Raymund and Elden's wife were the first to try. They'd always been kept from looking at each other by the arbitrary rule against adultery. But who said it was wrong? What if that rule just melted away in the heat and grace of a miracle? Until that moment, Elden's wife, Betty, hadn't realized how lonely she felt with a bony man like her husband. What would it be like to know the weight of a man as big as Raymund on her? A man who knew how to ask questions, who wasn't afraid to challenge the pastor? A man who'd lived and suffered and had lost a finger to prove it?

Betty took brother Raymund by the hand. She led him down to the hollow where the congregation lawn sloped towards the woods and the wetlands. They faced each other with naked terror in their eyes.

"It ain't going to be easy," Raymund said.

"We've got to be strong," Betty agreed. "We're not doing this just for ourselves. We're part of the miracle, too. You and me. We're going to bring in a brand-new world, and it's going to belong to us!"

Betty closed her eyes. She threw her arms around Raymund's back. He was as strong as an ox. She clenched her fists and set her teeth.

"We've got to be strong. It's a whole new world we're making."

That was her credo. Her catechism. It made doing this thing possible.

But not all the congregation celebrated that night. Some slunk away from the crowd and made themselves scarce in the conveniently nearby forest. Maybe they didn't have the spiritual strength to join in the new miracle. Maybe they didn't have the taste for olive oil. Or maybe they remembered something they'd heard: when the Messiah comes, it can be living hell for those who've been touched.

From the very start, people were divided that way.

In the edgy silver moonlight, in the wee hours, Sabbitha Hunter and Gazarra the peddler lay side by side in the back of his truck without touching. Both of them were exhausted. Neither could sleep. Gazarra's heart raced with astonishment. The longed-for event had finally arrived, even if it hadn't arrived on his terms. Even if he'd been waylaid by a miracle.

Sabbitha's concerns were more down-to-earth. Her skin ached from the labor of being worshiped by so many strangers, and her ears rang from their commotion. In the chaos that followed her miracle, everyone had celebrated, but no one had paid any mind to her. No one had lifted a hand to caress her, no one had spoken to her. It was as if her miracle had made her half-human, off-limits.

I got all those people out of themselves, she thought. And what did I get in return? Chafed skin. I was just an instrument. That's not exactly what I had in mind.

On the pallet next to her, the peddler silently wondered what had gone on out there on the lawn and in the fields, and if Sabbitha had joined in the rule-breaking. He would never know. He hadn't participated in the ecstasy. When the miracle hit, he retreated to his truck and put his hands over his ears and closed his eyes tight.

He rose and climbed out to lash down the rear canvas flap to keep out the chill. He noticed unhappily that one of the taillights had been cracked during the course of the evening's celebration. When it came to transgression, he would have preferred it not touch him personally.

Sabbitha sat up on her pallet, put her hand to her head and pulled off the snakeskin hairband. The fresh elastic left a crosshatch of tiny lines on her forehead.

"That's enough of that for one night."

"I didn't think," he began, "I never thought they would believe me."

"Nothing personal, but I don't think it was you they believed."

A ragged cry reached them from the woods. Human or bobcat, they couldn't say.

"I didn't imagine it would turn into such a battlefield."

"A bed," she corrected him.

He hoped that was only a parable.

"I suppose it has to be this way," he admitted. "You study, you wait, but when it comes . . ."

"A bed of illicit lovers, disorderly and full of rage and eagerness."

She savored the words and how they tortured Gazarra. "You're afraid of that," she told him.

"No, not afraid."

"Yes," she corrected him. "Afraid."

"All right, afraid. If you insist. But I've always wanted it."

"And now it's left you in its dust. I didn't see you out there."

"You live your whole life according to an ideal," he said, ignoring the accusation. "You think you know what it is, but your grasp of it is just poetry. Just a picture. You can't imagine what change might really mean, with all its power and cruelty. You don't know what to do when it comes."

Not very long ago, Sabbitha would have pitied him. The way she'd pitied Uncle Tommy when his good-bye letter showed up. It was touching to see a man come face to face with something he'd always yearned for, then find he couldn't look it in the eye.

But now that she was the Messiah, she clearly and painfully saw how much of herself she'd lost by pitying the men who had hurt her. This whole Messiah business had been given to her to erase the wrongs of the past. It would be a life's work. Tonight, in Alma, she'd made some first, giant steps.

"You wanted it," she told Gazarra. "You'll have to learn to live with it."

He nodded.

"The thing is loose in the land. People are hungry for it."

"I am, too," he assured her. "But the problem is with the imagination. You can spend your life calling down retribution on your enemy. But when you see him writhing in front of you, physically, sickening in the dust, then you see what your words really meant."

"I wouldn't have any trouble with that," Sabbitha told him.

Gazarra shook his head. "That's why you are who you are. And why I'm not."

She rearranged the squirrel-fur cover, freeing a swarm of fresh smells, the sweat and longing of her new followers.

"Maybe you're jealous," she probed. "I suppose that would be natural. A lot of people laid their hands on me. Sometimes I couldn't even connect the hand and the touch."

"No," he said flatly. "I'm not jealous. It has to be like that. You must taste everything. Every whoredom. That's what's been written."

"You do live your life by the book, Mr. Peddler."

"You must descend into darkness."

"Well, I suppose I did that tonight. But somehow I get the feeling it was only one step on the stairway."

She laughed a brittle, artificial, flirtatious, self-conscious laugh, then pulled the cover over her bare shoulders.

IX

The Most to Lose

*D*READED, DREADFUL MORNING rose over the moral wreckage of Alma. Sabbitha Hunter's head buzzed from lack of sleep. She felt hungover, then remembered she hadn't had anything to drink — at least, she didn't recall drinking. Her body felt as though it had been shut up in a garbage can and kicked down a very long, steep, bumpy hill. So many believers, so much longing and awkward discretion and childlike eagerness. So much terror and disgust at being pawed that way. And so hard to turn away that kind of adoration.

Now came the difficult part: living with her creation. A creation made against my will, she noted. I never asked for a miracle, the way everyone else is always doing. The damned thing just happened to me. It didn't even ask my permission. It just moved in.

The hardest part is re-entering the world of breakfast cereal after you've been the Messiah the night before. You discover that not every moment can be one of spiritual excitement. There are times of inactivity, and they can be terrible to bear. It gets harder and harder to live without the intensity.

The Messiah, if she really is who people say, wants to get back into action before the backlash of doubt can set in. Other people's doubts, and her own. She wants to be her true self at all times, wholly and completely. There's no room for ordinary things in her life, and no room for her past self either. That makes her an incurable romantic. The most vicious attacks from non-believers are preferable to having to choose between Corn Flakes and Rice Krispies the morning after a miracle.

In the back of the truck, Sabbitha sat up and shed the squirrel-fur cover. She inspected the bite marks and stubble burn on her biceps and shoulders. Gazarra didn't want to look, but he couldn't not look either.

"They tried to grasp my heart," Sabbitha explained, probing at the tender spots, checking to see if the skin had been broken, wondering whether she should get a tetanus or a rabies shot, or both, "but it stayed one step ahead of them."

She caught Gazarra staring at her, and smiled. He looked away, then swung himself down from the pallet and reached for his boots. He didn't care for sleeping in his clothes, but last night he had.

"Maybe we should have breakfast outside of town."

"Are we ashamed?"

"We don't want to expose you too much, too soon."

"We've already done that," she pointed out. "But it was nothing compared to the congregation. In their own town, in front of their own people, they took a stand. They were brave. Braver than me. Much braver than you. They have more to lose than we do."

"You showed them a miracle."

"One you told them not to expect."

"Yes," he admitted. "I had illusions we could do without."

"And you claim you know this country?"

Gazarra shrugged. "So I'm an idealist."

A redbird landed on the top edge of the pick-up's tailgate, unconcerned with the humans inside. In its beak it held a strip of yellow cloth. A bit of some believer's dress.

Sabbitha considered that bird and the tiny flag it carried.

"I don't know how it happened. Maybe I should feel used, or raped, like in one of your Good Book stories."

"Please stop saying that word," Gazarra told her.

"Should I be proud of the distinction, or should I demand my old self back?" she wondered. "That is, if I can get it back."

Gazarra wasn't interested in the petty psychology of the individual.

"What did it feel like?" he wanted to know.

"That's the wrong question."

"It is?"

"It's not what *it* feels like. It's what *I* feel. That's the one question everyone is forgetting to ask. And it's starting to piss me off."

Then she insisted on returning to the place where they'd had chicken dinner the night before. Gazarra was against it.

"It's a test," she told him. "I want to go back and see a place I was before. I want to see if there's been a change."

"For the better, or the worse?"

"Isn't change always for the better?"

Neither of them was willing to take that one on.

With her aching muscles giving her a stiff, dignified-looking walk, Sabbitha pulled open the screen door to the take-out hut. Gazarra followed, on the lookout for adversaries of all descriptions. Once the Messiah is known, she becomes the enemy of a thousand different people. Some you can anticipate, like the ones who object to her immoral goings-on. The ones who want to take her place are more dangerous. Messiahs are like potato chips or cockroaches: when you have one, you can't have just one.

On this first morning after the outbreak, there was one material change anyone could appreciate. When Sabbitha and the peddler approached the counter to place their order, the woman who ran the place started piling everything she had onto a tray, from Sugar Frosted Flakes with heavy cream to a chicken-fried steak.

The black grill cook hovered anxiously in the kitchen behind her, gauging Sabbitha's reaction. The blacks in Alma had no use for the foolishness that had gone on in and around the congregation hall last night. Like everyone else, they were waiting for their day of liberation. But their waiting was cautious. They didn't want to get fooled and have to pay dearly for their enthusiasm later, once the wave had passed. Like Brenner the Jew, they didn't want to be blamed for anybody else's excesses.

Sabbitha was ravenous with post-hangover hunger. She tore through her lumberjack breakfast, much to the relief of the grill cook.

"You don't have to pay," the owner told them once she and Gazarra had finished.

"Ever?" Sabbitha inquired.

The owner thought that one over. *Ever* was a long time, especially in this game. But she wanted to be on the Messiah's good side — you never know. She couldn't afford fire insurance, or to pay her cook a living wage, but hospitality to the one who might turn out to be the light of the world was within her means.

"Until the end of your reign," she decided.

With overfull bellies, Sabbitha and Gazarra made their way out of the restaurant, slowed by the effort of digesting a breakfast that had been fried to an inch of its life.

A woman was waiting for them on the lawn. She had been

standing there for some time, judging by the twin ruts she'd scuffed into the sandy ground. A colorless, frayed, bony Salvation Coast woman. Sabbitha didn't give her a second glance.

Gazarra knew who she was. The last person he wanted to see.

"Miss Sabbitha?"

Sabbitha eyed her blankly. "How do you know my name?"

"Don't be playing coy on me now," Thelma Cruice warned her. "We've met before. We even talked out in front of my house."

"I can't be expected to remember everybody's name," Sabbitha said in her own defence. "Names don't matter now anyway."

Gazarra stepped between her and the Cruice woman. The woman didn't look to be toting her shotgun, but you can't be too careful. He'd rather take the bullet than let Sabbitha die. Though what she would become without him, he couldn't imagine.

"I want to go with you," Thelma Cruice announced in a loud, toneless voice, "wherever it is you're going."

She clamped her chapped hands on her bony hips, where not an ounce of man-comforting flesh had had a chance to accumulate.

"I need changing as much as anybody else around here," she stated the obvious. "More than most, I'm willing to wager. And I can prove it."

"Everyone's needs are great," Gazarra philosophized. "Who can say whose are the greatest?"

The Cruice woman looked at him like he wasn't there.

"How do you do that thing?" she asked Sabbitha.

"What thing? You mean the miracle?"

The Cruice woman laughed. "No, you fool. How do you let those men touch you?"

"I don't know." The question was a good one, and Sabbitha had no ready answer. "They just do it. I don't have to do anything. They do it for me."

"How come I can't?" she wondered bitterly.

"You can. There's nothing to it. It just happens. You stop thinking about yourself."

Mrs. Cruice shook her head. "I couldn't. I never even tried. I never learned pleasure. Take a look at me. I learned the opposite." She spat on the dispirited grass. "I ain't no apostle of pleasure."

She gave Sabbitha a look of envy and hate. Sabbitha answered it.

"Either am I," she told the Cruice woman, "no matter what you might think. This thing isn't about pleasure. Not the way you imagine it."

Day One of the outbreak. Ground Zero: Alma. Being a reputedly unfettered rule-breaker and the moral lightning rod for so many needy people was turning out to be a complicated business. The demands of the job were positively inhuman. It would take super-human strength to shoulder the burden, and Gazarra knew it, having studied the great failures of the past.

Inside the truck, once they'd gotten rid of the Cruice woman, for the time being at least, Gazarra consulted the road map for the quickest way out of Alma. The map's crisscross of red lines looked like the bloodshot eyes of a believer.

"I thought we were through selling on the road," Sabbitha said.

"Why would we be?"

"'Cause of me being, you know, who I am."

"People still need things. Where else will they find them? They depend on me."

Sabbitha rolled her eyes heavenward.

"Is this what the Messiah's come to? Peddling baling wire and Hills Brothers coffee? That might be okay for the humble Messiah, you know, the one some of us used to have. I assume he's one of the failed ones you referred to. But that's not my style. You can't tell me humility and transgression go hand in hand."

"No," Gazarra admitted. "Not usually."

He fired up the engine. What a place the Salvation Coast was! Everybody was a theologian. A radical liberation theologian at that. With everybody wanting to lead, it was amazing there was anybody left to follow.

"It's a way of spreading your word," he told Sabbitha, manufacturing an excuse as he put the truck in gear.

"My word will spread itself."

"Not entirely. Not everywhere. Not yet."

Gazarra wrestled the pick-up into a wide U-turn in front of the take-out shack. The Cruice woman watched, as spiteful as a wallflower, from the sidewalk.

"Some places they don't know yet," Gazarra told Sabbitha. "Like Axom Springs. No word about anything ever reaches there. That's why it's such a happy place."

Which was why they were going there now. A quiet destination off everyone's route. An innocent place, Gazarra hoped, where there'd be no expectations, no demands for a better miracle than the last.

Damned miracles! Gazarra growled to himself. They'll ruin your life every time.

Sabbitha dozed away her false hangover and let her stomach work on her breakfast as Gazarra drove. He passed by the turn-off for Old Leno, a ghost town that even he didn't sell to. Legend had it that a gambling mayor had bet and lost his town in a card game. The beneficiary of the foolish wager, to teach the gambler a lesson, had let the place run to ruin. Too bad about Old Leno, Gazarra thought. Not that he had any prejudices against ghost towns and their ghosts. On the contrary. Yiddish was his mother tongue, and wasn't it classified as a dead language?

Old Leno's setting was splendid, in the midst of an oak grove, with magnolia and bay and stands of tall pines on the hammock. The river that flowed among the trees twisted and turned on itself, then took it into its perverse head to disappear right into the side of a limestone bluff. The river traveled on underground for a few miles, then reappeared, apparently none the worse for wear.

The sign for Old Leno fell away in his side-view mirror, disappearing like the old peddlers who used to rendezvous there. The place had been perfect until a local fraternity dedicated to hating blacks and Catholics caught them trespassing in the ghost town that belonged to no one but history. When there was none of the above varieties on hand to hate, peddlers would do just fine. Before that unpleasantness had arisen, now and again they would meet there to drop their lines in the water. In the pool that the river formed in front of the limestone bluff, chub and bream and bass gathered in good numbers. Spooked by the trick their river was playing on them, they'd swim to top water and get interested in the peddlers' dangling crickets.

On one such afternoon, Gazarra brought up the subject.

It had started innocently enough, as a way of telling his troubles to the fraternity. He was only looking for a few words of encouragement, some way of enduring another day. It was early in his career and he wasn't yet hardened to the solitude, the endless trek down the clay and sand roads of the Salvation Coast with nothing but mirages ahead of him and half-formed memories behind to keep him company.

The hooks dangled in the water. A fire was burning down into coals in optimistic preparation for the fish that would come. Old Gabriel Freedman, gone now, tuned up his fiddle. Every man had a thimble-sized drinking glass for their liquor. *Kornschnapps*, they called it, laughing revengefully at how they'd perverted the language of their new country. When it came to drink, they were excellent at pacing themselves. In this life, you didn't want to get too generous with yourself. If you got too tipsy too fast, you might start asking the world for too much.

The men chewed on indestructible ropes of reputedly kosher jerked beef as they drank. There were peaches, too, to counter the salt of the dried meat, Gazarra recalled, so it must have been summer, probably after one of those brief hot-weather downpours, since it had been child's play to dig the worms and crickets that would lure the fish.

"Say, brothers, what do you think of the Messiah coming?" Nathan Gazarra launched in after his first drink. "I mean, here?"

Everyone laughed, a laugh of recognition, the kind that greets an old family joke a thousand times told. Everyone except Brenner, who took the question badly even then. Old Freedman played a tragic old-country trill on his fiddle and gestured to the newly washed sky.

"Look around you, Gazarra, you young fool, and open your eyes. The leaves are all cleaned and pressed like your poor mama's tablecloth. The sky has been relieved of its burden and the fish can't wait to jump onto our plates. The peaches are so sweet they don't need cream, which is good because we don't have any. Okay, it's not paradise, but what would the Messiah do here?"

"Maybe bring us some women," Jacob Mayer Wolf piped up — he was gone now, too.

"Ah, but there are always women, even in a strange land. In a strange land there are strange women. And there are more of them than men, and this is a scientific fact I have been able to prove!"

To support that allegation, Freedman caressed the fiddle's curvaceous body with his hand.

"The music man, the *artiste*, always gets the girl," Wolf complained good-naturedly. "But honestly, sometimes I get tired of just being a peddler. I don't mind being that, it's a living, but I don't want to be just that. I'm not just that to myself — why should I be just that to them?"

No one needed to ask who *them* was.

"That's what I'm talking about!" Gazarra jumped in. "You know, if there were something that could lift us above ourselves . . ."

His words didn't make sense and he knew it. But it wasn't his fault. He was after something beyond words.

Freedman looked at him with compassion in his eyes.

"We all get tired of being who we are, and what we are," he told the younger man. "But is this a call for the Messiah? Maybe we are confusing our personal miseries with something greater."

Brenner spoke up in his harsh, unmelodious voice. "I left all that nonsense back in the muddy little village where I come from. You think I traveled all this way to be tormented by that stuff all over again? No, thanks!"

He looked into the same sky Freedman had, but did not see the same thing.

"How could the Messiah come to a place that's not worthy of redemption?"

The spite in his voice took everyone aback. Some misfortune must have befallen him since the last month's rendezvous, the peddlers concluded silently. Maybe his mule had gone lame. Maybe he'd caught a dose from an unclean woman.

One of his brothers might have inquired as to what was the matter if Fialkov the ace fisherman hadn't begun howling with predatory delight. Fish had attached themselves to all his hooks, and not just the slimy, slow-moving, bottom-feeding catfish. No, they were bass, the best the Old Leno River had to offer. Freedman set down his fiddle and unsheathed a knife so sharp a man could shave an hour-old beard with it.

Fresh bass fillets grilled over a fire of resinous pine boughs were the ultimate argument when it came to speculation about the world's fate. The peddlers' hungry mouths were too full of fish to take up Gazarra's question again. Now they were all deceased, gone from this earth, though not from his memory, where they would live and fish and quarrel on for as long as he was here to remember them. All were gone but the one who should have died of spite a long time ago.

Mrs. Anne Scoggins of Axom Springs was waving her flour sack like a flag from her stout front porch that commanded a view of the road. Her wave was expansive, untroubled, innocent, happy. Her face was radiant, her hair was bobbed and neat and not too long, and her apron freshly ironed. Obviously word hadn't reached the Springs. Gazarra was still an ordinary peddler, and Sabbitha Hunter was still his improbable, but not yet miraculous, assistant.

As he filled her flour sack from his barrel, Gazarra asked the woman, "I suppose you're still short of a preacher?"

"Our eternal problem! We have the circuit preacher, but we hardly see him, and when he does come . . ."

Whenever Mrs. Scoggins rubbed the freckles on her wrist, the peddler had noticed over the years, it meant she was hiding something. He wondered whether her husband, Bud, Axom Springs's top tobacco grower, had discovered that detail yet.

"I guess we're too small to rate. That must be it," she added.

"Is that what he told you, the circuit preacher?"

"Not exactly." Mrs. Scoggins shifted inside her clothes, nervous about telling tales. "Actually, he said our hearts were too full of comfort and contentment to have any room in them for the Lord."

"You mean the camel and the eye of the needle, that sort of thing?"

"He didn't exactly say we were rich," Mrs. Scoggins explained. "I didn't really get what he meant." Her forehead wrinkled with the enigma of it all. It was a forehead unused to care. "I think he was accusing us of being too happy."

Gazarra struck his breastbone with his fist. "A terrible charge! Being happy — a terrible sin!" he wailed.

He and Mrs. Scoggins dissolved in laughter. The woman's laughter was pure gold.

"If you like," Gazarra offered, "I can maybe make a little service at the congregation building this evening."

"I'm sure we'd all like that!"

"Then I will tell people about it, and you do the same," Gazarra replied, his voice low and rapid and confidential. "I'll be going by your husband's fields later, and I'll tell him, too. I guarantee nothing, but lately the congregations I have been tending have been transformed. People might not believe it if they're not there."

"Really?"

Mrs. Scoggins was caught. Gazarra smiled at his conquest.

"They might not believe it even if they are there," he added.

Their laughter was full of complicity, but there was a shadow on the woman's face. What a charmed life, Gazarra thought, to be able to have a face that shows everything!

"I suppose you brought some of those crazy, mixed-up stories of yours with you?" she queried.

"I don't make them up," Gazarra said modestly. "I just read them."

"That's not what I heard. That's not what the circuit preacher said. The last time he was through here, he was accusing you of twisting the word of God all out of shape. He was raising all kinds of suspicions about your intent."

"Jealousy. Plain, unadorned, professional jealousy. I get better crowds than he does."

"Is that how you men of the cloth measure success?" Mrs. Scoggins teased.

"No one can be sure what the Lord's word says — unless he's

talked to Him personally," Gazarra pointed out, serious now. "And I don't think your preacher has. I know I haven't. Everything we're able to read was written down by man. Our job is to interpret it, isn't that so?"

Mrs. Scoggins put both hands in the air, as if a weapon were being pointed at her.

"Don't ask me, Mr. Gazarra, I'm not a philosopher like you. I'm not one to be debating the fine points. I just come for the entertainment, and you know that."

"Entertainment? Is that what you call it?"

Anne Scoggins's throat flushed.

"Oh, stop that, Mr. Gazarra! Now you're sounding all self-righteous like that preacher you were making fun of a minute ago. It doesn't become you! People like the songs and the stories and the what-not. And you know it. Now, if it offends you to call that entertainment, then I'll call it worship, because I like you too much to offend you. I wouldn't want to get that beard of yours all out of joint!"

Mrs. Scoggins gave his gray whiskers a pull.

"As rough and tough as a rusty old Brillo pad! You could scrub out my pots with it!" She blushed crimson. "Now don't go and tell anyone I said that."

"Who would I tell?"

"That's a good point! Now, how much do I owe you, Mr. Peddler? Name your price!"

Gazarra did. It was barely above cost.

There's a high-spirited, unbroken Axom Springs woman for you, Gazarra thought as he watched her go back into her house, noting with admiration how she filled out her clothes. The circuit preacher was right. There was comfort in this place. The people here didn't have that starved need that he'd observed everywhere else on the Coast.

Later in the day, Gazarra made it his business to stop by Bud Scoggins's acreage. Gazarra took out the books on tobacco husbandry he'd been saving for him and invited him to choose among them, using the hood of the truck as a table. Once Scoggins had made his choice, and paid for them, Gazarra brought up the subject of the service he was preparing for that same evening.

"Anyone who dares come to the congregation building tonight," he boasted, "might have their lives changed forever."

Scoggins listened patiently, a look of polite incredulity on his smooth-shaven, unlined, dark face. Then he took off his cap, pushed his wavy black hair off his forehead and stuffed his pipe with the tobacco he'd grown and cured himself. From the edge of the road where he stood, he gestured out at his orderly fields, with the young plants standing proudly above the rich, silty bottom land.

"I don't know as my life needs changing just yet," he told Gazarra. "I am fortunate enough to have received the riches of the land, and to know how to use them, and to have the blessing of a pretty young wife under my roof. Why would I want to change all that?"

He lit his pipe, then let a sweet, satisfying cloud of smoke rise up into the clement blue heavens.

Gazarra took a chance.

"You might not want to change it today," he agreed. "But tomorrow, maybe, you might."

Scoggins's tanned, handsome face darkened. He gave Gazarra a sidelong glance, as if the peddler knew something he didn't. His position as Axom Springs's top grower provoked endless jealousy, and he couldn't afford to have people around him knowing things that he didn't. There was a challenge in Gazarra's invitation. A dare. Even a threat. The kind of thing that won't let you back down.

The spring at Axom Springs was one of extraordinary beauty. The water bubbled out blue as iris flower from fissures in the submerged limestone and between the roots of trees. It formed a pool as warm as a baby's bath, shadowed by oak and watched over by willow. In it, lilies turned slow, hypnotizing circles, their flowers dizzying violet and lavender, and every whisker on every fish was visible through the eight feet of crystal water. If you drank of that spring, so the local legend ran, prosperity and a healthy liver would be yours for all eternity.

The people of Axom Springs made sure the place remained a secret. There were no signs and no paved roads down to it. They had planted stiff, sharp-stalked broom-flower to mask the track that ran there.

At the end of the path was a building unlike anything on the Salvation Coast. It was shaped like a crescent moon, and it hugged the edge of the spring. There were no walls. Walls weren't needed, just a sharply slanting roof to keep the weather off the worshipers' backs. You could sit on a bench and spend all day watching blue lilies turn on blue water, with nothing but the voice of the spring and the calling birds to keep you company.

That's where Gazarra took his second stand, in the building financed and partly built by Bud Scoggins and his loving wife, Anne.

That evening, the people of Axom Springs weren't treated to one of Gazarra's more memorable attempts at pastoring. He was too anxious to find out whether Sabbitha Hunter would produce a repeat of Alma and imprison them both deeper in the miracle game. Gazarra preached at top speed. The great Patriarchs glanced off latter-day minor prophets like hail off a garbage can lid. As he twisted and warped and interpreted the Good Book, his Book, he listened to the mess he was making of it. He had that nightmare feeling that he'd been standing in front of the congregation for hours.

"Accept the one who permits all things forbidden!" he shouted at the lilypads turning perfect, silent circles in Axom Springs.

On their skillfully wrought varnished oak benches, the congregation looked left, then right. They were honestly confused. Who could such a person be? And what was forbidden them? They certainly didn't want anything they couldn't have.

By then, Sabbitha was among them. They felt her presence before they saw her — that's how they told it later, those who would admit to having been there. The scent of wet heat, like warm rain falling on rich earth, and then she was there. She had the snakeskin on and her hair poured over her bare shoulders that were streaked with clay, as if the Lord had just finished forming her out of chaos. *I know something you don't*, her eyes said. Everyone wanted to know what that was.

Swelling, luminous drops of oil blossomed on her forehead like jewels beneath her crown of rattler skin. Scoggins the tobacco-grower stood up and snatched off his cap. His hand was trembling. That hadn't happened to him since his first night with his wife. He stepped up to Sabbitha and touched a drop of oil. It attached itself to his fingertip like metal to a magnet. He brought it to his mouth in plain sight of his neighbors.

"What's it taste like, Bud," a congregation member called to him, "raspberry or strawberry, or tutti-frutti?"

Scoggins tried another drop. His skin turned as white as unsmudged paper.

"I don't know. There's no name for it."

"Try sweat," someone advised him.

"No. Unfortunately for us, it's not sweat. Not at all. It tastes like fruit. Ripe, wonderful fruit."

He listened to his own words and heard the madness contained in them. He briefly caught sight of Anne; she was frowning. He considered what a miracle would mean for him, and for his community, both too content to know God up until now.

"We don't need this here," he told the congregation who sat on the benches that he'd planed down to smoothness, in the shelter of the roof he'd paid for. "We don't. But it's here, come to us, unbidden and unwelcome, but undeniable. It pains me to have to say that."

He looked into Sabbitha's eyes. It was like looking down a well.

"I have to know what that taste is."

"I'm all bathed in it," she lied.

He bent to kiss her forehead. His hands slipped under the fabric of her blouse and touched her shoulders. Her skin was wet, but he couldn't tell whether it was from sweat or miracle oil, or whose sweat it was.

The congregation looked on in a hush. This kind of thing had been seen before, though not necessarily in Axom Springs. The chaste kiss of peace on the forehead. The laying on of hands. The swoon of sudden, sharp religious fervor. It was part of the local idiom. But no one would have figured Bud Scoggins to fall victim to the conversion experience, right out in front of everybody. A few of his neighbors cast their eyes towards his wife. If this kept up, there'd be no sugar for Bud tonight when he got home.

He stepped away from Sabbitha's embrace, but she grabbed him by the silky black hair of his forearms and held him. Despite its wealth and contentment, Axom Springs was nothing more than a society of adulterers, and she was going to prove that truth to them tonight. She was going to serve them all up her personal vintage of the grapes of moral wrath. There was no better place to begin than with this star couple.

The buttons of her blouse winked open. He wondered who had done that, and was shocked to think it had been him, undressing this woman in public, in front of spouse and community, something he wouldn't have even dared do with his own wife in the darkness of the bedroom.

He turned and looked into the congregation. Somewhere in that small crowd was his wife. The woman who would save him from what he was about to do. He scanned the building, row by row, bench by bench, seat by seat, until he realized he couldn't recognize her face any more, he couldn't have named the color of her hair or the kind of dress she was wearing tonight. Weightless and sick, he turned back to Sabbitha Hunter's care.

The people of Axom Springs could have separated them. They could have torn them apart or drowned them. But they didn't. When Bud Scoggins and Sabbitha Hunter threw themselves naked into the spring in a lascivious imitation of baptism, they followed. Sabbitha had a big smile on, and it wasn't religious ecstasy. There was no more spectacular vengeance than this. From now on, people would have to pay personal attention to the new Messiah.

Bud Scoggins finished in a big hurry. It must have been emotion that made him shoot off as quick as a boy, Sabbitha thought briefly. He slipped out of her and went floating like a dead man towards the shallow end of the spring pool, a lilypad beached on his chest. A new suitor took his place. Sabbitha felt no pleasure outside of the pleasure of anonymity and the sheer destructiveness of what she had started, and the superiority of being above it all, as the couples pumped and thrashed in the iris-blue water around her, their limbs separated from their bodies by its refraction, the ropes of sperm twisting up to the surface next to her face, driven upwards by the force of the spring beneath them, and the drops of her miracle oil astride the water like a slick. She loved tearing asunder what the Lord had so painstakingly pieced together.

No one spoke. The only sound was the splash of bodies in water.

From a rear bench, entirely dry, who should be watching the proceedings but Grady Rainbow, the snake-tanner, all the way from Doctortown. His lips were pressed together and his teeth were on edge. It looked like he was working very hard to stifle a scream.

His eyes met Gazarra's. Immediately, Gazarra looked away.

It is ridiculous, the peddler chided himself, being ashamed. But he couln't bring himself to look back at Grady again. He knew this must be hell on the man.

"Is that you?" Gazarra spoke from his shallow sleep.

Aching, still not in game shape, Sabbitha hoisted herself into the back of the pick-up and felt her way towards her pallet.

"Don't you know me by now? Everybody else does."

The peddler sat up in darkness. The same chilly, gleaming moon, increased by a quarter, made the dew stand out silver on the fields of Sabbitha's exhaustion.

"I didn't mean it that way," he mumbled.

She missed her pallet and sat down heavily on his. She carried a shoe in each hand, but they weren't her shoes. Hers had been snatched up by relic-hunters.

"They love me," she reported.

"Of course they do."

"They love me. But they shouldn't. I sure as hell don't have any loving intentions towards them. They're going to have to readjust their self-definitions after this evening."

She laughed hoarsely, proud of her work. Then she turned on Gazarra.

"They love me. But you don't."

"I do. Believe me, I do. I did first, remember?"

"Vaguely."

"But I have to love you differently from the others now, if people are to believe. Otherwise, I'm just taking advantage. Like a . . ."

Gazarra didn't know the word. If he had, he wouldn't have said it. Sabbitha helped him out.

"Like a pimp. Thanks a lot, Mr. Peddler."

She pulled the snakeskin off her forehead and tossed it into a corner with the hardware.

"They love me, but I don't love them. I'm just doing this to prove a point. I'm making war on love."

"You're doing what you have to. Because of who you are," he reminded her.

"That doesn't mean anything: 'because of who I am.' Who am I?"

"Because of your mission. Try and love them a little in return," Gazarra counseled her gently. "Maybe not one by one, you know, but as a cause. There is nothing worse than being loved unrequitedly."

"How would you know?"

"I don't. I read that in a book."

Sabbitha propped herself up on one elbow, then leaned over him. Her hair fell across his face and bare chest. Her breath was hot and fermented.

"You know very well about unrequited love, you liar," Sabbitha told him.

"I do?"

"Yes. From personal experience. From me loving you."

She found his dry lips among his wiry whiskers and softened them with her kisses. She climbed on top of him, but didn't touch him. She let her closeness do all the work.

"I suppose you have no loving intentions towards me either," he said.

"The monster always kills its creator — didn't you read the book?"

He hadn't. That particular monster, the one Dr. Frankenstein made, was out of his tradition, which was too bad for him. Sabbitha bent low over him, her breasts against his chest, matted with hair and bitten by mosquitoes.

All right, just this once, he contracted with himself. It's not dishonorable if it helps her.

No one in Axom Springs saw them. All the good citizens of the place were dead to the world. He cast his eyes upwards to gauge whether the Lord was spying on him, but he could see nothing. Sabbitha's hair had blocked out the firmament.

Later, they lay side by side on their pallets in the dark, the man who preached transgression and the woman who actually did the hard part. Gray dawn was pushing up over the heads of the saplings. Sabbitha's breath came strong and even. Gazarra took some comfort in that. She was sleeping. He had soothed her. That gave an unpalatable deed some grace.

Then her voice rang out, clear and composed.

"You didn't love me like before."

Gazarra sighed. "It's not before," he told her with weary logic.

"You just nibbled around the edges."

Gazarra didn't have an answer. He didn't know what she meant. It was better not to ask.

"Your body is a busy place," he reminded her.

"My body tricked me. The miracle you wanted, the one you ended up getting — that was just my body playing tricks on me. I don't know if I like it."

"It's the change everyone is longing for."

"Do I have to do this every night, like a circus animal? Is that what the world needs to be redeemed? A sluttish dancing bear with the predictability of Old Faithful?"

"It happens when it's needed. That's all we know."

"Don't I get any time off to be human?"

No. You don't, he thought. But he kept quiet. The answer was too obvious and too cruel. She was the Lord's plaything. She belonged to two realms and was at ease in neither. The Messiah, when her miracles inhabit her, is not completely human. No human could do what she did.

X

Occultation

*T*HE STORIES RAN north from Alma and south from Axom Springs. They ran east to the water and west all the way inland, to where the land was rich and black, to Ebenezer where the Messiah was really from — though that was the best kept of all secrets. People who would have sworn Sabbitha Hunter and her strange works were their personal revelation discovered that what they had to tell was old news. The prosperous men and women of Axom Springs with their white fences to keep their horses in and their artificial ponds to water them had known her, and so had the superstitious, clay-bound farmers of Doctortown and Alma. Sabbitha was for everyone.

Everyone but herself. That began to weigh on her. Her miracles had made her a prisoner of Salvation Coast expectations; her powers were becoming her own worst enemy. She began plotting her escape from them. It wasn't the kind of thing she could talk about out loud to anyone. The very suggestion that she might desert could have caused fatal disappointment among the people who had the most to lose. By now, there were more than a few of them.

As she contemplated escape, her fame spread, making escape less and less possible. Not long ago, she'd taken bitter pleasure in bringing down the society of petty-minded, convention-bound adulterers. That hadn't been too difficult. The trouble was, she was turning into a casualty of her war against them.

Meanwhile, she was becoming more miraculous and more scandalous every time someone told her story. There were variations to it, but the same truths emerged from every mouth. We all long for redemption. Call it change, call it the new age, call it being born again. Whatever you call it, the time had come to take the leap. Sabbitha Hunter could do the job of change on our behalf, but to make the world ripe for her, we had to load it down with trespasses and rule-breaking of all kinds so it would absolutely have to change. It would have no choice — it simply wouldn't be able to stand itself any more.

All along the Salvation Coast, all through the state, in ever-expanding circles, people listened to the story of Sabbitha's works. Some didn't understand. Some didn't have the gift for belief. Some thought they knew what it was all about and laughed lasciviously. There was no shortage of doubters, but every time a doubter voiced an objection, there was one powerful reply. Sabbitha Hunter wasn't just another used-salvation salesgirl. She'd performed real miracles, at least twice.

Everyone wanted to see what a miracle looked like. As far as they knew, the thing existed only in books, old books written in ways you could scarcely understand any more. They began to drop whatever they were doing for their day's work and head for the Coast. The Salvation Coast, not the West Coast. It must have been the first time people actually went east since America was invented.

Brenner the ex-peddler heard the news, too. He got it from the slow, jocular voices of the gentlemen of leisure who sat on the verandah outside as he strenuously practiced onanism behind the closed blinds of his shop. He glared spitefully at his gnarled, purplish organ that often refused to give him satisfaction, considered his undignified position there in the dim and dusty light and blamed it all on that prideful Jew, that Messiah-monger, that Gazarra. Could liberation and its attendant joy come to a place where he was so miserable? The very idea was a personal insult. If this was the place and the time, I'd know about it, he thought.

In Statesville and Statesboro, in New Pond and Race Union, in Rincon and Hopewell and Hopeful and Hope Corners and Hope Valley and Black Ankle, citizens began discovering vocations in their hearts they never knew existed. They packed their kits and descended on Sabbitha Hunter. Some to worship her, others to supplant her. Some came just to be part of the show.

These were dangerous times. The competition would be murder. Other miracle workers with better miracles could well show up. Gazarra repeated his monotonous lament: if only people could have believed without the crutch of miracles. He was only a poor pure-hearted peddler, but he did know how vulnerable a single miracle makes you — let alone two. People will start demanding blood, not oil, then gold dust, then 3-D movies projected on the Messiah's forehead. They'll accuse her of using smoke and mirrors. They'll sneak into the truck at the first opportunity to rifle through her meager belongings and see what makes her miraculous, stealing some of his precious merchandise in the process. If they can't find anything material, in their frustration they'll tear the heart right out of her generous, perfect white breast.

It's her own damned fault — her and her miracles, Gazarra brooded as he stood outside the truck that early morning in Axom Springs, staring at the pool, chilled by the mist that hovered over it.

A lady's straw hat all decorated with jonquils turned on the water in front of him. A fancy store-bought hat, top of the line, a hat he hadn't sold her — whoever the lady was. The lilies closed their eyes to its dizzying circuit. A slow-motion, heaven-blue maelstrom — for all its beauty, that's what a spring was. That lady's hat would be held prisoner there for all eternity, or until some crow stabbed it with its black beak and carried it away to shred for its nest.

Gazarra pulled himself away from the spring and went back inside the truck. He found the Messiah lying on her pallet. Something had happened to her overnight. Her puffy eyes slowly opened, her gaze as blank as a reptile's. Her hair flared out on the pillow in greasy strings. Her lips were cracked and her skin was flat and lightless. She turned her eyes laboriously in his direction.

"We're leaving," he announced.

"It's all the same to me. This nowhere or the next."

"It's a sign of a great soul to know darkness," he told her.

There was no response. She didn't want to know about her soul this morning.

"That's what history teaches us," he added.

"The history of the other failures who went before me?"

"You're in your own shadow now. That's proof you are who you are."

"You have an answer for everything. I've never seen anything like it. You couldn't say shit if your mouth was full of it."

Gazarra swung himself down from the truckbed and got in behind the wheel. It was time to clear out. Hide her, for she is in hiding. No one would be willing to believe in a depressed Messiah. A suffering one, yes. A depressed one, no. It's too common. Too damned human.

He gunned the engine and bounced down the rough track. That kind of reckless driving wasn't like him.

Untrue to habit, Axom Springs awoke late that morning. Alone, Bud Scoggins made his way unsteadily along the banks of the stream that flowed out of the spring. The slashing stalks of the broom-flower made the going tough. Pallor undermined his dark complexion, and new wrinkles had been carved into his face overnight. He had come to confess his love for Sabbitha Hunter. He had done it last night, of course, but with others, so many others, in a kind of chaos he had never believed possible, and certainly had never wished for.

Scoggins wanted more than love. He wanted knowledge. He wanted to know exactly what Sabbitha Hunter felt, and what she'd gotten out of letting him, a perfect stranger, though an honorable one, make love to her. For a woman to perform that kind of act was unnatural, he believed.

Is it any more natural for a man? he wondered. He would have talked that question over with her. If he'd found her. But fresh tire tracks, a few stalks of torn broom-flower and the revolving straw hat were all that remained by the spring.

With his stomach vibrating anxiously, he stared at the hat. It belonged to his wife, Scoggins slowly realized. He broke off a dry tree branch and gaffed it back to the bank.

He gathered it up with love and regret. It was hardly wearable now. It had been her favorite hat, too, a present he'd given her for their last anniversary. He'd gone all the way into the city to find her something fancy like that.

Now I wonder how she could have lost it? he asked himself. That kind of carelessness isn't like her.

Then it all came back to him. How bad it really had been. The unbelievable things he and his neighbors had done, and that he'd started. Suddenly he remembered everything in glaring detail, but could hardly believe his memories.

He had no choice but to become one of Sabbitha's followers. There was nowhere else to go.

Gazarra drove all morning, watching the gas-gauge needle drop, clutching the steering wheel, the only stable thing left in his world. From time to time, in some back-road settlement, people tried to flag him down, but he pretended not to see.

Sabbitha was in darkness — that was normal. The Messiah has to pass through darkness. She has to take on every man and every woman's pain as her own in order to lift them out of themselves. But what do you do with darkness when all the world is clamoring for you?

In the early afternoon, his old bladder bursting, Gazarra stopped in a grove of hickory to water the ground. Squirrels amused themselves by aiming the stout green nuts at his member. Songbirds rustled through the brush on the far side of the grove, graceful birds the color of sunshine whose names he had never learned. Nature, apparently, was unconcerned with the problem of whether the world was going to change. And he, in turn, was blind to its lessons.

The peddler zipped up, then went around to the back of the truck and threw open the canvas flap. Raw, cruel sunlight streamed in and engulfed Sabbitha Hunter.

"Are you here to tell me what I am?" she inquired.

"A great soul must pass — "

"Stop flattering me. And stop interpreting, would you? Interpreting and instructing and explaining. It's like being in a house of mirrors. The funhouse kind, except it's no fun. A house of mirrors on wheels! I'm right on schedule, it's all ticking down according to the master's plan. If I fuck someone and then forget his name, or if I never knew it in the first place, that's all been written down. If I don't have the strength to get off this pallet, that's been written, too. If I destroy myself destroying others, that's just dandy! What happens if I jump the track and go tearing through the fields? What happens to the master's plan?"

"There is no master plan. No one has ever been this thing before."

"Then how come you keep telling me about the way I'm supposed to be, and why it's all right? That sounds like a master plan to me. It sounds like predetermination! Do you know anyone who wants to be predetermined?"

"It isn't a plan," he refuted her wearily. "No one knew you would perform miracles. No one knew what would come from them. And no one knows what will happen next."

"You're wearing thin, Mr. Peddler."

"Yes, I am," he confessed.

Sabbitha threw her head hard back onto the pillows. "Can't you see how tired I am of all this?" she wailed.

"It must be exhausting," Gazarra admitted. "Even for me it is, and I'm not in the middle."

"The worst thing is the demands."

"Whose demands?"

"The followers' — who else's? Yours?"

"Oh, yes. Them."

"You never consider them," she said reproachfully. "You don't care about real people."

"You're right. I'm not a democrat. The realm of souls is not a democracy."

"They're just walk-ons to you. You don't feel what they feel when they're under the spell. You don't feel their courage. You think it's easy for them to do what they do in front of everyone?"

"If they make demands," Gazarra told her, "just ignore them."

"Ignore the people who believe in me? Who sacrifice for me? They made me who I am!"

"Nonsense!" Gazarra thundered. This was one blasphemy too many. "They didn't make you who you are!"

"Then you did. Because I'm no one. A sponge of identities. A woman without papers. A blank slate where people write their anxieties. An accidental creation!"

"You can't say that!" Gazarra wailed under the hickory trees.

Sabbitha's voice went cold. "I can say anything I want to because I'm the Messiah. And if I'm not, then I'm just some crazy woman lost in the fields, so it doesn't matter anyway."

A green nut struck the tailgate and ricocheted away. The squirrels were adding insult to injury.

"After the celebration, I sink into darkness while the others rejoice in their freedom. They skate on top of me like water-striders on a pond. I don't know if I like the deal."

"They only think they're celebrating. Deep down, they're suffering."

"Is that what you call it? You're not there to see them. Maybe you should show up some night in the middle of the festivities and remind them that they're suffering."

"I don't need to tell them. Sooner or later they'll find out for themselves."

"You're just so superior, aren't you, Mr. Peddler?"

Sabbitha closed her eyes and drew her cloak around her. Gazarra understood that the interview was over. He replaced the canvas flap and tied it down tightly.

"You just stay nice and cozy in there with your darkness," he told her from outside.

He wandered through the grove of hickories, then bent down and filled his hand with green nuts that had fallen prematurely from the trees. He spotted a squirrel on a low branch just above his head and let fly with his ammunition. Predictably, he missed the animal and the nuts fell back down on his head. The squirrel made a mocking, rasping noise in its throat and darted off to a higher limb.

He hadn't had a real argument with a woman for years. My God, Gazarra realized, it's like a marriage. It *is* a marriage: me, this woman and the Messiah. Sometimes the two are the same. Sometimes they're not. However many they are, they certainly make a crowd.

He sat down behind the wheel, but found he didn't have the energy to turn the key. Push on, he ordered himself. Go back on the road, get out there, sell something. On the road things can always happen. Anything is better than pitching green hickory nuts at the sky.

But the key stayed in the ignition, unturned.

"The Messiah is sad. Depressed, as they put it these days," he said aloud. "That's what the matter is."

He put his hand on the key, then drew it away.

"No," he answered himself a moment later. "The Messiah can't be depressed because of who she is. She must be above common depression. She is passing through darkness, like a star devouring its own light. Something grand-sounding like 'occultation' is fit for the Messiah. I, on the other hand, am an ordinary man, so I can be depressed."

Gazarra wondered if he was finally losing his will. That could happen to a peddler. It had happened to others he knew, and he'd come close to it any number of times himself. But that had been long ago, back when he was young and new in the country and a student of every one of the infinite shades of blue.

He hadn't started out as a blue man. He'd come to the Salvation Coast as a stoic stranger to emotion, starting with his own. Emotions arrived as he mastered the English language. Well, not mastered it — at least wrestled sections of it to the ground. In Yiddish, the closest thing he had to a native language, the word for "happy" in his mind referred to a certain fast tempo in music that allowed people to dance at weddings. But English had so many emotions in it, and the people who spoke that language naturally seemed unafraid to use them. Thousands of strains and shades of the same feeling suddenly became available to him. No wonder he caught some of them.

Sometimes, on a lightly traveled road, he would take his foot off the gas pedal and slip the shift lever into neutral. The truck would drift to a stop in the loose, deep sand of the shoulder, and he would sit there without the will to go on. Why should he? Where was there to go? If he'd had the energy to walk around to the back of the truck to where his loaded shotgun waited, he would have used it on himself. He could stay that way for hours, for a whole day at a time, entombed in the cab of his pick-up, neither awake nor asleep, alone on the road. A farmer might pass and slow by his open window. Seeing it was just the peddler, if he reacted at all, the farmer would wave discreetly then move on, not wanting to look like he was minding another man's business.

With Sabbitha Hunter in his life, Gazarra had hoped he wouldn't have a spare moment to be blue. But it wasn't working out that way. The Messiah had changed him, but he was still himself.

They knew about Sabbitha in the crossroads communities outside Midway, the closest thing to a city that the Salvation Coast had. There weren't many places left where they hadn't heard about her and her works.

In one of those small settlements, Gazarra swung himself up into the back of his truck to fetch a head for a claw hammer and a pound sack of coffee beans for a customer. Sabbitha was cowering on her pallet. On both pallets, he noted. She lay on her back, arms at her sides, palms up, legs slightly spread under her cloak as if she'd been etherized. She tensed when he barged in, as if she were an inmate in a soldiers' brothel.

Once the customer paid for his order, he asked Gazarra, "Where's that sinning Messiah of yours got to?"

"She is hidden."

The customer chewed on that for a while.

"Too bad. I was looking forward to getting in on some of the fun."

"Fun?" Gazarra questioned him sternly. "I don't think it's very much fun. Bringing forth a miracle is a travail akin to childbirth. Sabbitha Hunter is a woman of pains."

"Aw, you're just saying that!" The man waved his new steel claw in the air. "You men of God never want us to kick up our heels. We're supposed to sin, but it's not supposed to be any fun — is that it? We've got to have a reason for it, right? I don't see how all this sinning is supposed to lead us out of sin anyway," he confessed.

"It will lead to a time when the world will change."

"It doesn't make any sense to me, and I don't mind admitting it. But I sure want to be around when it happens."

"You will. But you might not like it. It might not be fun. You might wish you hadn't come. Your flesh might crawl."

No one could resist a challenge like that. That quickly, another follower was made. In this country, people were too proud to back down on a dare, especially one of a spiritual nature.

By the end of the day, Gazarra reached the center of Midway. He parked on the wide, soggy, grassy plot of land that occupied the heart of the town. A great brick hotel built by the railroad had stood there once, but one night some common drunks had set fire to their beds as they lay in them. By the time the fire burned out, the drunks were reduced to cones of white ash, and so was the hotel.

No one had ever come up with the capital to rebuild the place. Slowly, grass and wildflowers had taken over the spot. Now it served as a park, fairgrounds, sports field — it was common land.

Gazarra parked his truck there and waited to be discovered. That didn't take long.

The Messiah turned out to be good for business. Everyone wanted to see her, and a purchase was the best excuse to get close to the truck. Only they couldn't see her, since she was in hiding — at least that's what the peddler claimed. Her being hidden turned out to be good for business, too. Everyone who wanted to taste her miracle oil was left thirsting. They had no choice but to come back the next day and make another purchase.

"She has put on a cloak of darkness. She cannot be looked upon," Gazarra told the curious and eager would-be believers.

That obscure language was poetry to Midway ears. He might as well have been speaking Hebrew. No one understood what his words meant, they sounded like a bad translation from some lost language, but people felt they'd gotten closer to some big mystery when Gazarra talked that way.

"When's she going to take off that cloak?" the crowd wanted to know.

Gazarra shrugged his philosopher's shrug.

"You have to do something," they pleaded. "Do it for us. We need her."

"I wish I could," Gazarra said. "But I can't. I'm just like you — hoping and powerless."

Gambling was among the conventional vices in Midway. The betting men congregated around Gazarra's truck, and they soon got down to business. The event was too good not to put money on; it was better than a college bowl game. But problems sprung up. Gazarra would have warned them if they'd included him in their plans, but they didn't. Jews, the popular knowledge ran, were too pure-hearted to place a wager on anything.

Just exactly what would they wager on? That Sabbitha Hunter was the Messiah? That she would emerge from darkness, and when, and to what effect? Whether their funning would turn to suffering, or vice versa? The potential for side bets of all kinds was stunning.

The pleasure-into-pain side was unpopular. No one was ready to wager that their flesh would end up crawling off their bones. On the other hand, the side that held that sinning would lead to a great day of liberation attracted few serious bettors, since everyone wanted to put their money on that horse.

The system was having trouble getting off the ground. The most popular option was that Sabbitha Hunter was, or was not, the Messiah. At first, that seemed like a pretty clean bet with two clearly delineated sides. But some wet blanket popped up and wanted to know how they were going to determine whether she was or wasn't the one all were waiting for.

"I mean, how are we going to tell? Who's going to judge? Is it as simple as win, place or show?" the bettor wanted to know, waving a roll of tens in the air to help make his point.

No one could answer the man's question. The wagerers agreed that the situation had to be studied further. But not too much further, since anything could happen at any time.

Gazarra's stomach was grumbling by the time darkness began to gather over the treetops — real darkness, not the spiritual kind. He'd been too busy to eat. Business had been so frenetic that he'd nearly forgotten his anxieties about Sabbitha. After the day's last article was sold, he burst into the back of the pick-up with manic optimism to report to Sabbitha what the rest of the world was saying about her.

"They're waiting for you," he told her. "They really are. They're ready. They need you."

"I know."

Her voice was steady, dry, unimpressed. Gazarra realized she had heard every word through the canvas walls of the truckbed. He made a mental note to watch his tongue in the future.

"Which side are you putting your money on?" she wanted to know.

"That's the only way some people have of showing they're concerned."

Sabbitha laughed derisively. "Spare me from that kind of love!"

"Don't think about them. Think about yourself. If you're in darkness, it's not because of them."

"How do you know? Their expectations make me sick, physically sick! Who do they think I am? What do they want out of me? I can't do anything for them — let them do it for themselves! I told you I wasn't here to prove anything to anybody. Anyway, they're not the only ones around here who need changing!"

"They don't count. They're not your mirror. They don't define you."

"I suppose you do?"

She slammed the pallet with her fist. The nuts and bolts rattled in their containers. That way she had of sprawling across both pallets — that was no invitation. It was a No Trespassing sign. Like a hapless husband, he was forced from the common bedchamber.

"But it's my truck," he grumbled softly, very softly, as he stood in the dew-soaked field at dusk.

As Sabbitha's darkness wore on, Gazarra's sales dropped off, though it wasn't from lack of customers. Midway's population had doubled, then tripled. Trailers and campers were pulling in from everywhere, setting up camp wherever they could. There was a hobo jungle out by the exit off the Interstate. The sports fields by the high school were no longer available for young ballplayers because people had pitched their tents there. No vacant lot was vacant any more.

People were getting edgier by the day. They were ready to get on with the sinning, but no one wanted to get taken. No one wanted Midway's name going down in the history of gullibility.

"You know about Jews and money," the doubters pointed out. "He could be making up the whole damned thing just to sell more of those trinkets he's got."

Night after night, Gazarra sat in the front seat as if he was driving. But he wasn't. He was sitting on the passenger's side. Sabbitha was doing the driving now. For the first time, he allowed himself to wonder what would happen if his Messiah never emerged from a darkness he judged to be entirely too comfortable.

"So what?" he tried to encourage himself as he gazed through the bug-spattered windshield. "Some Messiahs have been in hiding for centuries, and their followers have gotten along just fine."

He prayed it wouldn't take that long. He'd been waiting long enough — at least, that's how it felt to him. Actually, his wait wasn't even a drop in the great sea of hoping.

XI

The Crab Man

SABBITHA HUNTER and Gazarra the peddler awoke one morning to the insistent thudding of sledgehammers sending wooden posts into the soft earth. Some carnival owner must have done his homework. He'd spotted the crowds hovering around the outskirts of Midway anxiously waiting for something to happen, and he'd decided to move in his freaks and animals and shooting galleries and cotton-candy wheels and take advantage of the people's pressing need for entertainment.

"Our competition," Gazarra said to himself as he stepped out of the truck and stood in the cool meadow.

Across the field spongy with water-loving plants, tents were going up with practiced ease. A flock of carnival tents rising at dawn is one of the finer sights on the Salvation Coast, but it put the peddler in a foul mood.

He stuck his head into the back of the truck.

"Maybe you want to go for a ride on a rollercoaster?" he called to Sabbitha.

"I'm already on one," she reported.

The back of the truck had filled up with the stagnant smell of her confinement. He didn't like the complacency in her voice.

"I think," Gazarra said carefully to his Messiah, "that you are treating your darkness with too much respect. You are enjoying it, even."

"Well, I am a sensualist." She paused. "I thought I was supposed to inhabit it. That's what you've been telling everybody."

"I was only trying to protect you from them. Anyway, I said 'pass through,' not inhabit. No one can inhabit darkness forever. Not even you."

"Oh, no?" Sabbitha sounded like a precocious child who's just discovered the power of blackmail. "Why not?"

"Because I won't let you!"

Sabbitha laughed at him. Gazarra reached into the back of the truck and grabbed his dusty cap off a nail. He went stalking off across the meadow's soft ground. But when he came to the other side of the common where the town's streets began again, with their welcoming, shady canopy of trees and white wooden fences, he stopped. He was afraid to let the truck out of his sight. He stood there and glared at it the way a prisoner glares at a wall.

His Messiah was bullying him. And he had no way to defend himself.

But Sabbitha Hunter wasn't playing games. She was in no shape to. She had fallen victim to the curse of the modern-day Messiah: performance anxiety. Fear of success and fear of failure fought for control of her mind. Sabbitha was a modern woman in the midst of a medieval outbreak.

Her anxiety had attacked at the worst possible time, the way anxiety always does. There were plenty of contributors to it: the thousands of followers crawling over Midway like lice, crowded into vacant lots and overnight trailer parks, waiting for a sign. She could feel them there, urging her on into anything, as long as it was action. The air buzzed with their hateful expectations and unrequited love.

There in the back of the pick-up truck on that fitful day, she tried to puzzle it all out. I became the Messiah because I wanted to get some business done, she reasoned, the kind of business every person in this lousy society must have. I was after revenge against certain people, and the world that let those people exist. I wanted to write myself a brand-new personal history. I wanted total control over myself, and to lose myself, and both those things, simultaneously. Everybody wants that these days, so everybody could be the Messiah if they only had the guts. All it takes is a heightened sense of responsibility.

There were no doctors of the mind or therapists in Midway to help her out, and tell her whether she'd accomplished the difficult missions she'd set for herself. She'd have to figure it out on her own.

Late that evening, Sabbitha emerged from her sickroom. There was no danger of waking Gazarra. He was sleeping in the cab, length-wise across the bench seat, the gearshift lever stuck in his gut, his despair temporarily stilled by whisky he'd actually bought at retail.

Sabbitha glided down from the back of the pick-up, shook out her hair and noted that the air had grown considerably milder since the last night she'd been out this late. She wondered idly how much time she'd wasted on the pallet inside the truck.

The stars swam overhead. A little ground fog crept across the grassy meadow that separated the truck from the carnival. Their competition, according to the peddler. She'd see about that! She felt the warm humidity on her bare legs and feet, and smiled a Mona Lisa smile. She could do anything. The Messiahship was an enormous blank check.

A bonfire burned through the mist on the far side of the field where the carnival tents sent up their dark shapes. The voices came from that direction. She crossed the meadow and stopped just outside the circle of firelight. The carnival workers were enjoying a moment of camaraderie, the way the peddlers had in Gazarra's stories. These workers were outsiders, too, of the most striking sort.

A man and a woman shared a single body, though each retained his and her head. My God, Sabbitha thought, love's ideal made flesh. Two minds united in one body. By the lovers' side sat a man who seemed unnaturally compact. He was occupied at nailing nails into a board with his head. His compulsion didn't attract much attention; his companions were used to it by now. Next to him, a woman faced the fire, but only with her face, since her body was turned completely in the other direction, towards the shadows where Sabbitha stood. Sabbitha wondered whether her body could see her.

The normal-looking man sitting among them must have been their manager, their pimp and taskmaster. Sabbitha disliked him immediately. Then he shifted his position slowly and awkwardly, and she saw he was among kindred spirits after all. He was perched in something that looked like a modified dentist's chair with an oversized footpiece. The pink of his skin wasn't due to fire-glow. It looked as though he'd been thrust into boiling water and held there. His arms and legs ended in claws.

Sorry for thinking you were normal, Mr. Crab, Sabbitha said to him softly. Then she stepped into the firelight.

The cohorts looked up. The Crab looked at the Two-Direction Woman. The Fused Lovers looked at each other. The Human Hammer went on doing what he did best. Visitors were rarely a happy occasion.

"We know you," said the Crab.

His voice was reedy and straw-like, as if whatever had affected his extremities had done something to his voicebox, too.

"We've heard all about the ruckus you've been raising. We figured we'd be running into you sooner or later. In fact, to tell the truth, that's why we came."

"You're the new Messiah, that's what I heard," the Two-Direction Woman added. "Well, I got nothing against that. Everybody's got to earn their daily bread. We're the living proof of that."

"You work miracles," the Crab Man challenged her. "Work one on me."

"I will," Sabbitha promised him.

"We could all use a fucking miracle around here," the Two-Direction Woman said. "That's what I see when I look around."

"I need one, too," Sabbitha confessed. "I'm just like you that way."

"Now wait just a goddamned minute," the woman burst out. "Just because you fucked half a church in Alma and the other half in Axom Springs doesn't mean you're one of us."

"I think that's a pretty freaky thing to do, personally," the Human Hammer put in.

"Sure, it is. But we've got an identity to protect," the woman protested.

"You can keep your identity," the Crab Man said glumly. "I'd rather have a miracle."

"All that was forbidden is now permitted," Sabbitha announced. "Transgression will bring in a ripe new age."

"We *are* transgression," the Fused Man and Wife said darkly. "So tell us something new."

"I need your help," Sabbitha wailed suddenly.

She caught everyone completely off guard. No one had ever visited freaks in search of help. In fact, nobody ever asked anything of them at all, except to be exactly what they were.

"Help?" the Two-Direction Woman echoed her. "You're barking up the wrong tree, sister."

"I need to get back outside myself, where I belong."

The sensation-workers, for that's what they called themselves now, puzzled over that for a while. The word "freaks" was forbidden, and they never used it unless they were alone, in the secrecy of their own society.

"I get it," the Crab Man said. "This Messiah thing is like therapy for you."

"Therapy? What's therapy?" the Hammer burst out.

"Therapy," the Fused Man explained proudly, "is when you try and get better."

"No, it's not," the Fused Wife contradicted her mate. "It means when they try and get *you* better."

"But we're not getting better," the Two-Direction Woman pointed out. "We're staying just the way we are. It's a vocation."

"No," said the Crab Man, "it's a profession."

The sensation-workers were a quarrelsome lot, noisy and profane and forever overcompensating, but it was hard to blame them, considering the hand nature had dealt them. Their greatest pleasure and most popular pastime was claiming that their infirmities were worse than anybody else's.

"You don't understand," Sabbitha protested. "The Messiah has nothing to do with therapy. It has nothing to do with getting better."

"Well, that's a relief," the Two-Direction Woman said sarcastically.

"When you're the Messiah," Sabbitha tried to explain, "you can do anything you want to. But it takes more effort than you can possibly imagine."

"We can do anything we want to, too," the Crab Man answered her, "except what everybody else does."

Sabbitha took a step towards the fire. Her foot landed directly on the sharp edge of a sardine can. Everyone had seen it coming.

But they wanted to find out whether the Messiah shed real blood. It turned out that she did.

She sank slowly to the ground by the flames with both hands around her sliced-open foot.

The Crab Man was beside her in no time. His embrace was ham-handed and horny, but expert.

"I'm no doctor," he told her, "but you're going to get can poisoning unless I do something."

He grasped her foot tightly between his claws and took to sucking out the wound as if she'd been snakebit.

That's how the romance between the Messiah and the Crab Man began. Because of a sardine can. And him saving her life, or at least her health. The Fused Wife looked away; she was jealous. The Fused Man didn't; he was jealous, too. He would have gotten a hard-on if he could have. The Human Hammer went back to his repetitive business.

As usual, the Two-Direction Woman had to have the last word.

"You can stick around, girl," she said to Sabbitha, "on one condition. Don't you ever, ever say you're like us."

Then she turned both face and body away from the scene of burgeoning romance, which was not an easy maneuver for her. What the fuck, she thought as she moved on a careful diagonal towards her trailer, she never really wanted the Crab Man anyway. She liked the Fused Husband — now there was a soulful gentleman who understood what a woman needed. He understood from the inside, and that was special.

But that was the whole problem. He didn't have what it takes for a man to be a man. Fucked-up androgyny! she swore to herself. It sounds great at first, on paper, but when it comes down to brass tacks, you're useless in the sack.

The Crab Man shared his trailer with the Human Hammer, but the latter considerately stayed out of sight. He was unheard, too, except for the occasional soft plop a rubber mallet might make. On his side of the partition, the Crab Man struggled to take hold of the hem of Sabbitha's black dress with his pincers. It was like trying to grasp a marble with chopsticks. She didn't help him, and he didn't ask for help. He worked with meticulous application and a kind of artist's concentration that made it possible to look at his face without revulsion. His transformation was what the followers were hoping for: through the effort of belief, they would become beautiful. When he finally succeeded, Sabbitha shared in his sense of triumph.

Gratefully, he discovered that she wore nothing underneath her dress. He couldn't have faced a thin strip of elastic on his own.

"Are you going to work a miracle on me now?" he asked with wary hope.

"You just watch."

"If you cure me of my infirmities, how am I going to make a living? I don't know how to do anything else but be myself."

"Don't worry. I won't go that far."

"What kind of miracle are you going to do?"

"The usual one."

She sloughed off her dress and showed him the full extent of what he didn't deserve.

"I don't get to see a body like that every day," the Crab Man admitted. "You can't buy something that good. I don't exactly measure up, and I know it."

"That's the point."

"Sorry, I don't get it."

"The Messiah must taste every glory, and every humiliation," she told him.

"You been rehearsing that line for a long time? It sounds like something out of the Good Book."

"More or less."

"Good Book says a lot of bad things, doesn't it? And as stretchy as a damn rubber band, too."

"Something in it for everyone," Sabbitha agreed.

Using his well-calloused elbows and knees, the Crab Man climbed on top of Sabbitha Hunter. She proceeded to work the usual man-woman miracle on him, as she promised she would. With word and deed, she reached down and drew out his soul, a piece of property he never even knew he owned. He never thought he possessed anything but his infirmities. In the process, she made him into the most fervent of followers. As far as he was concerned, she'd never have to work another public miracle again, and he was willing to tell that to anyone who'd listen.

Nathan Gazarra awoke at dawn. It had been a long time since he'd slept that way, like the poorest of peddlers, with a gear-shift lever in his belly.

The sky to the east was the color of sheet metal. A gray panel of mist tangy with campfire smoke hung over the field. He tried sitting up in the cab, and succeeded after a time. Then he bailed out the driver's-side door and half-stood in the dew-soaked meadow.

His hangover buzzed mercilessly in his ears like a cloud of blood-crazed mosquitoes as he negotiated his way to the back of the truck. He found what he expected he might. The canvas door was gaping wide open, waving tentatively in the breeze. There was no Messiah inside.

Gazarra had a pretty fair idea where she might be. It would be just like her to consort with the competition.

He came upon a campfire still smoldering, untended, by the carnival trailers. He stood staring at the ashy fire when an inhuman cry startled him. The bile of fear sprang into his throat. Then he realized why the noise was inhuman. An animal had made it. A carnival animal.

Gazarra stumbled over the lumpy ground towards the trailers where the carnival workers bunked. He was shivering, sick to his gut and his head, and no more coherent than a child in revolt against its parents.

"Why me?" he lamented out loud. "Why do I have to do this thing?"

His complaint was among the most unoriginal ever recorded. The proof? No being, superior or inferior, bothered to answer him.

Gazarra leaned against the rounded edge of an Airstream trailer. Peeping in people's windows was wrong. He knew that and he didn't care. He expected to see any number of things except what was there: a picture of conjugal perfection. On the other side of the dirt-streaked window, two heads lay on a pillow, turned away one from the other like old marrieds, in perfect repose. Under the gray sheet, the two heads were attached to a single body, but Gazarra couldn't see that.

He tried the window of the next trailer. Behind it, a sleeping hydrocephalic was clutching a piece of board in his arms.

He got lucky the third time.

Sabbitha was locked in embrace with an animal. A crab. A crab with a human face. A human being with little crab pincers. The crab's abbreviated body was thrown back, and he was being attended to by the Messiah herself.

Gazarra stepped back carefully from the window and deposited a liquid circle of whisky-brown puke by the trailer tires. Damned retail drink, he thought to himself.

Both he and Sabbitha were trapped beyond recognition. The worse things got, the harder he had to believe. It was a commitment, reality-denying and ennobling. And isn't commitment what gives grandeur to a man's life?

XII

The Midway Blessing

SUNRISE on the Crab Man's boiled pink skin. This is a defining moment in my personal history, Sabbitha told herself as her eyes moved over the surprising topography of his body. Not everybody could do this. It's not just the fruit of a poor self-concept, or some baroque form of suicide, or the result of something bad that happened to my childhood. This is above the laws of human behavior. It's an act with a purpose, an end. I wanted to see how far I could go, and now I know. If I can do this, I can do anything. You're my liberation, my proof. Thank you, Mr. Crab.

Sabbitha laughed softly. She didn't even know why. Her laughter was becoming a nervous tic.

The Crab Man slept on beside her, undisturbed, besotted with love. Delicate, reedy sounds issued from his throat with every breath he took. He wasn't ugly to Sabbitha, as he was to the rest of the world. He'd never been ugly to her. He'd just been her means of self-expression.

She was pretty proud of herself as she threw on her jacket and stepped out of the sensation-workers' trailer. Plop! went the Human Hammer on the other side of the partition. He was an early riser.

A llama was tethered to a post by the trailer.

"Aren't you a long way from home, Mr. Llama?" Sabbitha commiserated.

The llama sniffed at the unfamiliar woman and the sour grass at its feet, then spat.

"I don't blame you a minute for doing that. I'm doing the same in my own way," she told the animal. "I don't know why you're here, but I'm here on a mission. Nobody else knows that. I'm a kind of secret agent. Everybody's here to see me, the way they used to line up to gape at you. It's a form of love, so I'm told. They need me. I'm like you: a foreign beast on a short leash. I'll hang around as long as I need to serve my mission."

The llama made a llama noise, then spat again, hitting Sabbitha on the ankle.

She found Gazarra lying on his pallet in the back of the truck, eyes open, a bad smell on his breath.

"I suppose you're ready now for whatever comes next," he said.

She was too proud and elated to hear the spite in his voice.

"You have good intuition," she congratulated him, "for a man."

"It's not purely intuition," he assured her.

"Really? Well, good for you."

Sabbitha pulled off her jacket and lay down next to him.

"I'll hang out here till the evening. Then we'll have the Midway blessing."

She laughed, then turned and tried to kiss him. She came away with a mouthful of wiry beard. He smelled crab spunk on her breath.

"Jealous?" she teased him.

Gazarra didn't answer.

"Everything that was forbidden is now permitted," she reminded him.

"I'm not up to the level of my ideas this morning."

"That's too bad. Because now's the time to be strong."

Then Sabbitha went tumbling backwards, skull-first, into something like sleep. But it wasn't sleep; she didn't need sleep any more. It was unconsciousness. Whatever it was, God knows she'd earned it.

Gazarra redeemed the tortured, cramped night and the nauseous, sour dawn with a good day's business. The doubters and hesitaters who'd been hovering out by the Midway exit off the Interstate must have received a sign. Who knows how these things work? They began moving into town. Many of them had come from a long way. The dried mud that streaked the sides of their cars, trucks and trailers in aerodynamic patterns came in colors the likes of which Gazarra had never seen. Rich, deep black dirt from far inland, where the farmland was generous and the people established. There were licence plates from states and provinces he never knew existed.

His customers lingered by the back of the truck after they'd made their purchases, trying to steal a peek of the Messiah like schoolboys outside a strip show. Midway was definitely running a fever. The would-be believers had pent-up fury in their eyes. One misunderstanding, one more frustrated expectation and they'd tear him and his truck to bits. Against his better judgment, forgetting that Sabbitha could hear everything, Gazarra made desperate promises for the night ahead. Anything to keep these barbarians at a safe distance.

The customers responded by buying everything they could get their hands on. They buy like fools, then blame me afterwards, Gazarra thought. He couldn't imagine what these trailer-dwellers and campers would need with roofing nails. Maybe they were preparing a crucifixion. It occurred to him that it was wrong to make money off a spiritual outbreak, but he was so busy with people who wanted to buy something from the man who'd known the Messiah, whether they needed anything or not, that he didn't have time to get to the bottom of the question. It probably has no bottom, he grumbled.

Towards the end of the afternoon, a familiar voice inquired whether the peddler might not have a tin coffeepot that would do well over a camp stove.

"Mr. Rainbow! Am I ever glad!"

"You look awful, no offence, Mr. Gazarra. A damned sight worse than you did at Axom Springs. And you looked pretty bad there."

Gazarra ran his hand through his beard.

"I feel like I look, Grady. These days have been . . . unspeakable."

"They're what you were lusting after, old friend. Any regrets?"

"How could I say I have any?"

"I understand the problem. What about the great transparent soul?"

Gazarra remembered just in time that a canvas tarp doesn't shut out human voices.

"She's resting," he said guardedly, and cast a quick nod towards the truckbed.

"I see."

They paused to listen to a series of homesick, other-worldly cries. Llamas, big cats on short leashes, monkeys on chains. The whole exotic carnival set-up. Mr. Rainbow showily consulted his non-existent watch.

"Say, Mr. Gazarra, it seems to me like it's cocktail hour." He pulled a flask from his pocket. "Grab your cash register and let's go and lean against that tree over there so it won't fall down. Maybe it'll do the same for us. This is good hooch."

"My customers," the peddler protested weakly.

"You've done well enough. That's what people say."

"They do?"

Gazarra hated to be talked about. It was in the bones, or deeper: the genes. Identify a man and misfortune will find him. It was Old World wisdom that worked just as well in the New.

He walked along at Grady Rainbow's heels, holding the small leather stringbag that passed as a cash register. Once they were out of what the snake-tanner judged to be the Messiah's earshot, he said, "It looks like you got a tiger by the tail, Mr. Gazarra."

"It's a sacrifice. I knew it would be hard for her. That much has been written. I didn't know it would be this hard for me."

"That's only fair," Rainbow observed.

"I'm sorry, I sound selfish." He kicked at an exposed tree root. "I know pain is necessary if things are to change. Pain for her and, yes, for me, too. I can see the question in your eyes, so I won't make you ask it out loud. Yes, I still believe, harder than ever. I believe that when this world becomes so heavy with iniquity, a giant overthrow will take place, and all things will change. That's been written in a thousand places, a thousand times, in a thousand different ways, by people better than us. Why should it be easy?"

"Well, friend, I wish I had your gift for belief. Not that I don't believe, you know, actively, like some people. I just can't get the handle of it. I wish someone would explain to me how it's done. Maybe it's like rhythm: you either got it or you don't. All I can do is hang around and hope I'll learn."

On those words, Grady Rainbow produced his flask and took a pull. One thing he'd always been strict about was never drinking whisky as long as the sun was in the sky. But since the world was entering a period of great rule-breaking, the least he could do was kick in his small, personal part.

That's what he told Nathan Gazarra.

"How's that hairband holding up?" he asked.

Gazarra took a short, nervous sip from the flask. He'd been waylaid by whisky last night, and was feeling a little skittish.

"All right, I suppose. It's suffered its share of abuse, too. The last time I saw it, she'd thrown it in the hardware bin."

"Was she wearing it in Alma and Axom Springs?"

"Of course. It was for effect, right?"

"For beauty. To advertise her. That's what we said."

"Yes, we did use those words. Without knowing."

"We knew, we knew," Grady Rainbow told him. "There must be something magic about that thing."

"I don't know about magic. She talked to a snake in Retreat, then I ran over it. You made a hairband out of the skin, and she performed a miracle. Two miracles. Maybe more. I can't believe in coincidence. What if I'd run over another snake in Retreat, or no snake, or had never gone there? Accidents are exactly what they seem — accidents. The life of the spirit can't depend on whether a snake gets run over by a pick-up truck in Retreat. That's not the kind of world I live in."

"You live in a world of belief. Everything is justified there. I envy you. Even if it does make you a little extreme."

"Believe me, for years it was a burden. It made me different from the rest of the easygoing people around here. Yourself included, no offense. Now I see that belief is like riches — blinding, incomparable riches."

Mr. Rainbow took another pull, then shook his head.

"I used to go to church. I used to believe in all the usual things, just to be polite. It was more out of habit, I guess."

"Habit and ferocity aren't the same thing," Gazarra stated proudly. A little too proudly, Rainbow thought.

"Well, if I can't believe, old friend, at least I can hang around and lend a hand. Talking about ferocity, you don't know everything this place can do to someone who takes a stand like yours."

"I've been working this country for years."

"I'm not disputing that, Mr. Gazarra. But like I say, both of you need taking care of. You need protecting from the world and from yourselves."

"I didn't know you had anything of the nurse in you," Gazarra told him.

"I didn't know that either, until now. I grew into it, what with the circumstances. That's my personal change. My attempt at emotion."

"You want to look after Sabbitha," he accused his friend, "because you're in love with her."

"Sure, I am," Grady agreed. "Like every other man. And woman, too, who knows? But there's one thing that sets me apart from all the other fellows."

"What's that?"

"I know I can't have her."

Mr. Rainbow burst out laughing. It was the laughter of sheer relief.

On the carnival grounds, not a single light was lit, even at the end of the afternoon. There were no strains of that happy, tinkling, idiot music that makes people want to part with their dollar bills. The rides all stood motionless. Nothing was stirring in the compound but the animals. They didn't like changes to their routine, and they expressed their feelings by howling.

A lone customer stood by the back of the pick-up truck. A man dressed in a dusty, formal black suit like an old-style Quaker.

It was Brenner. He pointed at the stringbag Gazarra held in his hand.

"You're making a good business?"

"How come? Thinking about going back on the road? There's room for the both of us."

"But not room for two messiahs. The true and the false."

"The true? The false?" Gazarra aped theological excitement. "You know something I don't?"

"No. We both know the same thing. Your Messiah's a whore."

"Take thee a wife of whoredoms," Gazarra quoted at him.

"I curse the day you ever learned to read. That's a figure of speech, you ass. It means a man must humble himself before the Lord. It doesn't mean a woman is supposed to spread her legs for half the Salvation Coast in order to become the Messiah. A mind that takes things literally is the mind of a child, or an idiot. And you finished your childhood a long time ago."

"You have a thing about whores," Gazarra said. "You ought to go to the big city, where you can patronize them to your heart's content. The Messiah must know pain and degradation before glory. That's what those words mean. It's been written everywhere, even you have to agree with that. It turned out that the Messiah is a woman — that's not my fault. What should she do? Stay home and knit tea-cozies?"

Brenner looked as though he'd explode.

"I didn't bring my pistol because I knew I'd shoot you if I had it — you and that whore of yours!"

"If you did," Gazarra replied coolly, "you'd have a lot to answer for to a lot of people. And I don't mean the sheriff."

"Those people? Those nobodies? You're just pandering to them! No wonder the carnival set up next door to you. What do those peasants know?"

"They have a thirst for redemption, brother, the same as you and me."

"Where is that whore? I want to question her!"

"Question her?" he asked lasciviously. "If you want to see her, you'll come to the congregation hall tonight, like everyone else."

"And surround myself with ecstatics? No, Gazarra, I'm telling you, it's time you stop this blasphemy of yours. Admit that your so-called miracles were made up, and tell how you did them. That woman will fade away, back to wherever she came from, and I'll help find you a new territory."

"Why should I do that? I like this territory."

"Because of them!"

Brenner made a sweeping wave with his hand, embracing the New World in its entirety. He leaned uncomfortably close to Gazarra and whispered harshly into his ear.

"Because of what they'll think of the Jews. They'll laugh at us! They'll say we're only making money off them. Worse, it's an invitation to a pogrom! You know what I'm talking about!"

For a moment Gazarra truly did not know. He had become a believer in Sabbitha Hunter. He was a new man. A completely experimental being. A Jew was a sad old thing from another continent, better off forgotten. He didn't want to be that mournful, mourning, rule-bound thing any more.

He explained all this to Brenner.

Brenner went stalking off across the field, raving about the vengeance of whores, and how a social disease would gnaw off his little schmuck, which would be divine justice finally. For good measure, he promised his own revenge.

"What's the matter? The Lord's isn't good enough for you?" Gazarra called after him.

Brenner didn't answer.

The revenge of a gelding! Gazarra scoffed as he watched the old merchant shouting and pacing in the middle of the soggy field. As Brenner's ravings receded into the background, Gazarra wondered what it really meant to be the experimental being that he claimed he was: a believer in Sabbitha Hunter. How could he say that he was scarcely a Jew any more, when Messiah-waiting was the Jewish sport?

My logic is deserting me, the peddler realized. *Good thing no one is paying attention to that sort of thing.*

In the field, Brenner slammed his car door so hard it wrenched off the frame and hung at a 45-degree angle from its oversprung hinges. That iniquity, too, was laid squarely at the feet of the blaspheming panderer and his clapped-out whore. Dragging the door in the mud, Brenner took off across the field, shooting out chunks of clay and clumps of crabgrass in Gazarra's direction.

I suppose you heard that, too, Gazarra addressed his Messiah, who lay behind the canvas veil of his truck, waiting for her hour to spring.

In the early evening, with the warm spring sun still high in the sky, Gazarra slipped into the congregation hall to commune with the empty room before Sabbitha and her followers filled it with strange works. But the hall wasn't empty. From the first row, a woman was watching him. How she managed to face him and keep her body turned towards the front was beyond Gazarra's powers of imagination.

The Lord certainly does give variety to His creation, he thought in awe.

He walked over to the woman who went in two directions at once. Next to her, the Crab Man was arrayed in his ambulating dentist's chair.

"Out of deference to Sabbitha Hunter," the Two-Direction Woman said to Gazarra, "us sensation-workers have gotten together and decided not to open the carnival tonight."

"It's my doing," the Crab Man said quarrelsomely. "I had to fight the owner tooth and nail."

"And claw," the Two-Direction Woman stated the obvious. "We want to see what's going to happen."

"She's going to work a miracle!" the Crab Man exalted.

"Just 'cause she worked one on you," the Fused Man said, "doesn't mean she's going to do the same for everybody else."

"And if she did," his Fused Wife put in, "you might not like it, if you know what I mean. A jealous little crab is a sorry sight."

"As long as she never, ever says she's like us," the Two-Direction Woman repeated her threat.

"You'd be surprised how many people want to be like us," the Crab Man confided to Gazarra.

At the end of the pew, the Human Hammer was executing his number in his heavy, compulsive way. He didn't need an audience the way the others did, which made him a real freak.

"Like us," the Crab Man added finely with a nod in the Hammer's direction, "not like him."

"We feel close to Sabbitha somehow," the Fused Man said.

"Which is why we got the best seats in the house," his female half continued, agreeing with him for once.

"I only hope we don't steal the show," the Two-Direction Woman said maliciously.

"You won't," the Crab Man swooned, his face illuminated with pink light, as if the sun was setting on him, "no matter how many contortions you put yourself through. The body's one thing. The spirit's another."

"Don't forget this is a temple," Gazarra cautioned them, "not a place for personal pride and advancement."

"You can't tell me Sabbitha Hunter isn't getting something out of this!" the Two-Direction Woman scoffed.

"Yes, she is," Gazarra answered. "The terror of passing through darkness. The rending pain of bringing forth a miracle from her body. The confusion of being an instrument of a higher purpose. Satisfied?"

"All right, all right. Then how come she's going to all that trouble?"

"To change the world."

The sensation-workers weren't very happy with that explanation. Except for the Crab Man, of course, who'd already been transformed by love. Their minds were too mercantile to contemplate anything in the way of a higher purpose.

"You can count on Crab Boy," he piped up in his reedy, unsteady voice. "Her gospel was made for me. I want to change!"

Understanding from a crab, Gazarra figured, was better than the selfish striving of these back-biting, commercial-minded sensationalists. He would have thanked the Crab Man if it wasn't for that little tableau he'd witnessed this morning through the trailer window.

But whose fault had that been? No one had jammed his face to the streaked glass and made him look. Gazarra had gone in search of knowledge. He'd come away with pain. The typical equation.

That was another one of Sabbitha's many innovations. In the old days, only the Messiah knew the pain and terror and loneliness of the calling. The followers could only watch with sadness and pity in their hearts. But this new democratic twentieth-century version spread the pain around. Everybody got a taste of what she was going through, whether they liked it or not.

That evening, as they moved into the hall, the people of Midway gave the sensation-workers a wide berth. If a miracle ever happened over there, in the front row, it could make a hell of a mess. What if the Fused Man lost hold of his Fused Wife, or the other way around? The good folk shivered with the possibilities.

Gazarra the peddler looked out upon the moving, uneasy sea of followers from his position on the platform. Once again, he crossed them up with his sermon. He served up a lecture thick with the ideas of duty and responsibility. To believe in Sabbitha was to serve the world, he told them. And to serve the world meant taking on the pains of every brother and sister. The approach was strangely puritanical coming from a Hebrew, and a great feat of daring in that lion's den, with the sensation-workers writhing showily in the front row and Midway's blood at the boiling point.

"It's not enough to break the rules," he warned the men and women who'd showed up for a sinning good time. "You have to believe in the cause of your transgression. Rule-breaking without belief is the worst abomination of all! It removes all the holiness from sinning. There would be no more reason to sin."

"Reason to sin?" a believer called out. "Who in hell needs a reason?"

The audience chuckled. A few people whispered to one another, newcomers unaccustomed to the peddler's logic. Sinning came as easy and natural as breathing, they thought. Nobody needed a reason.

"Sabbitha has permitted all that was forbidden — but only to make redemption possible. Don't think you can do what's forbidden just for its own sake. Without belief, your sins will turn sour in your mouth. Pleasure will evaporate and you'll be nothing more than a robot, pumping and flailing away meaninglessly. A machine that doesn't know why it's doing what it's doing."

Gazarra looked into the body of the crowd. So many unfamiliar faces. People he'd never seen before, people not from the Coast. He literally didn't know whom he was talking to any more. That worried him; the first thing any pastor has to know is his audience.

"Sabbitha needs your help to carry out her works," he pursued. "She can't do everything herself!"

Then he saw her, moving up the aisle like a bride with no one to give her away. Wearing black, her magic hairband keeping her hair at bay, on her way to the altar or the gallows. He closed his eyes. He was terrified. Something had to give.

And it did. All hell broke loose.

"Liars! Fakers! Blasphemers!"

Brenner's voice sounded painfully foreign and strident in the Midway hall. Quiet down, you talk like a Jew, Gazarra warned him under his breath.

"Your Messiah's a whore, a diseased whore! And you're all going to catch the disease, all of you that have porked her. You'll all catch the clap, and worse, you'll all look like fools for falling for her carnival tricks!"

Brenner leaped from his seat and lunged at Sabbitha as she glided up the aisle.

"I'll rip that silly thing off her head! Olive oil, my ass! There's not an olive tree anywhere around here. Olive trees are in books!"

But Brenner wasn't as fast on his feet as he thought he was. He grabbed for Sabbitha's hairband but missed. His horny yellow nails raked the side of her neck and raised three long bloody welts. He had to hang on to her dress to keep from falling into the aisle, and he ended up pulling it off her shoulder. The black fabric ripped and her breasts were exposed for all to see. Sabbitha didn't flinch. She didn't draw back. She certainly didn't try to cover herself.

"Save her! Rescue her!"

The Crab Man's reedy voice rose high-pitched above the congregation. He didn't care to hear the light of his life being called a diseased whore, especially since his cock was still slick with their love-making. All four of his pincers rattled convulsively with the kind of violence he didn't have the means to express. His spasms threw him from his chair and he rolled onto the floor, his skin flaring red. The blame for that sad spectacle was also laid at Brenner's feet.

The Midway congregation heeded the Crab Man's call. The little crab couldn't act; they would act for him. Hadn't the peddler just urged them to take on their brothers' and sisters' pain, and who displayed more pain than the Crab Man? They fell upon Brenner with no other weapon than their hands and nails and teeth, which turned out to be weapons enough.

A minute or two later, Brenner couldn't have even found a spot as a sensation-worker in the carnival, had he lived, which was out of the question.

The worshipers drew back to admire their work. They observed a momentary silence, broken only by the Crab Man's pincers flapping with ecstasy. Brenner's arms were bent at impossible angles behind his back, his eye sockets were two pools of gory jelly, his teeth were cracked off and pushed down his throat, his accusing tongue was torn out, his nose planed off and his genitals stomped to a mushy pulp. Above him, Sabbitha Hunter stood unmoving, splattered with the blood of Brenner's sacrifice.

The worshipers poured out the door and into the night, howling Sabbitha's praises. In their own way, they had paid good heed to Gazarra's short sermon. They had taken responsibility for the world and answered his accusations. You accuse us of wanting a superficial good time and sin for its own sake? Watch this! We're capable of more sober pleasures, too. Like murder.

That evening, Sabbitha Hunter did not work a miracle. There were no drops of miraculous oil. Her forehead was dry as a desert. But no one had noticed that.

XIII

The Praise-Singers

W HEN YOU KILL for something, the value of that thing automatically goes up. It's been written in all the love songs. I
love her so much I'll kill her, men are always singing. Anybody
who hadn't been convinced by the miracles at Alma and Axom
Springs were made believers by the events at Midway.

There wasn't anything particularly original about murder, but
the way it was done caught the imagination. Right out in front of
everybody. No one person could be separated from the mass and
accused. The body of the congregation had done the killing.
They'd all taken responsibility and changed something in the world
that had caused one of their number pain.

That was the problem the law faced when two men from the
sheriff's department showed up at the Midway congregation hall
the next morning to throw a sheet over Brenner's mess. Once the
murderous worshipers had fled, Gazarra righted one of the toppled
pews and sat down on it to keep watch over Brenner's remains. It

was a reproachful kind of shiva, an evaluation of a kind. One displaced Jew in the New World wilderness telling the other where he'd gone wrong, and both of them terribly far from any sort of Jerusalem.

"I *am* sorry," Gazarra assured Brenner's shattered corpse.

Gazarra would have preferred not to stare at the human wreckage, but he didn't dare cover him, or move the body. He'd always heard you weren't supposed to tamper with the evidence of a crime.

"At least I'm not leaving you alone," he said in his own defence. "I am sorry, but you should have known. Once a Jew, always a Jew. The minute I heard your voice, or should I say your accent, I knew you were making a big mistake. You shouldn't have forgotten the lesson of the zealots. We are always forgetting our history. We should remember all of it, not just the heroic, humanistic parts. Now that we're in America, we have a tendency to forget that we are not always a rational people. Okay, so America is making us into rationalists. She is trying very hard, and we are trying even harder than she is. Some of us, in any case. Like you."

Gazarra cleared the phlegm out of his throat. His frankness was coming dangerously close to violating the traditional respect for the dead.

"This is what becomes of the rationalist," he told what was left of Brenner. "I am sorry. May you be spared further suffering. In any case, your name," Gazarra promised him, "will certainly not be forgotten."

Outside the hall, a heavy car door slammed. A minute later the sheriff, who went by the unfortunate name of Slaughter, came and stood over Gazarra, considering him with some curiosity.

"We heard about you and the little lady. Where's she at now?"

"The light of the world," his deputy, named Traverse, specified.

"She's not in very good shape, I'm afraid."

"The fair sex," Slaughter concluded.

He nodded in the direction of Brenner's remains. "You've been sitting here since last night looking at that? It's a wonder you don't lose your mind."

"I always heard you weren't supposed to touch the victim of a crime. You know, so as not to spoil the evidence."

Traverse laughed, which struck Gazarra as sacrilegious.

"You see any evidence around here?" he questioned Gazarra.

The peddler shrugged. "I don't know, I'm not a policeman."

"I see someone who got beaten to a pulp in front of several hundred witnesses. But I don't see no evidence."

Then Traverse went outside to the car for a tarp.

"Why don't you tell me your story?" Slaughter suggested.

Gazarra did as he was told. It wasn't hard. He knew the victim, he had known him forever. Brenner used to be a peddler, now he was a storekeeper. Slaughter told him to skip the anecdotes. Gazarra excused himself and described how Brenner had gotten up and started insulting the congregation. He'd called them fakers and whores. Then he attacked Miss Hunter in an indecent manner by trying to tear her dress off. The Crab Man, who must have had a weakness for the young lady, called upon the congregation to defend her honor, seeing as though he couldn't do it himself. The congregation did his bidding in a completely shocking and unexpected way.

"Did this freak tell the others to kill Brenner?" Slaughter asked.

"No."

"What did he say?"

"I don't remember. It was hard to hear, and he has such a tiny voice . . . But he never said the word 'kill.' That much I know."

Slaughter gave Gazarra the look he gave all witnesses struck with temporary lapses of memory. Traverse came back with the tarp. It was plasticized, like a mattress cover in a cheap motel. He spread it over Brenner, tiptoeing around the clumps of tissue.

"Who were these people in the congregation last night?"

"Men and women I've never seen before. People from out of town. I know my customers, I've been working my routes for a long time. I've never seen anything like this."

"There were women, too?" Traverse asked Gazarra.

"Of course," Slaughter answered for him. "Don't you read the papers? Don't you know about women's liberation?"

"And they participated in the killing?"

"They might have. There were so many of them, like a cloud of locusts. It was a nightmare."

"I bet it was. What was your assistant, the light of the world, doing in the meantime?"

"She just stood there. She was in shock. She couldn't move."

"She didn't tell them to stop?"

"If she had, no one would have heard her. They wouldn't have obeyed her anyway. They had blood in their eyes."

The sheriff considered the truth of that claim for a moment or two.

"Just what kind of congregation is this?" he asked.

"Bible-reading," Gazarra answered with a hesitation so slight an ordinary sheriff wouldn't have been able to detect it, "for people who don't know how to read."

"There's nothing wrong with that," Slaughter admitted. "But if I hear about anything like this happening again, I'm going to have to dissolve your congregation. People'll just have to learn to read and study the Bible all on their own. We got freedom of religion around here, but not when it comes to disturbing the peace. And murder is definitely disturbing the peace. My peace."

Gazarra nodded in agreement. Traverse returned to the corpse and lifted the tarp with his boot-tip. Like the peddler, he wasn't afraid of gore.

"This is not a natural killing," Traverse stated. He smoothed the tarp with his boot. "Maybe we ought to question the lady."

"She didn't do it," Gazarra told them.

"So you say. Only problem is, the ones that did do it, they don't seem to be around any more, and you don't know them anyway. We have to start somewhere."

"They're out there." Gazarra pointed to the door. "Running wild in the woods. They'll come back."

"Why would they?"

"They're attracted to Sabbitha."

"Really? Well, you let me know when they do come back," Slaughter advised him. "If they do."

He bent over and picked up the head end of Brenner's remains, and Traverse took the foot end. They tipped the corpse onto the tarp, then wrapped the body gingerly in it, trying to keep their uniforms clean. That wasn't easy. There were bits of Brenner nearly everywhere.

At the door, Slaughter turned to Gazarra.

"I don't know what the hell kind of Bible you're reading, but it sure ain't the love-thy-neighbor version."

Then the sheriff and his deputy steered Brenner out towards the trunk of their car.

Another murder goes unpunished, Gazarra thought. It occurred to him that he was probably the only one in Midway who cared about the late storekeeper. That's the way it is with old enemies. You define yourself against them. You're sorry when they go. Poor Brenner, he wouldn't change, even when Sabbitha Hunter came. A small-hearted, quarreling, pessimistic rationalist. A Jew in Eulonia. What sadder fate could there be?

Gazarra shooed away the flies buzzing excitedly over the manna of Brenner's blood. One final indignity. He closed the door to the congregation hall and stepped outside.

"All right," he addressed his Messiah out loud, "you've fucked a crab and gotten a man killed, but has that brought us any closer to the new world? What are you going to do to us next?"

But she didn't do it, he reminded himself as he walked under the quiet elms and oaks through the town in the bright morning sunlight, so why did I say she did?

He started across the field where the carnival slept. Some part of him was beginning to rebel. Against Sabbitha Hunter, or against the Messiah? His mind was too exhausted to begin figuring out the differences, but he knew there had to be some.

By the time Gazarra got to his truck, he was practically sleep-walking. He was getting too old to be engaging in all-night vigils over the remains of a rival. But he didn't climb into the back of his truck the way he normally would have. The chances were good that Sabbitha would be inside. And since the dismemberment of Brenner, the thought of her inspired prudence.

His discretion turned out to be a wise thing. As he hesitated outside the back of the truck, he distinctly heard the Crab Man's voice coming from within. There was no mistaking it: reedy, feeble and metallic, but completely audible. Definitely the voice of a man in the horizontal position.

"You were great," he was telling Sabbitha. "Any of us would die for what you did. Making people act that way. We're just ordinary moths pinned to a board compared to you. But you, baby, you went out and moved them and showed them who's boss."

The Crab Man could have been a carnival barker, or a cornerman urging his bloodied fighter to answer the bell one last time. It wasn't enough for him to hoist his crippled pink body onto hers, Gazarra thought. He has to manage her, too.

"I heard about you, but I didn't believe it. I've heard about a lot of things in my line of work. Seeing is believing, I said to myself. But I saw, all right. Oh, boy, did I ever!"

The Crab Man paused to gulp his saliva.

"I don't know what you are, but I sure believe in you!"

There could be no greater compliment than that.

Sabbitha supplied no answer. Then, slowly and monotonously, gaining momentum, the reluctant, oversprung rear shocks of the pick-up began to rock as Gazarra looked on. Those springs were the sick seismograph of the Midway soul.

The peddler walked around to the front of the truck, where the shade was, and where the movement was not. He leaned his head against the left front tire and immediately fell into sleep.

Thirty blissful minutes later, the peddler was troubled by the feeling that he wasn't alone. Sheriff Slaughter had come to question the Messiah. "Are you really who you are?" In his dream, the word *really* tormented Gazarra. It was the thing that stood between you and you. There was always something separating us from ourselves. Even the Lord had to use a *that* between "I am" and "I am" when Moses asked Him to say who He was in Egypt. In the peddler's dream, Sabbitha had escaped. She began running flat out towards the black wall of pines at the edge of Midway. An escape attempt. A suicide attempt. She didn't want to be who she was any more. His cause was to stop her. But she was everywhere. Whenever he saved her from one collision she would rush again, craving the impact. He was too old, he was tiring, he couldn't keep saving her forever. Why did she want this, why wouldn't she stop, this wasn't who she was supposed to be!

When he finally failed, and her forehead struck the unmoving trunk of a pine at full force, her skull opened as if an axe-blade had split it. Gazarra gave a weak cry and flicked open his eyes in terror.

No Sheriff Slaughter. No Deputy Traverse. Grady Rainbow was standing in front of him. The snake-tanner looked the worse for wear, too.

"The tiger sure whipped her tail last night," Rainbow said.

"You saw it?" Gazarra asked.

"I'm afraid I did."

"What did it look like to you?"

"She didn't do wrong. She didn't whip up the crowd. She just stood there, for Christ's sake . . . She just has this effect, I guess."

"This gift."

"Some gift," Rainbow said darkly.

Gazarra leaned against the fender, then got to his feet.

"I suppose you're still rejoicing in her powers?" Rainbow asked.

"Why wouldn't I? Even you said she did no wrong."

"You know, Mr. Gazarra, it doesn't matter any more what she did or didn't do. That's just details now. Petty shit the sheriff can worry about if he feels like he's got to arrest somebody. From now on, you either accept it or you don't."

"It?"

"Yeah, it," Mr. Rainbow said. "The whole package. The way those people are acting. You know, transgression and all. Whatever happens now, you have to accept it. You set this thing loose. Now live with it!"

"I don't have to accept everything those people do, just because I believe in the idea. The need. The idea doesn't depend on us accepting it anyway. It's free of us. It doesn't depend on us. It's non-human!"

"It certainly is!"

Suddenly Grady Rainbow realized that the truck was rhythmically rocking beneath his rear end. It didn't take him long to figure out what that motion was due to.

"Holy Jesus!" he burst out.

He jumped off the fender as if it were on fire.

"The Crab Man," Gazarra told him.

"That freak?"

"You don't call them that any more. They want to be called sensation-workers."

Mr. Rainbow waved off the difference. "New bottles for old wine. A lot of oomph in that little crab."

"She's supposed to act that way," Gazarra said, heading off the usual question. "It's part of being what she is."

"It sounds like cruel and unusual punishment to me," Grady Rainbow objected. "Where's it going to take us? How long can it possibly go on?"

"Until it changes the world."

"The world's already changed for a lot of people," Mr. Rainbow said somberly. "It has for me, and I'm not sure I like it any more, on her account. I mean, think about it, from her point of view. What can it be like?"

He moved away from the truck.

"I've got some other things to tell you, but first you'll have to excuse me. My nerves won't allow me to hang around this vehicle any more, not with it doing what it's doing."

Grady and Gazarra walked together out into the field. Clumps of crabgrass lay here and there, scattered by Brenner's spinning wheels. The cheerful, generous sun poured down on the peddler's uncovered head. From where they stood, the pick-up truck's motion was ever so slight, like a leaf on a tree on a quiet summer day.

"That little crab's got staying power," Grady Rainbow observed.

Both men laughed. It was the tradition to laugh at such things. But neither put much conviction into it.

"Last night, after what happened to Brenner," Rainbow began, "I figured I'd better hightail it out of here. I didn't like what I saw, and I didn't want to end up in jail as accessory to murder."

"The sheriff didn't do anything," Gazarra told him, "except haul away the corpse."

"That's not the point, Mr. Gazarra. It wouldn't surprise me if he and his men have become followers now, too. Anyway, I made it home and I started to work, you know, I figured I'd pull a few snakes to get my mind off what I'd seen. One of the advantages of being self-employed. Anyway, during the night, when I was out in the tanning shed, a terrible racket rose up in the woods. Something inhuman was out there, wildcats fighting or some new breed of sow in heat. It froze my blood. I got out my shotgun, I wanted to shoot it but I didn't know where it was. And I didn't want to attract attention to myself."

"A wise choice."

"This morning I got out on the road to see what I could see. Everything's closed up. There's not a store or business of any kind open. They say everyone's come up here! Shit, I had to siphon gas just to get back myself. Then I realized I was doing exactly what everybody else is: I closed my shop and came up here for the big show."

"What about your wildcats?"

"I'm getting there. They say since last evening, after the murder, the people who did it have been prowling around the countryside, living off what they can steal and practicing the gospel according to Miss Hunter. You can imagine what that means. They call themselves the praise-singers. That didn't sound like singing to me, what I heard. It sounded like the Devil rattling the chains of hell!"

Gazarra smiled. "So you came straight back here, to the center of it all?"

"It doesn't make any sense, does it? But I figure that if things turn out the way Sabbitha Hunter says they will, it might be a good thing to be in with you."

Grady Rainbow laughed guiltily. Gazarra smiled, too, but over something completely different. "The way Sabbitha Hunter says," his friend had put it. But so far, Sabbitha hadn't said very much at all. She was playing the role of the cipher quite nicely.

"I'm happy to consider you my friend, Mr. Rainbow, and I'm glad you came back. I could use the company. But I don't know what good I'll be as an insurance policy."

The tailgate of Gazarra's truck rattled in its moorings. Both men turned to look. The Crab Man was lowering himself down from the bed, on his way to work. He hung briefly from the crook of both elbows, then dropped heavily onto the ground. He must have had padding in his butt like a football player.

Gazarra and Mr. Rainbow had wondered how the crab managed to make it in and out of the truck. Well, now they knew. And now that they'd seen it, they both wished they hadn't.

XIV

A Fabulous Loss

*O*NE EVENING, with Midway still hovering on the edge of the apocalypse, a man came looking for a certain Miss Sabbitha Hunter. Until then, no one knew her family name. The man was an older gentleman, though not as old as Gazarra. His face was criss-crossed with lines like a road map, and his eyes looked as though they had seen a few roads, too, but that was no particular distinction along the Salvation Coast. Despite the signs of age, he carried himself proudly, aware of his powers, the way a younger man would.

He had driven through Midway once, then twice, reconnoitering. He had seen the crowds and judged them to be disorderly. The car he was driving wasn't his, and he'd promised to return it to its owner, a friend who sold used vehicles, the day after next, in at least as good condition as when he'd taken it. He decided to leave the car in the parking lot of a shuttered gas station out by the Interstate, far from harm's reach, he hoped. He would walk in the rest of the way.

He wasn't afraid to put a little mileage on his legs. Exercise kept the body young, and staying young looking was one of his life objectives. The walk would get his mind percolating, and he figured he'd need that organ in top shape by the time he got to the center of Midway.

On the way in, he asked directions to where Miss Sabbitha Hunter might be, just to test the air. He discovered that using her last name offended people.

"No such thing as 'Hunter,'" he was told by a snaggle-toothed believer with a boil on his cheek, who looked as though he needed saving in the worst way.

"Is that so?" the man asked.

"Hunter's a family name. Family ain't what this is all about. This is about getting rid of your family."

"Well, what do you know?" he said to the man with the boil. "No family? I think you ought to know that that little girl's my favorite niece. My late brother's daughter, to be exact. I've known her ever since she was just a sweet little child. And sweet she was, my friend!"

The man's boil pulsed with conviction. He stood frozen with outrage on the strip of concrete that led into Midway from the Interstate. He ground his teeth and stared at Uncle Tommy as if he were out of his mind. For a second, Tommy thought the man would hit him. Or worse, bite him.

"The Messiah don't have no family."

"How can that be?" Uncle Tommy reasoned. "Everybody has family. She didn't just hatch."

"The Messiah ain't no natural person. She's above all that petty shit the rest of us have got to worry about. That's how come she's free to be who she's got to be, and do what she's got to do."

Then the man hurried away from Tommy as if fleeing the poisonous whisper of heresy.

No family, Tommy told himself. Then who the hell am I?

He pinched the creases back into his slacks and smoothed his gray brushcut. His baby had really become a somebody, that much was clear. If only he'd known . . . It could have been because of me, Tommy thought with mixed pride and guilt, the two conventional emotions that had defined him over the years. A man like me can have quite an effect on a woman, he concluded. Especially a wild young one like her.

Sabbitha Hunter, who could have had anything she wanted, chose to live in the back of an old pick-up truck with a tarp stretched high over the bed like a Wild West wagon. Those were the rumors that had reached Tommy. He didn't believe a single word of them. With sweet, stylized regret, he pictured his niece's pride, her natural elegance, her love of pretty things, her awareness of her own splendor. Some of that came from being an Ebenezer lady. The rest she'd improvised with her own genius. So why would she live in the back of a truck — unless she was making a point, which was something she excelled at, as he recalled.

As for the other rumors and testimonies he'd heard, which had made his flesh crawl, he'd given them enough credence to have driven two days in a car borrowed off a friend's used-car lot to see for himself.

The center of Midway was thick with people, but they weren't there to make inquiries, the way Tommy was. They'd already made up their minds about who and what Sabbitha was. Their public displays of rule-breaking made it hard for him to make much headway. He had to stop and gawk every few steps. He saw, but didn't believe what he saw. If these people were his baby's followers, he wondered, what the hell would their leader be like?

Tommy was no theologian, but he could detect two tendencies among the followers. The first believed in repentance. Sabbitha hadn't asked them to practice penance, but they couldn't help themselves. It was in the blood, it was a style they had been born into, the fruit of a generalized sense of guilt. They went wandering and staggering under the stately oaks and elms of Midway's gracious old streets, reciting all the woes that were bound to fall upon the town, if not sooner, then later. It wasn't clear whether their recital was designed to spur the arrival of those woes or ward them off. But one thing was sure: the repentance people took deep and lusty pleasure in ticking off the list of fleshly terrors that awaited everyone, themselves included.

Tommy wished he'd had a set of earplugs handy. In their apocalyptic warnings, he heard echoes of all the accusations a pleasure-loving man is ever likely to hear from the female mouth.

The other tendency wasn't that much more pleasant to observe, even if they did preach free and joyful rule-breaking. Imagine the kind of thing you'd do in private with the lights dimmed and the shades pulled down — if you'd do it at all. These people were doing it out in the open, by a clump of bushes or next to a mailbox, barely out of the way so you wouldn't step on them. He couldn't look, but he couldn't not look. The ugliness and commonness of their bodies struck Tommy. The flabby, hanging flesh, the clumps of random body hair, the warts and skin tags where the sun had punished them, the angry, bruised, purple color of their parts of pleasure — Tommy's romanticism took a real kick in the teeth.

"Jesus," he thought to himself, "is that what I look like when I make love? No wonder people turn out the lights."

He believed that love-making was reserved for the young and the strong and the beautiful — and that included himself, of course. The people in Midway seemed to hold the contrary belief; they were true democrats of the flesh. The worse you looked, the greater your obligation to expose yourself. From the man with the pulsing boil out by the Interstate on down, every one of them seemed disfavored by nature. They were all working furiously to remove the stigma of their ugliness by celebrating it in the crude light of day. And who knows, maybe they'd succeed.

If this school of followers was pursuing pleasure, they were a long way from their goal. Worse than the raw-meat color of their skin was the turn of their mouths and the set of their eyes. They lusted after pleasure, but to no avail. They'd done their best but they were exhausted, they'd hit a wall like amateurs trying to run the marathon.

Tommy had a despairing thought for his baby, that sweet girl who'd danced her way down with him so willingly to the soft, welcoming riverbank. Shit, she'd been a rule-breaker even then, but only with him, not with . . . He couldn't finish the sentence. Tommy was beyond jealousy. He cursed himself. His head swam with the enormity of his fabulous loss. He wanted her back. He'd tell her, finally, why he'd had to cut and run on her that way. Maybe she'd understand. Maybe she'd see the world his way again.

What did he have to lose?

Tommy came to a wide, grassy field and saw an old truck parked askew there, its tires half-sunk into the ground. He had to admit it looked very much like the truck in the rumors. There was a crowd hanging around it, and as Tommy came closer he saw that money and goods were changing hands at furious speed.

In the chaos, on the eve of the end of days, Gazarra was peddling his remaining merchandise. Not that he particularly wanted to. But he was besieged by customers, people he'd never seen before, and who didn't care what they bought or how much it cost them. Everyone wanted a souvenir from the old world before it went up in smoke. No one much wondered how they were going to carry that pound of sugar or length of fence wire or bar of perfumed purple soap across to the other side, to where the new world would begin, or what they would do with those things once they got there, whether those objects would even have meaning in the glorious future they were preparing, whether you would need to sugar your coffee or mark your property line or perfume your skin in the great changed time to come. Buying was a habit. A familiar thing to do in a world gone very unfamiliar.

By the truck, Tommy saw something he would have called a gang, except that all its members were white, and to him, gangs had to be black. Sabbitha hadn't asked for it, but it had sprung up anyway. Her posse, her security force: the praise-singers. After their first success with Brenner and their celebrations that ravaged the countryside, they returned to fester around the back of the pick-up truck, directionless, waiting for guidance. No one dared speculate out loud that their presence might not be required in a new and changed world. And that if it was needed, then the world would not have changed that much after all.

Their dirty fingernails, stained clothes and nervous, vacant eyes persuaded Tommy to get in line and wait his turn with the rest of the supplicants and customers. Shit, this is like the line-up to the whorehouse, Tommy thought idly.

But it was no whorehouse line. Everyone waiting with him was a woman.

The women were arguing furiously about a piece of news they'd heard. It was the sort of thing that could have happened only in Sabbitha's reign. Apparently there was some kind of miracle pill you could take that would keep you from getting pregnant.

"That must be how Sabbitha manages it," one of the women in the line concluded.

"I heard it lets you slough off their sperm like it was soap scum on a bathtub," a thin, jumpy woman reported.

That woman was Mrs. Cruice of the sorrowful sorority of Alma Road. A diet of too few calories and too much ecstasy had sharpened her bones down to a cutting edge. She'd tried to spread

Sabbitha's gospel back in Alma, but no one wanted to do it with her. She didn't have the charisma, and though she was willing to break any and all rules, she could never make it seem like much fun. But in Midway, in the crowd, she found strength and partners aplenty.

She shook her head in wonderment.

"No more staying power than bathtub ring when you rub it with cleanser. Rinse it right out of your system. Can you imagine that?"

"It sounds too good to be true," her Alma Road sisters agreed. "Science being on our side for once."

"If it's true, and why wouldn't it be, then what's holding us back?" Mrs. Cruice asked rhetorically. "Getting knocked up is the only thing keeping me from letting loose like Sabbitha does."

"You mean getting knocked up by the wrong man," one of her sisters teased her.

"No. I mean what I said — getting knocked up, period. They're all the wrong man as far as I can see."

"That, and a social disease!"

"The clap's for other people," the Cruice woman claimed. "Men can do it, so why not us? You know what I'm going to do? I'm going to get me that pill and cat around and get what I want when I want it, and be just as low-down as any man!"

"Well, that'll be some improvement in the world!"

"You just shush up, now," Mrs. Cruice told her sisters. "You know that's why we're here, all of us. Otherwise, you might as well go home and feed the chickens and get covered by Mr. Rooster!"

The women cackled happily.

Tommy gave his crotch a self-conscious hitch. He felt like he was being eyed. He wondered whether these women intended on skewering him on a spit and roasting him whole for all the wrong that men ever did to women, which was no small amount, by the look of these ones.

He felt he was being blamed for something, but he didn't know what. It's just because I'm a man, he deduced. That's all they've got against me. But being a man wasn't his fault. It was none of his personal responsibility. You can't blame a person for the way they were born, their sex or the color of their skin. That's racism, and Tommy was no racist, not like some people he knew.

"Just as soon as I get alone with her," Mrs. Cruice confided to the other women, "I'm going to ask Sabbitha about this pill."

"You think you can ask the Messiah about that kind of stuff? I mean, it's pretty personal."

"Why the fuck not?" Mrs. Cruice swore self-consciously. "What use is she if she's not for us?"

Tommy understood what it was about these women. With their showy, aggressive ways, especially that bony one who was doing all the talking, it was obvious that they considered him prey. He hitched up his pants again. Not that he minded a hot-blooded woman. He just wasn't used to predatory feelings from the other sex. He didn't know how prey is supposed to act.

He felt relieved when he was finally thrust to the front of the line, face to face with the grizzled old peddler.

"I've come to see Miss Hunter. We're family . . . She's my baby niece."

Gazarra scrutinized the man's neat gray brushcut and anxious, polite ways. Maybe there was a family resemblance. Something in the way manners were used to cover up madness. Family, though, is always bad business.

"The Messiah has no family," Gazarra told him flatly.

"Yeah, I got that already, on the way in. How do you think that makes me feel?"

Gazarra didn't particularly care. He smelled the warm stink of family trouble. He tried feeding the man more abstractions.

"The Messiah has sprung from herself. She has anointed herself to do the Lord's bidding."

Uncle Tommy had a logical mind. He didn't care for riddles. If this old geezer wants proof, he decided, I'll supply proof. He reached into his pocket and for a moment Gazarra thought he was going for his gun. He wouldn't have been surprised. People have been shot for a lot less.

But Tommy produced something more dangerous. He pulled out his wallet and flipped open a pocket-sized plastic-encased photo album, the kind people carry around to remind themselves what their husband or wife and kids look like. Gazarra considered the proof: a snapshot of Sabbitha asleep on the banks of the Sandspur River. She was lovingly framed by tree branches and covered with the pretty sheet she and Tommy used for their picnics and their pleasure. Anyone with eyes in their head could see that the Messiah was naked under that sheet.

"That's her, that's my niece," Tommy explained proudly. "We're family." He pointed at the truckbed. "I got a right."

Gazarra jammed his broad palm and stubby fingers over the image. The Messiah must have no family. Nothing banal or normal must be allowed to compromise her. How could that be? The Messiah's first birthday, the Messiah's first two-wheeler, the Messiah on ponyback. That's what family did: it made you ordinary. It gave everyone the same experience, and put them on the same level. That was bad for business.

"What do you want?" Gazarra whispered at Uncle Tommy. "Blackmail?"

"I already told you," Tommy answered, "so stop hissing at me. I want to see my niece, Miss Hunter. I'd lost track of her, and I'd just about given up hope of ever seeing her again when I heard tell of her and . . . you know, all those things people say she's doing."

"Do you believe what they say?" Gazarra stalled him.

"I don't believe, but I don't disbelieve. I'm just like everybody else. I want to see with my own eyes . . . You know, it's kind of unusual to have someone like her in your family, you just don't know what to make of it. You don't know what it says about yourself. Sabbitha always was an extraordinary girl, never afraid of anything. Kind of a wild child, you might say. I could tell you things . . ."

"Don't," the peddler advised him.

Gazarra had no choice. He let the man step past him and the praise-singers and enter the sanctuary of the pick-up truck. The women hanging around the line were starting to get interested in this handsome stranger's well-worn snapshots.

"Put those pictures away," Gazarra ordered Uncle Tommy in a low, urgent voice. "Graven images aren't allowed. Don't you know that? Haven't you read the Bible?"

"Not that part," Tommy admitted.

Gazarra held back the edge of the tarp, then closed it quickly behind him.

Inside the truck, Sabbitha basked in the private splendor of her power, knowing all of Midway awaited her next outrage. Her face glowed in the dim light, and heat poured off her skin in ripples like summer asphalt. Her blouse was half-open in theatrical disorder, and she had twisted her hair into a crown around her head.

Tommy had to bend double to fit inside the truck. His face was inches from hers. She looked up at him with dreamy, unconcerned eyes.

"Don't tell me you suffered a miracle, Mr. Crab," she inquired with mock care. "You look almost human. What are you going to do with yourself now? How will you make a living?"

"What the hell are you talking about crabs for, Sabbitha? You got them or something? I wouldn't be surprised, living this way . . . Don't look at me like that. It's your Uncle Tommy. Don't you remember me?"

She focused her eyes on him, but registered nothing.

"Don't tell me you've gone crazy," he pleaded. "Shit, maybe we shouldn't have done all that introverted stuff after all. Maybe that flipped some kind of switch in your head."

"Why, Uncle Tommy, it's you . . . I didn't recognize you at first. The light's not too good in here, you know. They keep it dark, like in a cocktail lounge. But I do recognize your way of talking. That Ebenezer way. You know, laugh it all away, everything's all right in this imperfect world, nothing's anybody's fault. Yes, mister, I remember your voice and everything it told me. And I remember believing every last one of those things. As for the switches in my head, Tommy, think of it like the chicken and the egg. Did we throw those switches by what we did, or were they already thrown, and that's why we did it?"

She laughed. Misplaced laughter, it seemed to Uncle Tommy. As misplaced as a squirrel-fur cover in a warm climate.

"We'll never know, will we?" she said. "To find out, we'd have to dig way down deep, and I don't have the shovel for that job, or the inclination. I'm doing this" — she motioned to her pick-up truck cloister — "instead of digging. It's the new psychology."

"Sabbitha, I've come to tell you the real reason — "

"That useless, chronic guilt of yours. You're the kind of man who thinks that admitting your wrongs is restitution enough. This new world we got going here doesn't work that way. It's more severe."

"I heard all about you, baby," he said, trying flattery. "I always knew you were something special."

"You wrecked my life," she told him. "But only for a while."

"I knew it was wrong. You knew it, too. But you wouldn't have stopped and either would I have, no matter what we knew. Our love was strong. But they *made* me go away. That's why I came to see you. I need to tell you what they did to us."

"You wrecked my life because you went away. You ever hear of loneliness?"

"I know all the varieties."

"You do not. You're mixing up 'lonely' and 'alone.'"

"They made me go away," he pleaded.

He launched into the whole sad, undignified story. Though it wasn't a story, it was an explanation, and explanations never elevated anyone in anyone else's eyes.

"Somebody saw us, you know, when we were together — you know what I mean. I don't know how it happened, but it did. There are always people skulking around the woods, and whoever it was, he told your daddy and your daddy told me. Told me to get out of town. I had to. It was either that or solve it with a gun, and that wouldn't have helped you any. Shoot my baby's daddy? My own brother? Though I was tempted to. What the hell! Why not add one crime to another?"

"He died," Sabbitha pointed out. "He was already dying. Everyone saw it but you. You could have come back once he was in the ground."

"I can't believe you're talking that way about your father. Your own flesh and blood!"

"You were fucking your own flesh and blood, so don't tell me how I can talk and how I can't. I can say anything I want to. Especially about my family. That's what this whole thing is all about. You get rid of your old family and trade it in for a new model. Or you replace it with a band of lunatics. That's what I found out since my miracles started: I can say any old truth I want to. All the truths, if I have to. Sometimes I can't even help it, like with the miracles. That's the advantage I have being who I am — or who they say I am, anyway, who I've become. I have power. The power to say whatever's on my mind. Like how you wrecked my life with your cowardice."

Tommy winced. "Is that such a great thing?"

"What?"

"Saying everything. Anything. The first thing that comes into your head. That sounds like what crazy people do."

"They call it honesty now," Sabbitha informed him, "though I don't believe the concept has made it to Ebenezer yet. You're afraid of it because you don't want to hear the truth, and how it concerns you."

Tommy shook his head. He was a conservative sinner with a sense of propriety. Sinning out in the open, and telling everyone about it, was against his code of conduct.

"I wish I could have you back, Sabbitha. I'd protect you."

She laughed harshly. Her laughter sounded lewd to his ears.

"From what, poor man? From myself? From my powers that have just about raped me? From my followers?"

Tommy sunk to the pallet next to her. Her body stiffened. He really had lost her.

"This can't be any way to live, baby."

"Which way is that?"

"Inside a goddamned truck, with all those crazy people out there!"

"Did you see the woman in the bramble dress?" Sabbitha asked, her eyes lighting up.

"I'm afraid I missed that one. But I saw all the others."

Then her voice dropped and her tone turned confidential. "Don't worry, Tommy, it can't go on forever. She can't go on forever and either can I. She'll bleed to death."

"What's going to stop them?"

"Come on, Tommy, use your imagination if you have one. Look around at what's happening out there. How long do you think they can last? Look at me. It's humanly impossible. We're living by an idea. That idea is inhuman."

"Then stop it, baby!" he pleaded. "Just walk! Walk with me!"

"Walking, and walking with you — those are two different

things. No," she said flatly, "the end of days has to come first. And we're certainly doing our best to hasten that time."

Tommy felt the cold hands of jealousy across his skin. The hands of Sabbitha's countless transgressors, real and imaginary. Even if he did win her back, he wondered briefly, how could a simple man like him measure up to the experiences she'd had as head rule-breaker?

"You really do want to get this thing over with, don't you, baby?" he tried one last time. "I could help you."

"No, you couldn't — nothing personal, you understand. You're just not the saving kind of man. You'd better go now. They'll be getting impatient outside. You don't want that."

Uncle Tommy jumped down from the truckbed. He kept his eyes fastened on the ground so no one would start in torturing him with questions. He was part of the spectators now. The crowd of suitors and admirers and supplanters. He joined Grady Rainbow, the Crab Man, Gazarra, the praise-singers and the rest of the millennium who were waiting to see whether Sabbitha would rise or fall, and them with her.

From the point of view of simple economics, the entire region was a mess, not just Midway and the towns of the Salvation Coast. Those places had opted out of respectability right after Sabbitha's first miracle. It hadn't taken much; that had always been outbreak country. Enter at the risk of your own trespasses. But now, even the rich black-dirt farm belt that stretched inland, and the cities and towns that exploited the land, had caught the disease. Their inhabitants flowed downstream like so much silt to join the poor and the exalted of the Salvation Coast.

Which is what explained all those chrome-silver aerodynamic Airstream trailers, and those extended-cab luxury pick-ups with the exotic licence plates that made Gazarra's truck look like a Radio Flyer.

Midway was the place to be for believers and non-believers alike. Some came to gawk, some came fleeing the world, some came to persecute Sabbitha's followers. Others came to write reportages for the big-city magazines whose job was to analyze the great popular movements. Everyone had a reason, and usually more than one. It got harder and harder to separate the observers from the partici-pants. The journalists from the rioters.

People couldn't work two jobs at once, and being part of the outbreak was a full-time occupation. The fields were neglected, the stores shuttered, the windows duct-taped like before a hurricane. Some people showed up in Midway intending to visit a day or two and take in the show but ended up staying on. They claimed they couldn't find the gas to fill their tanks and get safely out of town again. They soon merged into the movement they had come to gawk at or record, and discovered they had the believers' fire after all.

Meanwhile, Gazarra sold every article he had on hand, right down to the paper that had held the confectioner's sugar that had wrapped the hard candies he used to give away to poor children. He hadn't planned it that way. He'd hoped to hold back a store of essentials for Sabbitha and himself, just in case.

In case of what? he wondered.

He let the rest of his stock go. The praise-singers would have laid their hands on it sooner or later anyway. They'd killed openly once and gone unpunished. They knew Sheriff Slaughter and his deputy wouldn't be returning to this territory soon. Besides, it would have taken the National Guard to quell this riot. Looting a peddler's pick-up truck would have been nothing to them.

Just yesterday, suffering from hunger but more from boredom, the praise-singers marched on the last store in Midway that had managed to keep its doors open. Faced with dismemberment, the owner was only too happy to contribute everything on his shelves to their cause. But that wasn't enough. Their hunger was appeased, but not their boredom. Unfulfilled by a victory that had not spilled blood, they swept into the countryside in search of ripe fields to pillage. On the outskirts of Midway, they discovered that nature had betrayed them. It was too early in the season for the crops to have produced much. They harvested the fields anyway, if destruction can be called harvest. They ate the unripe stalks and the tight, green, sour fruit and immature kernels, vomiting it all up as soon as it hit their bellies. Liberation harvesting, they called it.

Where are the asylum-keepers brave enough to put them in cells? Gazarra wondered. When he realized he'd had a part in their creation, shame overtook him. Shame, and revolt.

In the ravaged fields that looked as though they had been rooted up by razor-snouted wild pigs, along the shuttered main streets, by the sheered-off trunks of trees that had been felled for fuel, in the yards where all the flowers had been picked to make crowns for Sabbitha, random acts of faith and moral vandalism occurred daily.

That was where the woman in the bramble dress could be found. She never gave her name or the name of the place she came from. She claimed she'd forgotten those details, and maybe she was right.

She was the finest specimen of womanhood they had ever seen; that was the only thing people were sure about. A pastor's wife, to judge by her language when she bothered to speak. Her skin was as smooth and perfect as the inside of a freshly opened almond. There must have been a West Indian trader in the family tree, because the woman in the bramble dress had the kind of aggressive rear end prized in the hot countries.

On beauty alone, she could have been a rival for Sabbitha's crown. But she didn't have Gazarra — prophet, peddler, advance man. And she lacked a natural sense of rhythm: when to speak, when to stay hidden, when to burst forth from herself. None of that bothered her. She didn't have the ambition it takes to want to remake the world; she just wanted to say her piece.

But she understood transgression as brilliantly as Sabbitha did. She had traveled to Midway on her own at the beginning of the outbreak, and gone to the edges of the woods and into the empty lots to gather her materials. She worked alone and didn't boast about what she was doing, toiling anonymously like a monk in a cave.

On the day after the praise-singers had dispatched Brenner, she appeared on the scrubby lawn outside the congregation hall. She dropped her clothes on the ground and declared that any man who wanted her could have her, then and there.

Every man was a candidate until they saw what she had devised. Once she was naked, she reached behind her, into a sack, and produced a dress woven out of brambles, a stiff, hostile model of her own body. The dress was the fruit of her labors in Midway. She put it on and fastened it with a rope clasp.

The men stood in a circle around her. No one would make the first move. They, too, were struck with performance anxiety, but of the male kind. For the first time since Sabbitha had come, an inhibition arose. Here was a thing every man wanted but that no man would take. Clothed in her transparent shield, the woman in the bramble dress drew the line past which the rest of the rule-breakers would not go.

No wonder they hated her. She summed up all the terrors of the outbreak without having to say a word or move a muscle. That made her an artist of the truest sort.

Somebody had to say something.

"Sorry, baby," one of the men spoke up. It was the man with the pounding boil on his cheek. "Not for me."

"Maybe some other time, when you take that dress off," another promised her.

"I never take it off," the woman told him in her fine, pastor's-wife enunciation.

A man came rolling out of the crowd and stepped up to her. He had a tool belt hanging low on his jeans, as if he'd been waylaid here on his way to raise a barn somewhere. He walked like a drunken sailor fresh off his ship, full of confidence, rum and hard currency.

He fingered the thorns of her dress. The brambles shone red in the sunlight, as if they were on fire. He tested the points of the thorns. They were razor-sharp.

"Shit!" He sucked a dot of blood off his finger. "How the hell do you make love to a porcupine?"

He laughed richly at his own joke, then proceeded to commit blasphemy. He pulled a tin-snips off his tool belt and began lopping off the sharp points from the woman's dress.

"You want to know how to make love to a porcupine? I'll tell you! You snip off her damned quills first, then you dive right in!"

He managed to dull a dozen of the woman's thorns before the praise-singers collared him.

"You trifled with her devotion," they told him. "That was your mistake. You were trying to take the easy way out. That's not allowed. Now you have to take on her pain. You have to know her suffering."

The praise-singers stripped the drunk man naked, down to his shoes and socks and tool belt.

"You're hers," they told him. "You wanted her."

The woman in the bramble dress raised her arms to embrace her conquest. The praise-singers urged him in her direction with an elbow between his shoulderblades. It wasn't a hard push, but it was just as effective.

To his credit, the man with the tool belt tried. Like the rape victim he was, he understood that the sooner it was over, the sooner he'd be free. The brambles tore at his and his new lover's body.

He looked into the woman's face. She was crying. He couldn't bear to see a woman cry.

"Act like you really want me," he whispered to her, "we'll get out of this thing quicker, and save both our skins."

His was a rare act of humanity in the Midway madhouse.

The woman in the bramble dress returned to the congregation lawn several more times. Everyone gave her a wide berth. Most men wouldn't even risk looking in her direction. Though they'd used her once, the praise-singers didn't know what to do with her now. Her performances had become a menace to morale. Nobody liked having their limits shown up in so graphic a fashion.

One day the woman stopped showing up, though her spirit still hung heavy over Midway. Some believers joined together and secretly resolved to turn their backs on their compulsive rule-breaking, but they found that wasn't so easy. It had become a habit. Life was lackluster without the thrill. Others wanted to keep up the transgressions, even up the ante, but they lacked the imagination. It's nothing to sin for a night or even a weekend. But day after day, week after week, in a fevered state? The effort exhausted people's resources. There are only so many ways and so many combinations. The body has only so many possibilities. There is a finite list of Commandments and laws to defile. The believers of Midway were nearing that border where pornography crosses into boredom.

Once it had been joyous and liberating. But now, rule-breaking had turned into a cruel, ideology-driven practice that crushed the individual. Systems like that had flourished in the drab, gray countries of Eastern Europe, but never in America. Never before, that is.

No one ever thought it would be so hard. Midway, once the capital of revolutionary rule-breaking, was now about as appealing as the paranoia wing in an insane asylum, with the prowling praise-singers playing the role of guards. Some of the believers sobbed with nostalgia for the good old days when all of this had been new and fun. *Fun* — now that was a word no one had heard in a while.

The Crab Man saw all this as he scrutinized the faces that came to stare at him in his cage at the carnival. Disgust and fascination are the normal human reactions at a freak show, and he'd always found comfort in them. They prove that people still have something decent and shockable in them. But when he saw the blank, unimpressed pairs of eyes on the other side of his wire mesh, he knew the town was in big trouble. The man with the boil had strolled by and looked right through him: "So what?" he'd asked in a loud, challenging voice. "Do better." The Crab Man was a sensation-worker through and through. Not only are sensation-workers quarrelsome and ambitious and self-serving, they also depend on the observance of a strict order of things to make a living. If he lost his power to shock, the Crab Man knew he'd soon be out of a job. That prospect scared him more than anything he'd seen in Midway.

Driven by the love of his trade — or self-interest, call it what you will — he set out on a journey from his trailer to Sabbitha's pick-up truck. If anyone could change the atmosphere of the town, she could. After all, she'd gotten the whole thing started.

Unaided and alone, it took him nearly an hour to cross the field and its few hundred yards of crabgrass. He traveled in fear. It was a feeling he hadn't had since joining the carnival and achieving the security it offered. He was afraid of Sabbitha's followers. Not only had they been outdoing the sensation-workers when it came to freaky things, they were trying to use them for their own base purposes.

Just the other day, they had attacked the Fused Man and Wife. Fortunately for the couple, when the praise-singers laid their eyes on the mess Nature had made by hesitating about the couple's gender, the crowd backed off fast. But it was a warning shot, all the same.

The Crab Man was more fortunate. He made the trip unmolested. But once his arduous journey was complete, he found the back of the pick-up truck lashed down tight. Gazarra was sitting stiffly in front, on the passenger's side, with the door closed. The Crab Man scratched at the rusty metal but the peddler wouldn't respond. When he started hanging off the door handle, Gazarra had no humane choice but to open up.

The Crab Man perched on the running board.

"I want to talk to Sabbitha," he declared.

"I'm sure you do. But you'll find her a poor conversationalist."

"What happened now?"

"She had a visit from her family. Or someone who said he was her family . . . No, he was. He had the snapshots to prove it."

The Crab Man put a pincer to his forehead.

"Her family?" he said with a pained expression. "You must never, ever let the family in! They'll mess up a person's concentration worse than anything else. It's impossible to do your act when your family's around."

"Act?"

"Art," the Crab Man corrected himself.

"I'm sorry now. But at the time I had no choice. The snapshots this man had . . ."

The Crab Man wasn't listening to Gazarra's excuses.

"I remember the first and last time my family came to see me. It was the only time I felt like a freak, a real, honest-to-goodness, bona fide, goddamned freak — I mean, sensation-worker! The family! How could you do that?"

"He forced my hand. I told you that already."

"Well, now we know why we say the Messiah has no family."

The Crab Man slid off his perch on the running board.

"I have to help her," he said manfully. "I'm going to talk to her."

"You're on your own," Gazarra warned him.

XV

Family Therapy

*I*T WASN'T THE FIRST TIME someone wanted to save Sabbitha Hunter from herself; the efforts had started back in her childhood. But this was the first time a human crab had tried his hand at that thankless task.

Dragging his pink-hued body across the field was nothing compared to the labor of scaling the back of the pick-up truck, hoisting himself over the raised tailgate, then vaulting into the chamber beyond the tarp. Only the most determined man deaf to the protests of pain could have pulled off that feat. With courage and perseverance, the Crab Man did it. But when he cast his eyes on the object of his efforts, he had to wonder whether his pilgrimage had been worth it. The look in Sabbitha's eyes could have frozen the sun.

The Crab Man was in over his head and he knew it. He wished he'd heeded Gazarra's advice and stayed away.

"Your family bugging you?"

"He was more than family," she answered.

The Crab Man elected not to bite at that bait.

"They're here to help, that's what they say," he told her. "But if they really wanted to help out, they should have done it a long time ago. Either treated us like humans or put us out of our misery. It's too late now. Family's the enemy. They make you self-conscious. I found that out a long time ago. You can trust me, I've been at this longer than you have."

Bad nerves and fear had the Crab Man boasting that way. Sabbitha looked at him blankly.

"You couldn't be. No one's ever been this thing before," she reminded him.

"You've got to shake them off. You can't let them throw you off stride." The Crab Man sounded like a college football coach running for Congress. "I saw you do things I've never seen anyone do before. You've got a gift, don't waste it. I can help you. I can take care of things for you. Everything you need, I got — and I mean everything. I'll keep the world out of your face so you can concentrate and do your art. They're nothing but a bunch of sand gnats anyway."

The naivety of a child, Sabbitha thought.

"What do you say?" he angled. "You and me as a team."

"You want to be my manager? Is that what you're getting at?"

The Crab Man would have blushed, but he already was blush color.

"If you want to put it that way. I was thinking of something a little more friendly."

Sabbitha laughed. "The Messiah's manager! That would be a pretty important position. I guess it's true what they say: there's some big opportunities opening up in the service sector."

The Crab Man fidgeted and wondered how long a decent interval was and when he could leave. He'd already forgotten the miracle she'd worked on him.

Sabbitha pointed to the world beyond the tarp. "I don't need managing," she told him, "they do!"

"That's what I'm getting at!" He slammed the metal floor with a pincer foot, and pain signals rocketed up his leg. "You've got to jerk their chain a little, dammit! They're eating each other up out there. It's not safe for us any more! They're out-freaking us!"

Sabbitha listened to the sensation-worker's insecure wail. It hurt her ears.

"It's true what the Two-Direction Woman said," she mused. "I'm not at all like you."

"Well, no kidding! You finally got around to seeing the obvious!"

The Crab Man was looking for an excuse to exit Sabbitha's company. Now he had it.

"Good for you, you got to see how that pervert God put me together! Shit, this is the last time I'm going to bed with a normal. I should have made you pay for it double!"

His pincers clicked against his sunken chest and his reedy voice trembled in its tiny cavity.

"When in doubt, throw a tantrum, elicit pity," she told him calmly. "That won't work on me, I didn't pay to get in and gape at you. The real difference between us is that you think only of your-self. Your management. Your promotion. Your performance. You're in business. I'm not. That's the difference."

The Crab Man had stopped paying attention. He was too busy scaling the tailgate and planning his descent to the ground below, hoping to do minimum damage to his carapace in the process. The rest of his thoughts ran towards revenge, but how? The woman was untouchable. He'd be lucky to get out of this in one piece.

From the cab, Gazarra heard the flat murmur of Sabbitha's voice and the urging, keening, insistent sound that the Crab Man made. Then came the thud of flesh against tailgate. Like Sabbitha,

Gazarra was unmoved. Why should this sensation-worker succeed in taming the Messiah when so many others, including himself, had failed?

He stepped out of the cab. Where was Grady Rainbow, where was anybody human? He needed a talk, a drink — any kind of escape from the end of days would do just fine. Above his head, storm clouds were boiling up in the evening sky against the luminous blue. Nature was deploying all the unnatural colors and spectacular effects she had at her disposal.

Gazarra strolled across the field towards the center of town to see how the popular apocalypse was holding up. He looked back once at the truck and made a mental note to check the tire pressure. The tires seemed low, but maybe it was just the pick-up sinking into the ground.

Based on what he saw in downtown Midway, Sabbitha's followers hardly needed her at all any more. He passed in front of a church where a woman was playing the organ with both elbows. All the portraits of Jesus were carefully placed face-up on the lawn outside. The most famous in the line of failed Messiahs stared in disbelief into the pagan sky. Like Sabbitha, he had never admitted to being anything else than what he was. He never made claims; he never overreached himself. He let other people worry about who he was. He just said his piece, even if that meant speaking in riddles.

Didn't it work for him? People still had his name on their lips to this day. You couldn't go out your front door without running into him in one incarnation or another, or one of his self-appointed representatives, even if he did fail, even if his death didn't bring about the great change everyone was hoping for, which meant that he had to come back again, or so some believers claimed. And since the world refused to change as a result of his dying, his followers, in their confusion, built churches around him.

On the lot between the church and its worn, rambling rectory, the woman in the bramble dress had built herself a lean-to out of cardboard boxes that once held home appliances. She called Gazarra over to her shelter and offered herself. Beneath her dress, her wounds had all but scabbed over, proof that no man had been man enough to take the challenge a second time.

"I'm sorry," Gazarra told her, "but I can't join the fun."

"Are you chicken, or are you queer?" she wanted to know.

"From a pastor's wife I would have expected better manners."

"Ha! You don't know my kind!"

Gazarra glanced furtively at her dress and what was underneath it.

"Where did you get such an idea?" he asked.

"It is written," she said in parody of the church language that filled every part of her. "It's written all over the place."

"I'm afraid I don't know where."

"Mortify the flesh," she yelled at him. "Don't you know that one?"

"Yes, of course . . . I'd forgotten."

"What about the living envying the dead?" she challenged him.

"I'm acquainted with that one," he admitted warily.

"Well, that makes two of us. And you don't understand it the way I do!"

The woman in the bramble dress began to wail and sob with all the despair of the believer who realizes she's sacrificed for nothing. Suddenly she became a pastor's wife again. Her prudery returned. She went to cover her sex, but stabbed herself in the palm.

Gazarra was too afraid of her thorns to comfort her.

"Keep doing what you're doing," he stammered, "whatever it is. You're an instrument of the apocalypse."

He hurried away. He had no love for Sabbitha's followers, only for Sabbitha. Or the idea of Sabbitha, now that she had veered off from the humanity the Messiah was supposed to represent. Her primitive, disorderly followers were walk-ons, tools, blunt instruments. How could you love an instrument if you weren't willing to play?

❧

"Hey, Jew peddlerman!"

It had been some time since Gazarra had heard that offensive cry. Since he'd sold off the last of his merchandise and stopped being a peddler. The Cruice woman was standing in front of him on the sidewalk by a tree whose bark had been gnawed off. She was rocking from side to side like a punch-drunk boxer. As emaciated and edgy as ever, but with an aggressive new self-assurance. The outbreak had given her that much.

Inside the church, someone began punishing the organ again.

"Now what?" Gazarra asked the Cruice woman.

"In Alma I wanted to come with you. You wouldn't let me. You wanted Sabbitha all to yourself. She showed you!"

"You had work to do there. Anyway, you're here now, so what's the difference?"

"Yeah, I'm here. I followed Sabbitha. I did what she told us to."

"You look freer to me," Gazarra complimented her.

The woman looked down at herself. "I do?"

"Much freer."

It wasn't easy devising compliments for Thelma Cruice.

"This was supposed to be the temple of my liberation." She grabbed a handful of flesh from her side, but there wasn't much to hold on to. "I was supposed to use this thing to get free. The thing that dragged me down was going to set me free. Sounds like one of your goddamned riddles. I don't get it."

"It *is* a little philosophical," Gazarra commiserated.

"I ended up at the bottom of a heap of men. It was like a football game, but I didn't have any shoulderpads. I got trampled. I couldn't breathe. I didn't like it and they didn't seem to like me very much either. Not a single one of them wanted to kiss me. I'll tell you something: this freedom thing was invented by men to get at women. I don't know a single woman who got anything out of it."

"Some have."

"Yeah? Who?" Mrs. Cruice nodded towards the deconsecrated church. "The organ player? The bramble-dress woman?"

"Those people had problems before," Gazarra reasoned.

Suddenly she fell to scratching herself.

"All we got was a social disease. Even I got one."

Thelma Cruice worked herself so industriously that in thirty seconds she'd raised welts up and down her bare arms and legs. From what he'd heard, Gazarra didn't think you could catch a social disease there.

"What about your kids?" he asked her.

"They finally burned the house down."

Gazarra chose to take that as a parable.

"You have to keep on," he encouraged her. "The world will change."

"It better," the Cruice woman warned him.

That evening, Gazarra took a chance and let himself into the back of the pick-up.

"Are you there?" he called softly into the darkness. "There, and alone?"

"Can't you tell?"

He sniffed the stuffy air. It smelled like slighted crab to him.

"Yes. But I can't see you. You're like a black cat in a coal bin."

Sabbitha didn't laugh. The Messiah had no sense of humor. She lacked the requisite ironic distance.

He felt his way onto the pallet next to her.

"I saw the Cruice woman," he reported.

"Who's that?"

Idly, Sabbitha began scratching at herself around the belt-line.

"No one. Just a believer."

For all her supposed caring about her followers, Sabbitha couldn't remember the name of a single one. Gazarra didn't push it. The relief of lying down on something more welcoming than the front seat of a truck was too strong. He was beyond exhaustion. The coming of the Messiah had turned out to be a long, extended nightmare, a three-day drunk, a party you couldn't leave, a bad trip that never ends, a vicious argument whose obscure motives have long since been forgotten. Yet it was necessary. Gazarra still believed that, though it was getting harder and harder for him. All this is necessary, he told himself. Change, or accept the cowardice of living and dying the way everybody else has. How could he lack courage now, after everything Sabbitha had done?

He put his arms around her from behind and felt her breasts under her stained jacket. She didn't push him away. She didn't warm to him either. That was just as well.

"Close your eyes and sleep," he told her softly.

He began to sing to her in his tuneless voice. A lullaby. He'd never sung a lullaby in his life. Lullabies were for children, and he knew nothing about children but their shoe sizes and the patches on their pants. *Sleep now, hush-a-bye, don't you cry.* Where this lullaby came from he could not say. *When you awake, you shall have cake, and all the pretty little horses.* That was all he knew of that one, so he sang one of his mother's songs, a song about almonds and raisins and all the sweet things no one has ever tasted but that everyone knows about, instinctively, through deprivation, the way everyone knew about olive oil on the Salvation Coast, where there were no olive trees.

Then he remembered the lullaby's next verse. It was a curious one, he thought, to be singing to a child or to anyone in need of comfort. A colt was out in the pasture, *bees and butterflies, pecking out his eyes, poor little thing cried, Mammy!*

But Sabbitha didn't mind. She hadn't heard. She had surrendered to sleep in the old man's chaste embrace. She'd even stopped scratching.

Her brief surrender was a miracle in itself. A private, authentic, miracle.

"Sabbitha!"

The praise-singers were like a swarm of maddened bees. Insanely occupied, mindless and self-important, drunk on their own noise.

"Queen Sabbitha!"

Gazarra opened his eyes in the darkness.

"I didn't create you," he cursed them under his breath. "Climb back to hell where you came from."

"Sabbitha, we have your tormentor. Open up and let us in!"

Outside, the praise-singers scuffed at the ground like feral pigs. Their noise woke Sabbitha. It came from everywhere. Around the truck. Under the truck. Atop the cab. She sat up and girlishly fixed her bangs so they'd fall just right on her forehead. Then she rose, opened the tarp and went to meet her madmen.

Gazarra came and stood behind her. He placed both hands on her shoulders. Sabbitha shrugged off his touch.

The praise-singers were milling around in the darkness beyond the tailgate, their clothes stained like butchers' smocks. Their voices were anxious and strained.

"The Messiah has no family. We're her family. We're above family and all its rules. That's what this thing is all about, right?"

"Yes," Sabbitha told them.

"He said he was your family. He took out his snapshots and waved them in our faces. He was so proud of himself."

"That kind of thing isn't allowed here."

"He was tormenting you, right, Sabbitha?"

The praise-singers awaited her answer. Not that it mattered much now.

"In a way," she told them.

"Then accept our offering!" they ordered her.

Did she have a choice? The praise-singers pulled themselves up onto the back bumper and pressed their gift into Sabbitha's hand. Not exactly Uncle Tommy's head — not all of it, in any case. That would have been too delicate for them. It was his face, with part of the skull attached. They'd left his face intact so Sabbitha could see it was him.

That was important to them. It proved that theirs wasn't just an ordinary murder. The victim wasn't just anybody. What they'd done wasn't murder any more, it was sacrifice.

Uncle Tommy wore an astonished, outraged expression. Not the look he usually had. He loved life. He found no reason to be outraged by it. He was a sensualist, not a brave man. His love for the Messiah got him killed.

Sabbitha cradled the piece of tissue against her belly where Uncle Tommy used to lay his head. He was a coward when he should have been brave, and foolhardy when he should have shut up, she thought. He boasted to strangers about how well he knew her, but never told her what she needed to hear. By the time he got around to showing her how much he loved her, it was too late. You can love that way only once, and not forever. When love is spurned or not recognized, it sours into violence.

Good-bye, former life. Good-bye, girlhood. It had been a short, oblique childhood, but with its share of pride and mystery.

She felt nauseated. It wasn't just the gore. It was that weightless feeling you get when the past drops out of your life.

Then she remembered the praise-singers. They must have

wanted something from her — everyone else did. Her approval, no doubt. Her blessing. How could she give them that? But if that's what it took to get rid of them, so be it.

"I can do anything now," she told them. "I'm free. You have murdered my past."

They took that as her benediction and howled in triumph. They were a new law for a new age. They turned and spread out through Midway like a plague of locusts. Their madness was the new proof. They'd taken the place of Sabbitha's miracles.

"I can do anything now," Sabbitha added softly in the whirlpool of their departing voices, "including make you disappear. Or better yet, disappear myself."

XVI

The Schismatics

*T*HAT EVENING, Sabbitha Hunter put on her magic hairband and informed the peddler that she was going out to view the apocalypse, and did he want to come along with her. Gazarra declined the invitation. He'd had enough of the Midway jungle. She shook her hair prettily, called him a coward, then stepped out of the truck.

The sky was leaden blue and shimmering with humidity. It's going to rain soon, she decided. Just as well.

Sabbitha was feeling so detached and determined that at first she didn't notice the day-old piece of Uncle Tommy in her right hand. She was in the middle of crossing the meadow when she saw it there. She began to sing him a love song. It was full of blame, a modern love song. You said a gun wouldn't settle it, she addressed her departed lover, but it would have. Whoever that dog was that spied on us, leave him in the woods to rot. You'd have never gotten caught. It would have been one more sweet crime between us. Think how much closer we would have been! But you chose order and seemliness, and look where it got you. You took me too lightly, that was your mistake. You were never much for feelings yourself, so how could you expect to know what a woman like me can feel?

Sabbitha reached the carnival, where her followers were taking time off from rule-breaking by going on the rides, the Whirligig and the Mad Mouse. None of them dared stop her, not with what she was carrying in her hand.

She passed the lot where the carnival-workers' trailers were parked.

"Sorry about the misunderstanding, Mr. Crab," she said, stopping by the trailer where she'd spent a night. "You might look strange, but you turned out to be an ordinary man after all. Just wanting to run the show and make a profit and control everybody. What a disappointment, coming from you! I had higher hopes for someone in your situation."

By the time she'd walked through the meadow and reached the streets of Midway, a steady, unhurried, dispirited rain began to fall. She approved. That rain would suit her purpose.

The apocalyptic campers, on the other hand, were unprepared for bad weather. They'd forgotten all about rain, and how miserable it can make outdoor living. Betrayed by the heavens, which they figured would remain blue forever, they pressed together under the spotty shelter of the remaining trees, pulled out their pocketknives and began splitting open the sides of green garbage bags to make tarps.

In a vacant lot, Sabbitha saw two long iron posts driven into the ground. They weren't part of some unspeakable transgressive procedure, as it turned out. The believers had hammered them in to play horseshoes.

Sabbitha came across the ubiquitous Cruice woman on the sidewalk. The rain hadn't sent her scurrying for shelter; maybe she didn't know it was raining. She was wearing a rusty horseshoe around her fleshless upper arm like a piece of exotic jewelry.

They stood face to face, two antagonists. Thelma Cruice stared at what was in Sabbitha's right hand.

Sabbitha reached up with her left and touched the snakeskin hairband.

"You want this thing? I'll trade it for that horseshoe."

The Cruice woman panicked. She shook her head. Greasy strands of lank hair flew in her face.

"You could be like me," Sabbitha offered. "Free."

Even Mrs. Cruice got that irony.

"Bullshit! You told us we'd get free if we were bad. All we got was more of the same."

"Freedom doesn't become you. That's your problem."

"We didn't get anything out of it, not like we thought we would."

"Who's *we*?"

"Women — who do you think?"

"You got to act like men. That's what you wanted. I was there when you said it. You didn't know I was listening."

"I was expecting more," the Cruice woman admitted.

"Well, you got what you were lusting after."

"What about you? What did you get out of it?"

"I got power," Sabbitha answered with no hesitation. "I got to kill my past through you. You were my instruments."

"Dream on! Your past will kill you before you can kill it. You were just being used, too!"

"Time will tell," she said, turning her back on Thelma Cruice, "but at least I'm not blaming anybody else for my troubles."

Sabbitha Hunter was full of those sorts of judgments on that sodden late afternoon. She was out to dismantle the cult that had been erected to herself. It was the only way, she calculated, to get free of the Midway monster. She walked bare-headed among the believers who huddled unhappily under torn drop cloths, scratching themselves through holes they'd pierced in the plastic. The followers needed their illusions deflated in the worst way. To let them go on believing in her would be an act of cruelty, and there had been too many of those committed in her name already.

She came upon the praise-singers who had appropriated the driest shelter for themselves under the branches of a giant oak.

"Queen Sabbitha, we need a miracle!" they called out as she went past.

She stopped. They were soaked, mud-stained, demoralized. She remembered how afraid of them she'd been, just last night.

"I'm fresh out," she reported.

They wouldn't believe her.

"Real belief doesn't need miracles," she teased them.

That mystery was beyond their understanding.

"We're too tired to believe. We need a miracle, and fast."

"Try bringing back Uncle Tommy. Here," she said, thrusting the piece of skull at them, "start with this. Build the rest of him out of it. Then we'll see."

The praise-singers recoiled. They wouldn't take the skull. They claimed they never heard of the man.

"We're having bad dreams, Sabbitha," one of them told her.

"I should hope so."

The youngest of them peeled away from the group and stood in front of Sabbitha in the rain. He couldn't have been more than eighteen. Like a soldier in some undeveloped country, murder had made him a man, or so he thought.

"I've been having the same dream all my life. I came here trying to get rid of it."

She looked him over. The boy hadn't even started shaving yet.

"All your life? Aren't you a little young to be talking like that?"

"I did something wrong, see, and now they're running me down for it."

The boy was intent on telling her his dream. He'd been hoping for this moment with Sabbitha since he'd come to Midway.

"A fat man is chasing me. He's got these great big rolls of white fat like a pig, and tiny little jiggling hairless privates. He wants to get me because I signed the petition against fat people. He's chasing me, and he's gaining on me, even though he's fat and I'm young and fast, and while I'm running hard I'm trying to explain to him why I had to sign the petition. I don't have anything against him personally, see, I only signed it because I was alone, you know, lonely, and I wanted to join something. So I shouldn't be judged, right? But all that talking ruins my wind, and he catches me."

"And?"

"And . . . I don't know. I wake up, I guess."

"Like you're waking up now, sonny."

The boy trotted alongside Sabbitha, a kid running after a grown woman.

"Maybe we did do some wrong things, okay? All right, so we did. But we're still good people underneath. We did them because we are good people . . . Can't that be taken into account?"

Sabbitha stopped. So did the boy.

"Taken into account?"

The boy nodded eagerly.

"By whom?" she asked.

She knew he had no answer.

She turned and walked away from the boy. He stood in the rain and screamed at her.

"We don't need you to believe, you know! You can't stop us!"

At the end of the street, the congregation hall stood before her, doors open. Torn off their hinges, actually. The entrance gaped like a bad wound.

Right now, Sabbitha thought, a little deus ex machina would do just fine. I'd use it to spirit me away, far from here, to safety.

By the time she entered the hall, all of Midway that could still ambulate had fallen in behind her. Except for the sensation-workers, who were boycotting her with vengeance in their mercantile hearts. They'd shed no tears over the dissolution of the love affair between her and the Crab Man. But when the spiteful, slighted crab explained how she was going to put them out of business with her hijinks, they launched a conspiracy to unseat her.

But everyone else was there. Including one face in the crowd that Sabbitha didn't pick out. It belonged to Grady Rainbow, her guardian angel. A pretty ragged, stained-tooth angel, and looking more and more like a follower every day. He admired her strength and her courage, but he knew that even the strongest human can't endure forever. Grady made sure she wouldn't recognize him; he'd positioned himself behind a pillar. He was too wise to show himself just yet.

Sabbitha considered the moving sea of believers. She discovered she had nothing more to say to them. She'd delivered the judgments that concerned her: to the Cruice woman and her cult of victimhood, and the praise-singers and their cult of violence. "I quit!" she could have declared to the congregation. But that might have proved hazardous to her health; those were the only words not permitted by the followers of a religion that permitted everything else. She said nothing instead. The crowd didn't mind. They were completely satisfied. That still-recognizable clump of human flesh in her hand was eloquence enough for them. There's something inspirational about unpunished crimes.

Sheriff Slaughter and his deputy hadn't even bothered to show up and spread a blanket over Uncle Tommy's remains. There weren't enough of them to make the trip worth any lawman's while. Sabbitha's followers had acceded to a state of utter freedom, right out in plain sight. They hadn't needed to go into exile like the Puritans who founded the country, or cower unseen in some desert or forest that had been pressed into service as a utopia. They'd built their own savage wilderness in Midway, on prime real estate, right on Main Street, underneath the sheltering elms and oaks.

It was the American dream in its rawest state: to carve out a deeper, darker wilderness from the wilderness that surrounded you.

It used to be said among the pure-hearted that every man was his own church. Sabbitha Hunter came along and changed all that. Now, every man was his own wilderness. And every woman, too.

Beneath the platform, at her feet, the praise-singers sprawled upon each other like winded young wolves after strenuous play. Maybe I could get them to tear me to bits, too, she speculated. That's one way out of this thing. I wonder if it would hurt much.

Golden drops of oil blossomed on her forehead. The third and final public miracle authored by Sabbitha Hunter. Too bad her followers didn't notice. They were too exhausted for miracles. As such, they were already dead.

But one man in the congregation saw those drops of oil, and he took them as a sign of how deep her distress was. He'd read the Good Book. He knew that miracles are the last resort of a desperate being. That man, who had traveled to Midway with a plan, rose to his feet.

Big men weren't rare in that part of the country, but this one was a tree. Six-foot-six, a graying crewcut, brown-skinned, with short gray stubble on his cheeks and a pair of old-fashioned steel-framed glasses. Each of his hands was as broad as a flagstone.

"The time has come for Sabbitha to be saved!" he announced in his big voice.

The praise-singers stirred murderously. Those were blasphemous words. The Messiah can't need saving. It was the kind of paradox they weren't equipped to appreciate.

At the back of the hall, behind his pillar, Grady Rainbow stood on his toes to get a better look at the man — before he got torn to pieces. He'd seen him before. Seen him, but not seen him personally. He had an athlete's grace despite his huge size. His whole body had described a single, uninterrupted arc as he got to his feet, and he'd done it in the wink of an eye. The man had to be a professional.

Then it dawned on Grady. The man was Felix Culpa. Culpa had gotten famous for swimming across the Straits of Florida, from Cuba to the Keys, because he wanted to be a catcher in the American League. He'd been a sensation when he hit the Majors, and not just because he was so good. No one knew Cubans could get that huge. The man played baseball like it was football, and when it was in his hand, the ball felt puny and insignificant.

What the hell was Felix Culpa doing in Midway? Grady wondered. Had word traveled so far that it could have reached him in Miami, or San Diego, or whatever warm place old ballplayers retired to? How bad had this thing gotten?

"Your ears would burn," he told Sabbitha, "if you heard the things people are saying about you out there."

"My ears would burn?" she scoffed. "Is that all that would happen? Do you think we're doing this just to get our ears burned?"

The congregation laughed along with her, pleased with itself. Culpa stepped out of his row and moved up the aisle towards her.

"People say you've come up from hell to corrupt us. I don't believe a word of it. I'm like you. I believe the world needs a good shaking up. And you've done that. But shaking it up isn't all there is to change."

The insane bee-buzzing swelled in volume. The praise-singers were pulling themselves to their feet. They didn't know who Felix Culpa was and they didn't care. Sure, he was big — but there was only one of him. They had at least two murders on their scorecard, and Sabbitha's dominion was the only thing keeping them from having to pay.

Sabbitha looked down at the praise-singers.

"No," she ordered them. "Not this time, you won't."

They sank back into a resentful crouch at the base of the platform.

"Be satisfied with this."

She threw them a bone: the piece of Uncle Tommy's head. It went over the edge of the platform and into their midst. They had no choice but to contemplate their works.

"You started a war in this land," Felix Culpa pushed on. He didn't even know he'd just had his life spared by the woman he was trying to save. "It's the men against the women, and they've just about ripped each other to shreds. If we don't do something to stop it, there won't be any survivors left to speak of. Okay, you've shaken up this old world. Amen — your work is done. I've heard a lot of talk about souls, but one soul has been neglected. Yours. Who's going to look after you?"

Culpa jumped onto the stage. He moved so gracefully it looked as though Sabbitha were manipulating invisible chains to draw him to her side.

"Who will heal you? Someone's got to do that. Someone's got to heal you with love."

In front of hundreds of witnesses, he took her hand.

"I know all about rule-breaking and sin," he boasted to the crowd. "I was an All-Star transgressor myself. So when I say love, I don't mean a woman's ordinary kind of love either — I had so much of that I couldn't tell Sally from Sue. I was a drinker, I gambled on my own games, I fought my friends, I cheated, I was a whoremonger, I doublecrossed my teammates. I became everything a poor boy turns into when riches are thrust upon his plate, and when that plate is used to being empty."

"You're mighty proud for a converted sinner," Sabbitha told him. "You'd better watch out for your pride. It's a sin."

"Love cured me," he replied in splendid non sequitur. "It can cure you, too."

"Are you trying to love-bomb me?" she inquired. Culpa didn't know the meaning of the word. "I hear the explosions falling all around me, but there haven't been any direct hits yet. Besides, your sins are all pretty minor league, if you ask me."

"I knew you'd resist. But believe me, love can change a person."

"We've heard entirely too much about change around here. You ask any of these people." Sabbitha motioned to the crowd. "Besides," she told him, "I'm not here to listen to other people's problems. Especially boring, run-of-the-mill ones like yours. Can't you do any better? Take a look at the audience — they've seen and done ten times better than you have."

"You need to heal."

"'Heel' is more like it. You want me to heel, like a dog. Obedience school. Woof-woof."

The congregation laughed. They were enjoying the moment. There hadn't been much laughter between these four walls lately.

"I suppose you're the one who's going to do the healing?" Sabbitha pursued.

"Yes," Culpa answered without a shred of embarrassment, "I am. But the message is what counts, not the messenger."

There was more scoffing from the congregation. The praise-singers glared at Culpa, measuring him for a coffin. The ballplayer had made a claim for himself, and that was the first step to being refuted. Refutation, in Midway, could be pretty harsh.

Culpa turned on the audience. He saw the weakness and self-loathing behind their taunts and catcalls. They were easy marks.

"Do you think you can live in promiscuity and disorder all your lives?" he harangued them. "How long can you go on like this, waking up every morning hungover, sticky, besotted, stinking, aching, ulcerated, confused and full of self-hatred and disgust for whatever poor creature is sharing your misadventure?"

In the silence, a few followers began scratching idly at the snugger places on their bodies. The belt line, the armpits, behind their ears, around their crotch. When one person scratched, they all did. It was like saying the word "louse" in a crowded room. Pretty soon their arms and legs and necks were covered with welts.

"The experiment is over!" he railed at them. "All you've proved is that it's impossible to live like this. I could have told you that from the start."

The believers' fervor had been dampened lately by a pest that liked to lay its eggs under human skin. When the egg sacs burst and the parasites eagerly chewed their way to the surface, it was pure hell for the host.

"I was a Major League sinner," Culpa told Sabbitha again. "That's how I knew I had to come when I first heard word of what you were doing. Word always reaches those who need it. You need to heal."

"I suppose you want me to repent?"

"No." His voice was soft and low and comforting. It had the gift of persuasion. "What you've done is penance enough. You're suffering enough as it is. You don't have to suffer any more. That's my word."

"Would you like to know what happened to the other man who wanted the Messiah all to himself?"

"No. I don't know, and I don't want to know. My love isn't the jealous kind."

Culpa put his arm around her waist. As chastely as he could manage, he kissed her lips and touched the golden drops of miraculous oil with his fingertip. The congregation was dumbfounded. They hadn't witnessed a proper kiss since they'd come to Midway. They'd forgotten all about the man-woman romance. A few of them began to remember in spite of themselves.

It was too much for Thelma Cruice. Her voice rose up, as harmonious as a grackle's.

"He's just another man! He just wants her in his bed!"

"He wants her miracles all to himself," an Alma Road sister complained. "That ain't fair! We've got to share here! That's what this thing is all about!"

"He wants to control her!" Mrs. Cruice called out as she tried to fight her way to the stage. "Sabbitha, listen to me! Do you want to be controlled?"

Sabbitha looked into Culpa's face. It was the color of cured leather, like an old baseball glove, or a glass of bourbon in the sunlight. His eyes were gray and mild and trusting. He had a smell about him like freshly laundered shirts.

"You win," she told him under the uproar of the congregation. "Heal me. Take me somewhere, anywhere — as long as it's off this damned stage."

Alarm bells, not church bells, would have rung in a more experienced man's mind. Felix Culpa had been a rule-breaker in his time. But all his peccadilloes hadn't made him any less innocent.

He jumped down from the stage, then whisked Sabbitha past the paralyzed praise-singers. He set her gently on the floor. Together they walked down the aisle towards the door, hand in hand.

The Cruice woman tried to block their path, but she didn't add up to much.

"Go ahead, try and have her all to yourself!" she cursed Culpa. "You'll never make it! She's not like anything you could ever know about!"

Culpa looked genuinely confused. He considered the welts on Thelma Cruice's arms.

"You need to heal, too," he told her.

Furious, she grabbed at Sabbitha's clothes and missed. A moment later, the Messiah was gone. Her step had been positively businesslike as she went out the door.

By the time the praise-singers roused themselves and decided they didn't need Sabbitha's permission to rescue her from this new tormentor, it was too late. They poured out of the hall in time to see the taillights of Felix Culpa's comfortable sedan driving their hopes away in the rain.

They reported this to the rest of the congregation.

"The Messiah eloped," one of them declared, water running off his cap.

"Ran off with that guy," the boy with the bad dream said, his soaked shirt clinging to his scrawny chest.

"And we let her!"

"Well, she told us not to do anything," the boy protested.

Grady Rainbow stood in the midst of the crowd, as stunned as the rest of the congregation. He didn't think a man could lead a woman around like that in this day and age. Especially not a woman like Sabbitha Hunter.

But Grady interpreted the event differently than everyone else. At least Sabbitha's off the stage, he reasoned. Now, at least, it's just one-on-one. Her and that ballplayer. And I'm putting my money on her.

The wailing and bickering of the believers began to hurt his ears. He slipped out of the hall as discreetly as possible. The hard rain was preferable to their voices.

244

"Stop right up there," Sabbitha ordered Felix Culpa. "By the bridge."

Culpa braked tentatively. They were on the outskirts of Midway, exactly where, he couldn't tell. What a night! His windshield wipers could hardly keep up with the sheets of water. He didn't want to run his wipers on High; their anxious movement across his field of vision might give his overexcited brain fits. His tires felt for the shoulder, but there was nothing but ditch. Somewhere below was a treacherous riverbank.

Culpa was careful. This was the greatest night of his life. The victory was better than any he'd tasted on the ballfield, and he wasn't about to take any chances with it.

"Stop," Sabbitha said again.

He did, on the road, in the middle of nowhere. He checked his mirrors. They were black.

Sabbitha flung open the door.

"Here's where we part company, Mr. Love-Bomber," she told him. "You were a temporary shelter. An emergency therapy. You did your part well. Very well, and I thank you for it."

Felix Culpa opened his mouth. No sound came out. He stared dumbly at the streams of rain falling on the upholstered front seat of his fine sedan, and felt the emptiness of everything being pulled away from him.

"But it's raining," he protested weakly.

Sabbitha laughed. "You did save me, I'll grant you that much. 'Save' as in rescue. But you can't heal me. That's out of the question, since I don't need healing, at least not any more. Jesus, I never thought I'd get out of that place alive. I was about to say something that wouldn't have been appreciated by those murderers when you showed up. I'll be forever grateful to you."

"What about love?" he wailed. "We kissed, remember?"

"Free-floating, disincarnate, no-risk, reduced-fat, objectless love,"

Sabbitha shot back. "That's your brand. It sounds like sublimation to me. There's not enough meat on the bones. You don't mind if I decline?"

"My love is Christian love," he insisted.

"So what? Everyone's a damned Christian around here, except Gazarra. You sound like the kind of radio program I shut off if I accidentally turn it on."

"But where will you go?"

Culpa looked as though he'd just lost a foot off his height.

"That is a problem," Sabbitha admitted. "I'm walking out on my followers. I don't believe any Messiah has ever done that before! It's a first — I quit!"

She laughed giddily, carelessly, then stepped out of the car and slammed the door hard. She wheeled away into darkness, slid down the steep bank towards the river and was gone, into the pounding rain. She had no idea how she'd make her way, any more than she'd known in Retreat.

Back when he was a bad man, Culpa would have run after her and grabbed her by the hair, thrown her over his shoulder like a sack of potatoes and brought her back. Dead or alive. Taught her a lesson about possession. Now he wished he still had that option.

"*Mierda*!" he swore, and slammed the steering wheel with his palm.

Sabbitha sloshed diagonally down the slope in sheer darkness, counting on the god of fools not to put a cliff in her path. At the bottom, she found a weed-choked creek. The water was running high and fast in the rain. But it wasn't going to jump its banks and flood Midway. That kind of apocalypse would have been too easy.

She pulled the snakeskin hairband out of her mass of soaked hair and threw it in a high arc into the creek. It floated a minute or two, then blended into nature.

There, she decreed. We'll call it Hairband Creek. See, I get to rename places, just like Jacob in the story. I bet they'll be talking about me for generations to come, too!

Up above her, on the bridge, Felix Culpa's car still idled, a cloud of exhaust hanging motionless in the humid air. She knew he couldn't see her down below, in this darkness. She was free.

Now what?

XVII

Wisdom from Above

J UST AS COUNTRIES dissolve after the great charismatic leader dies, all the cracks were free to appear after Sabbitha's disappearance. It seems unthinkable that just one personality could hold so much chaos at bay, but it's happened with whole nations, and it happened in the much smaller dominion of Sabbitha Hunter's followers. Schisms appeared. Sects split off. The affliction of doubt took hold.

The problem is one of investment. If you are the woman in the bramble dress, or any of the others, if you have invested, as Grady Rainbow put it, and invested unspeakably, what do you do with yourself now?

The dilemma wasn't a new one. The first Christians faced it after their Messiah died and the world continued on unchanged. In the end, they recovered quite nicely from the disappointment.

The next morning, once the wailing and gnashing of teeth had subsided a little, a contingent of believers went to see Nathan Gazarra for advice. He'd talked long and hard about the world changing, and for them, it really had — but not the way they'd been hoping for. They'd been turned into followers without a Messiah, and they didn't appreciate the irony.

Gazarra, their old expert in spiritual matters, was of little help.

They found him sitting on the soaked ground in the hazy sunlight left by the previous night's storm, his back against the rusting fender of his truck, consumed with dejection and guilt. If only he'd accepted Sabbitha's invitation last evening when she wandered into town! He swore at his own stupidity and lack of vigilance. When you've got a Messiah on your hands, you must never, ever let her out of your sight.

At first, he had nothing to say to the believers.

"Come on, help us," they cajoled him. "You speak God's language."

"What has that got to do with it?" he mumbled.

"You've read the Good Book inside out and backwards," they flattered him. "Tell us something. Something to tide us over."

It took all his energy to appease the followers' anguish.

"This is the darkest of all journeys for Sabbitha," he told them wearily, with the feeling he was turning into a broken record. "We must travel with her through our prayers and deeds. I know you're tired. But we must not desert Sabbitha. She needs us. Make sure we don't lose her."

"But she deserted us," the believers lamented.

"She hasn't deserted us. She's gone into darkness. It's the final test she'll have to face. She's just using that man."

The believers were unsatisfied. Gazarra watched them wander away from the truck, worrying their hair and their crotches. The humanist in him was in full rebellion. He had started remembering that he was a decent man after all, and that he was locked in an indecent business. He felt something for the followers, whom he'd once called instruments — if not love, at least pity.

Grady Rainbow's pick-up was parked a stone's throw away. Grady hovered around the peddler's truck and listened to Gazarra's explanations.

"We live off hope, brother," he laughed richly and shook his head once the believers departed.

"It's a disease," the peddler agreed.

"If your pants were on fire, you'd find some way to justify the smoke."

"Don't mock me," the peddler told the snake-tanner. "I'm exhausted from comforting these people. Do you think they'd ever ask about me? Do you think they'd care? They never have, ever!"

"Whoa, there, you sound like Felix Culpa, with all this caring and sharing and comforting stuff! I'm not making fun of you. On the contrary — I'm in blunt admiration."

The praise-singers came by and unveiled their plan. They would find Felix Culpa wherever he was and tear him to shreds. Not a single recognizable piece would remain.

Gazarra dissuaded them with theology. He could not have tolerated any more blood.

"You are free to do that," he told them. "But if you do, she won't be able to face the final test and come through triumphant. Don't try to stop the process. It's necessary. That man is a necessary instrument. She'll beat him. But on her terms, not yours."

The praise-singers retreated in frustration, then went in search of lesser targets for their violence. They hadn't forgiven themselves for letting Felix Culpa remove the Messiah as they looked on impotently.

What they didn't know was that Culpa was close at hand — a few miles away at most, inside a silver Airstream trailer along the access road by the Interstate, in the improvised campground there. From inside his luxury trailer that had more appointments than many people's houses, Culpa gazed out through the real lace curtains he had ordered from Belgium and watched the progress of Sabbitha's believers through the pretty patterns. Their conduct disgusted him. Love, redemption, healing, all the things he'd learned to hold precious at great cost to his instincts — these people were having a hell of a good time mocking them.

"She loves her misery," he said out loud. "Take away her misery and there wouldn't be anything left. There wasn't a single part of her that wanted to heal."

At one point during his bitter observations, he did something forbidden. He reached into the oak veneer cupboard above the genuine porcelain sink in the galley kitchen. There, behind the insulin, he found a bottle. He poured a tumbler full of whisky, then drank it off. It boiled and fumed in his empty stomach. He repeated the operation a time or two. What was that bottle of whisky doing there in the first place, in the trailer of a man with severe diabetes? Awaiting its hour, no doubt, when it would take revenge against the ex-sinner who'd had to swear off drink. In his moral disarray, Felix Culpa momentarily forgot his condition and the discipline he needed to keep surviving it. One more casualty of the outbreak, he fell to the carpeted floor in a hypoglycemic coma with the realization that love doesn't conquer all.

Groups of deserters began to slip out of Midway and head home, hoping to return to their old lives in their former towns. They put on innocent faces and showed up in the convenience stores and poolrooms and video rental outlets, and acted as though they'd never strayed from the straight-and-narrow. They didn't fool anyone. Their old lives wouldn't take them back. They had that look about them — as tell-tale as the thorn scars on the bramble-dress woman's skin. When they wandered home, besotted and confused, even their dogs growled at them, not to mention what the rest of the town wanted to do, and sometimes did.

The deserters were forced back to the chaos of Midway and the persecutions of the praise-singers, who pursued them the way the Army tracks down AWOL soldiers. Their old lives were off-limits, and now Midway was, too, since they'd committed the sin of doubt and desertion. They ended up building camps in the deepest tangles of the woods and living off what they could steal. Soon they resembled their enemies the praise-singers, who had preceded them into chaos.

The rest of the believers remained in Midway and made their camp in the congregation hall. They turned the spot where the Messiah had been taken from them into a shrine. They tried to heed Gazarra's advice and accompany the Messiah with their prayers and deeds, but they didn't know how to pray for Sabbitha. "Come back, we're nothing," they wailed, as prayer and self-loathing wedded. As for deeds, attacks of impotence made many of them unfeasible, not to mention the incessant scratching. After dark, their worship hall sounded like a monkeyhouse on a full-moon night.

The carnival packed up and left town after the petting zoo llama was slaughtered and roasted. Any mammal can be eaten, the followers discovered. Though he was only half-mammal, the Crab Man wondered whether his turn might come next. Sooner or later, one of the praise-singers, jealous of his love affair with Sabbitha, was bound to crack a vindictive joke about liking steamed crab, and the joke would be taken literally. Literalism was a disease among these people. Of all the carnival employees, the sensation-workers were the happiest to be waving that freaky town good-bye.

Several days after Sabbitha's departure, the woman in the bramble dress hung herself in her shield of thorns. Gazarra and

Rainbow discovered her swinging gently from a sturdy dogwood branch out in front of her house of cardboard. Ever hopeful in the face of beauty, Grady checked her pulse despite the evidence.

"Look at her. She was beautiful."

Gazarra mumbled something. He didn't much feel like looking.

"Excuse me for saying it at a time like this, but this woman, even in that ridiculous get-up, even dead, is the most splendid specimen of female creation any man could ever hope to see. And that includes the ones in the movies!"

"Mr. Rainbow, please," Gazarra said.

Rainbow's voice rose in outrage.

"I want to know why she wasn't happy with a gift like that! Tell me! Some people would die for that kind of grace."

"Well, she did," Gazarra reminded his friend.

Grady cut her down with his fishing knife. They pondered over where to bury her. Neither man knew her original religion. They chose the Methodist churchyard because it was furthest from the center of town, and less likely to be profaned.

"I'll stay with the body so nothing worse should happen to her," Gazarra told Rainbow. "You're younger, you're better with the shovel. Go dig her grave."

The old peddler lowered himself down next to her. My second shiva, he realized. The first on a tipped-over pew, the second flush on the ground. I am moving closer to the earth. That is as it should be.

He had nothing to cover her body with. Vines grew thick around a telephone pole across the street, but he didn't want to leave her alone, not even for that long. He had sold her the rope, weeks before, and the thought tortured him. Of course it wasn't directly his fault, but he should have foreseen how she might use it. And if he had? What would he have told her? "I'm sorry, ma'am, but I can't sell you my last coil of rope because I'm afraid you'll hang yourself with it if this thing doesn't work out." That, in the middle of an outbreak?

Gazarra stripped off his shirt and covered what he could of her. He took her hand. It was cool, rubbery, lifeless. He released it.

"I don't know where people like you go after death," he admitted.

Grady Rainbow had to ration his whisky just when they needed it most. He and Gazarra sat taking tiny sips from Grady's snakeskin-covered flask after laying the woman in the bramble dress to rest. The companionship of survivors was their final consolation.

"Tell me, Mr. Gazarra," Rainbow said, "do you really believe? Do you still believe?"

"Those are two separate questions."

"Take them in any order you want."

"Yes," Gazarra answered.

Rainbow put his palm to his forehead. "You're as impossible as ever!"

"And I still believe, too."

"Okay — in what?" Rainbow pounced.

"In the need to be free."

"That sounds like good old-fashioned patriotism. Or something from one of those folksongs that guitar-players sing. Sufficiently vague as to be true."

"You want specifically? Free from poverty. Free from your neighbor's violence, even if he's never raised his hand against you."

"If you want to get rid of that stuff, all you have to do is build a better society," Rainbow chuckled. "Or change neighborhoods if that doesn't work."

"We all came to this country, some of us more recently than others, to get your better society. We had to give up a lot of things for it. All the old beliefs from the old places we came out of. Before

I was a Sabbithite I was a Jew, remember? My people worked like slaves to stop believing in what they used to, and start believing in this new American society. That was the only way to fit in."

"People can believe anything they want to here," Rainbow pointed out. "That's why we have this country."

Gazarra took the last nourishing pull on the flask. He sighed.

"Okay, let's say you're right. Which you are not, no offence, Mr. Good American. Even if you have the better society, some things will never change."

"For instance?"

"People will still need to be freed from themselves," Gazarra declared.

"I don't know if I can follow you down that road."

"You already have." Gazarra made a wide sweep of his hand, across the field where the carnival had been. "All the pettiness in me that comes from having to accept second best, all the desires that go unfulfilled every day, every week, every year for a lifetime — it's like a cancer! That's what we need to be freed from."

"Show me a person who has everything he wants," Rainbow said weakly, by way of disagreement.

"You're too reasonable, old friend."

"It's only because I never learned to talk like you do. I don't have the words to justify the kinds of things that are going on here. I mean, weren't you there when we buried that woman?"

"They're not just words. Don't forget the ideas, and the longing."

"Longing?" Grady Rainbow laughed. "It sounds like something out of a love song!"

"So it does," the peddler agreed. "It is a love song."

Grady took back the empty flask from Gazarra and looked into it. It was dark as the grave inside. He blew on it to warm the glass and coax out a few last drops.

"In every town there's bound to be a few natural sinners, you know, pleasure-loving types. What my father used to call sporting men. But I've never seen so many in one place. And women, too! The inmates have taken over the asylum. The monkeys are running the zoo. The most beautiful woman I ever saw — outside of Sabbitha, of course — hung herself from a goddamned dogwood tree. That baseball player was right. People can't go on living this way. They don't need to be freed from themselves — they need to be rescued from themselves!"

"It's the same thing."

"It certainly is not."

The whisky was gone and the sun had set. Rainbow and Gazarra were old enough friends to be able to bid each other good night on a note of discord.

Grady retired to his truck, where, to his shame, he kept another bottle stashed that he had decided not to break out with his friend Gazarra. The peddler might be the instigator of a lunatic band that practiced murder and self-murder, Rainbow chided himself. But he'd never hold back a drop from his friend.

Oh, well, the snake-tanner excused himself, settling back with his mild, contemplative sin. Nobody's perfect.

In that mood of whimsical inquiry inspired by whisky, Grady Rainbow considered Mr. Gazarra's apocalypse. The whole business about the world changing had him fretful. Would there be whisky after the Messiah changed everything? Would there be lonesome guitars and football and his tanning work that he enjoyed so much because it got his mind off his troubles? Would he even need to get his mind off his troubles after the Messiah triumphed? Rainbow knew he was being far too down-to-earth, but he couldn't help it. He wanted to know what would happen to all the steel-stringed guitars once the new world dawned. He wasn't going to sign up for it until he had that particular question ironed out.

ᚥ

To fill their days of waiting, Gazarra and Rainbow conversed. Their disputations began at breakfast, around the Coleman stove. Not only is waiting for the Messiah an endless task, talking about her is, too. Which made the topic a good one to have on hand.

"If I understand correctly, you still maintain that we have to make this old world as bad as we can so a new, better one will come," Rainbow inquired of Gazarra as the time dragged on.

Gazarra nodded.

"Don't you think you're trying to force the Almighty's hand a little? Don't you think He might get a little peeved?"

"I'm petitioning. I'm praying, in my own way. People have always done that."

"But what if you don't get the world you wanted? Doesn't that worry you?"

"We have to take that chance," Gazarra said.

Grady Rainbow frowned. The peddler's answers sounded ready-made to him. Maybe he's actually running out of answers, Grady mused. Won't that be a day?

"We have pictures of what we want," the peddler admitted a while later, "but of course we have no assurances. Maybe we'll all feel fondness for the time before. But I doubt it."

Grady Rainbow shook his head in wonderment. "It's amazing how you do it. I mean, how you believe. It's . . . well, it's down-right noble."

"It's in the blood. It's a gift I spent most of my life thinking was a curse."

"Are you feeding me more riddles, or just running out of answers?"

"Absolutely not." Gazarra's voice hardened. "You're down, you're alone, you don't even have the words to say how bad you feel, you're standing in the middle of an empty road that goes nowhere. You can't believe that your life is just this: riding from one stranger's door to the next, pleading for a sale, peeking in on the warmth of other people's lives. Is this what I was born for? If you say yes, you kill yourself. If you say no, you believe."

Rainbow's silence said he understood that much.

"I wonder," he ventured, "what would have happened if you'd never met her back there in Retreat."

"Every fool knows you can't turn back the hands of time."

"And I know that, too," Grady assured Gazarra. "But let's just say, you know . . ."

"She'd have remained in the realm of possibilities," the peddler answered with no hesitation, his voice steely. "Like a viper under a rock. Like a razor blade in an apple. An abscessed tooth in a whore's mouth."

"Whoa, there, Mr. Gazarra! Is that any way to talk about the light of the world? All this waiting is starting to take its toll on you."

"Since when have you started defending her, Grady? You're no believer."

"Nor am I a disbeliever. You know I've been following her ever since her career began, ever since you brought her into the shop. I like it when she's around. Life is — I don't know — fuller somehow."

"You're just in love with her, like everybody else."

The snake-tanner thrust his hands in the air as if Gazarra were training his shotgun on him.

"Just in love? Is that what you said? Lord, I stand accused!"

"You think you can do better than the Crab Man, and that uncle of hers, and all the others?"

Mr. Rainbow's eyes narrowed.

"I like to think I'm a better man than they are. And I like to think that you think so, too."

He lowered his hands. His palms struck his thighs with a sharp report.

"You should relax a little, Mr. Gazarra. You're starting to say things you don't mean. Now, after this excellent cup of coffee, which is actually three-quarters chicory and one-quarter sawdust, and some shredded wheat biscuits in cold water, I'm going downtown to pitch a few horseshoes with the congregation folks. You should come with me. It'll do wonders for your nerves. You can't live on a fever pitch every minute of your life."

"Horseshoes?" Gazarra echoed. "Did you say horseshoes?"

Grady put a cup of brown water in Gazarra's hand.

"Life goes on, friend. People need a little amusement."

Gazarra wandered away from Rainbow's outpost with the coffee cup in his hand. He had nowhere to go. Sabbitha occupied him entirely, but he could do nothing about her but wait. There was nothing left in his truck to sell. No one had any money anyway. The idleness was killing him.

And now there were horseshoes. Horseshoes on the eve of the end of days. Horseshoes on the cusp of a new age. The instruments of the apocalypse were pitching horseshoes to pass the time. How could something so ordinary be happening at such an extraordinary time? He would not have it.

Gazarra crossed the soggy meadow. A fine curtain of humidity rose out of it, drawn upwards by the sun. The wildflowers there had been trampled into mush at the height of the outbreak. But with fewer believers now, and the remaining ones so dispirited, the flowers had grown back. The magnificence of the ordinary; Gazarra didn't appreciate it. He lopped off the top of a weedy daisy with one swing of his curled boot-tip.

Meanwhile, the holy sinners, the blunt instruments, were pitching horseshoes. He dropped his coffee cup with its load of brown water and looked heavenward.

"Lord," he spoke, "spare me from horseshoes!"

For once, when a man spoke to the sky, the sky decided to answer. This hadn't happened in living memory, at least not to anyone reputable.

What's wrong with horseshoes? I made horseshoes. Horseshoes are useful, especially if you have horses.

The voice was wistful and gentle, with more than a touch of blame in its sadness. The opposite of hellfire and thunder. But the explosion it made inside Gazarra's ears threw him to the ground.

When he opened his eyes, he was face to face with the daisy he'd decapitated.

You can get up now. The prophets were famous for falling on the ground and hiding their faces, but don't put on any airs.

Gazarra the peddler raised himself to the sitting position, but could get no further. His knee joints wouldn't cooperate. This time he was careful not to curse them.

I look down and wonder how you people can live this way. And here I'd worked so hard to separate things. Darkness and light. Man and woman. Clean and unclean.

One question, Gazarra said to himself. Just think of one question to ask.

He spotted a strip of lady's undergarment beaten into the dirt of the field among the meek, nameless wildflowers. A souvenir of the transgressors. He put his hand over it and slipped it into his pocket before the Almighty could see.

Then he thought of his question.

"Tell me," Gazarra begged, "will it change? Will the world ever change?"

The answer was slow in coming.

I don't understand this endless praise and commotion that rises up from you below. It's too rich for me. My tastes run towards the elemental things. Besides, your constant squalling for change is beyond my comprehension. If this thing I made is so great, and if I'm every-thing you say I am, so wondrous and fair, then why is everyone always trying to change what I made?

Anyway, it's not mine to change any more. It's yours. Enjoy it.

A sweat-bee landed on Gazarra's leathery arm to sup on the cold sweat of his awe. The cut-off daisy gazed at him reproachfully with its single eye.

A flock of blackbirds flitted from branch to branch in a tall pine he'd never noticed before. The tree wasn't there yesterday, he would have sworn. The birds were jet-black, so black they were purple, their calls were more melodious than he knew blackbirds to be, and they rose and fell in a single harmonious line like some-thing an expert painter's brush might leave.

Gazarra picked himself off the ground. He rubbed the humidity off the seat of his pants. A peacock was moving in its stately, self-important way across the meadow, pecking at grubs. An escapee from someone's menagerie. It fanned its tail threateningly at Gazarra as it went past.

He couldn't tell anyone about this — that was the worst part. Whom could he tell? Nearly everyone toughing it out in Midway was receiving messages from above, and those messages were as garbled and meaningless as the sentence at the end of the tele-phone game.

He imagined the scene.

"The sky has spoken to me," Gazarra would announce to the first person he met.

"So what?" the reply would come. "It speaks to all of us. What's so special about you?"

And if, by some miracle, the person was concerned or curious enough to ask, "What did the sky tell you to do?" Gazarra would not be able to answer.

It wasn't fair.

A simple peddler is spoken to from above. But he can't relate the experience for fear of sounding like one of the multitude of Midway madmen to whom the heavens babbled on a constant basis.

No one would listen anyway. They were all too busy talking.

"But it really *did* happen to me," he protested to no one in particular, there in the middle of the field.

Every believer and every madman has had the same lament.

That was the point the sky was making, in its own oblique way. What had happened to Gazarra was untellable.

That night, the peddler was confined to the back of his truck. The rain was falling in sheets.

Sticky patches on the metal floor grabbed at the soles of his boots. The sensation revolted him, but he couldn't spare any clean water to wash away the blood and clumps of tissue that belonged to the praise-singers' second victim. The man who claimed to be the Messiah's uncle. Who probably was. It took real hard-headedness and a keen sense of self-destruction to make that claim in Midway. Now, there was a real believer!

He scoffed at the word, which had once sounded so noble to him.

When the sky speaks to you, he thought, but you can't tell anyone it has for fear of becoming someone you don't want to be, then it's time to evaluate your circle of acquaintances.

That's how the sky works — nowadays, at least. Not through commandments and showy miracles. It uses oblique lessons to make its point. It has to adapt to the spirit of the age if it wants to be understood.

As he paced and turned and contemplated the mess that his once-orderly store of goods had become, Gazarra tried to remember what the sky had actually told him to do. It hadn't *told* him anything; it had just spoken. He couldn't even remember the exact words. The tone was what had moved him. Resigned and gentle sadness, the peace of mind of One who has done all He can, and is content to do no more.

Gazarra's ears still rang from the intrusion of that voice in his ears. He lay down on his pallet, fully clothed, and took his head in both hands.

In the flattest part of the night, Gazarra woke up to rustling noises around the truck. He reached above the pallet for his shotgun and trained it on the back of the tarp. Somebody or something was being frog-marched across the field.

"Light a light," Gazarra ordered the darkness. "Let me see who you are and where you are, or my shotgun'll open the doors of hell for you."

The peddler had never uttered a threat in his life. He must not have sounded convincing, because there was no answer. He listened to the rain rolling off the edge of the cab. The canvas flap hung motionless.

He put his eye to a rip in the fabric.

"Sabbitha!" he shouted.

Silence answered. He called his Messiah's name again and threw open the canvas flap. The night was opaque and unreadable. He squinted into it and saw ropes of mist that could have been her hair, twisted and gray, as old as he was. The flap fell back in his face and blinded him. He lifted his shotgun and fired it without aiming, blowing a hole in the tarp. He shouted to drown out the deafening crash in his head.

"Gazarra! What the hell . . . ?"

It was Grady Rainbow's voice. The peddler raised what was left of the flap.

"It's nothing," he called across the field. "Nothing."

He spotted Rainbow crouching by the side of his truck, a lantern in one hand, a pistol in the other.

"Just bad nerves, that's all."

"Be careful you don't plug the Messiah like that!" Grady advised him through the drizzle. "Or even me!"

Gazarra tied down the shredded canvas flap and lay back on his pallet again. Immediately, his skin began to crawl. His squirrel-fur blanket was alive. Literally.

XVIII

The Error of the Ages

*J*UST BEFORE DAWN the next morning, Gazarra stepped out of his truck and lashed the tattered tarp shut. That's the last nightmare I'm ever going to have, he swore as he inspected the damage. Then he walked to the cab and got in behind the wheel. He'd missed that sense of control a steering wheel provides. He patted the dashboard to encourage the old machine, then turned the ignition key. Despite the weeks of idleness and the abuse, especially of its sensitive rear suspension, the truck's engine sprung immediately to life.

"A miracle it still runs," he said to himself. Then he regretted his use of the word. He was out of the miracle game now.

A black cloud of exhaust billowed out into the moist air. Once the humidity burned off, the engine idled remarkably smoothly. Those years of meticulous maintenance paid off at a time like this.

He threw the truck into first gear and began to ease it out of the ruts. The rear tires spun in the mud, then found purchase. After he'd covered a dozen feet or so, Gazarra stuck his head out the window into the mist and looked back. The grass described a pallid yellow rectangle.

That grass would grow back, just as the wildflowers had.

From under the aluminum cap of his pick-up truck, Grady Rainbow watched Gazarra drive away. He didn't think to intercede. He'd miss the peddler, his best and only friend, but it was clear that the man had taken the Messiah idea as far as he could, and now he was giving up.

Shalom, he wished him.

That was the only word of Jewish Grady knew. It must have been the right one, because Gazarra himself had taught it to him.

The peddler steered the truck carefully over the broken clumps of sod and around the low spots in the field. He picked up speed once he hit solid pavement. He glanced at his gas gauge. There was plenty of fuel. Amazing that no one had thought to siphon it out of his tank.

"I have made the error of the ages," he said out loud as Midway fell away in his side-view mirror.

His shelves and baskets and trays were empty, there was blood on the metal floor of the truckbed, the canvas was in shreds, but none of that mattered. He was free at last from an idea that had harassed him ever since he was old enough to ask questions. Cracked taillights and a torn tarp were a small price to pay for freedom from the Messiah. Not only from the Messiah — from the waiting, too. Gazarra had achieved the rarest of virtues: self-acceptance. He was simply one in a long line of people for whom the world had not changed. That was just as well. From what he'd seen in Midway, the world was better off staying exactly how it was, right down to the last humble wildflower.

With the whir of road noise rising in his ears, Gazarra had to own up to something scandalous: he was happy. It was the first time in his career in America that he'd known unfettered happiness. He was immensely light and outrageously free. And fortunate, too. The sky didn't speak to just anybody. Who cares if he couldn't spread the news — *he* knew. He had a steering wheel in his hand and a near-full tank of gas riding behind him. The open road, all over again, a source of endless optimism for anyone who knows how to use it. Nathan Gazarra turned out to be a good American after all.

He didn't think to blame Sabbitha Hunter for walking off the job. Sabbitha wasn't to blame — no one person was. The problem was in the waiting itself. It destroyed a man's life.

Gazarra came to the entrance to the Interstate. There were hitchhikers, as he figured there would be, making their exodus, so many it would have taken a schoolbus to accommodate them all. He didn't stop.

At first he was nervous as he merged onto the perfect concrete. He'd never driven the Interstate before. But the high-speed route did have its uses. There was nothing like it for making a fast getaway to somewhere far and anonymous. A place like that must still exist, he prayed.

When he went to spoon chicory into his coffeemaker that morning, after watching Gazarra make his escape, Grady Rainbow discovered he'd hit the shiny bottom of the aluminum can. All out of provisions, he thought. All out of friends, too. I believe this party really is over.

Gazarra was gone for good, he knew that. The peddler was a creature of the road, and the road would provide for him, somehow. Grady had that trust. But Sabbitha was still unaccounted for. She had disappeared, but she couldn't have gone far. That Cuban of hers was just a stepping-stone. Once she'd shaken him off, where would she go, how could she escape? There wasn't any way out of here for someone as notorious as her. She had to be hiding somewhere.

Grady Rainbow went looking for her. But without Gazarra, his guide and insurance policy, Midway frightened him. The obese, the scarred, the lonely, the unloved and unlovable — they'd all expected that belief in the Messiah would raise them out of their misfortune. Now it looked as though they'd fallen back into their troubles twice as hard. Rainbow felt painfully and visibly well maintained compared to them. He stood out like a white man in a black ghetto at nightfall. When he thought no one was looking, he bent down and scooped up a handful of mud from one of the village lawns and applied it to his face and clothes. But even filth didn't mask the fact that he'd never been a committed believer.

He began ranging out into the countryside in his pick-up, planning his route carefully to save gas. He never left the shelter of his truck, and when he was at the wheel, his pistol rode on the seat next to him with the safety off. He crisscrossed the sand and clay roads, peering into the damp, tangled scrub beyond the ditches. There were charred spots where campfires had been built, and middens of tin cans and liquor bottles, but nothing close to a human being, at least not the one he wanted to see. But he swore he wouldn't leave Midway until he'd found Sabbitha.

One evening cool with the beginnings of autumn, Grady Rainbow had the inspiration to go by the Continental Trailways bus terminal. It was a square box of a building next to a gas station by the Interstate, the same Phillips station where Uncle Tommy had left his car, which had long since been stripped for parts. Not only was the bus station closed, it had been boarded up, broken into, squatted in, burned out and boarded up again. That had been the praise-singers' work. Their way of marooning the believers in a world that more and more of them were trying to leave.

Boarded up again, but entered one last time, Grady saw. He had an eye for the critical detail; it was the craftsman in him. One of the plywood sheets had been pulled off its nails, then fitted back to look as though it hadn't been tampered with. Fitted back from the inside, he noted. It could be anybody. He stepped out of his truck. It could be her.

He reached in through the passenger window for his pistol.

He picked his way towards what was left of the terminal. The smell of the soaked, charred timbers gave him a headache. Rusty nails jutted out of split planks, and man-killing chunks of concrete were scattered everywhere. He tried the loose plywood sheet. It came away easily from the wall. He slipped into the building, gun barrel first.

In the evening light that filtered through the ruined roof, Grady saw someone huddled in a dry corner. Dead or alive, he couldn't tell. He lowered his gun and tried his luck.

"Stranded in paradise, Miss Hunter?"

The figure looked up. It was a woman, all right, but the only part of Sabbitha that Grady recognized was the color of her eyes, and even that was faded. All the rest had leached away.

"Should I be afraid?" she asked lifelessly.

"Frankly, yes. But not of me. It's Grady Rainbow, remember?"

He squatted next to her among the burnt beams and broken masonry. She was wearing something that looked like bleached-out drapes around her head. He lifted the fabric away. She'd tried to disguise herself by cutting her hair, and it looked as though she'd used a dull knife to do the job. Her skin was ashen, and her body was staying alive by feeding off itself. Sabbitha Hunter was starving to death, right here in the land of plenty.

"The peddler left," she reported.

"How do you know that?"

"I heard his truck. I could tell by the engine it was him. I'd know that sound anywhere."

"You feeling abandoned?"

Sabbitha shrugged. She looked too weary for anything in the way of emotions.

"He finally got some sense in his head," she answered.

"That's why I didn't try to stop him when he cut and run."

"A sign of a true friend."

"Splitting up was the best thing for both of you. Between the two of you, you were running this country ragged."

"It was doing the same to us. You can't imagine the pressure."

"You were probably pretty hard on each other, too. It must have been one hell of a marriage."

"Marriage?" Sabbitha coughed. "I didn't even know him outside of his . . . obsession. And he didn't know me. Despite all his fancy talk, he wasn't any different from the rest."

"You don't have to get to know someone to have a marriage like that. I'm telling you, you had the whole marital cycle. The honeymoon, the routine, the divorce. The rise and fall. The career."

Sabbitha smiled wanly and motioned to the debris. "The usual banal ending, too."

"I wouldn't say that. Not in your case. There's nothing banal about you."

"Well, that's a consolation."

Grady Rainbow stood up and dusted off his trousers.

"Are you in any shape to move?" he asked her. "We've got to get you out of this place. Some people are feeling pretty resentful about you deserting. You can imagine what that means."

She tried propping herself up, inch by inch, using a broken timber for support. It was too painful for Grady to watch. He slipped his hands under her backside and lifted her up.

"You don't weigh anywhere near enough, Miss Hunter."

He kicked down the sheet of plywood and they stepped out

into the evening. Grady was supremely happy. He'd been waiting to feel her weight in his arms for a long time.

"Over the threshold, like a proper bride and groom! Except we're moving out, not moving in."

"Such poetry, Mr. Rainbow. I didn't know it was in you."

"Oh, I'm a poet, all right. People are always underestimating me because I happen to work with snakes. Don't be one of those people," he told her. "But I'm the poet of everyday things, not of ideas, not like Mr. Gazarra."

The mention of the peddler's name threw a brief silence over the proceedings.

"I wonder where he's gotten to by now." Grady kept his eyes on the jutting rusty nails underfoot as he carried Sabbitha to his truck. "I don't suppose he can go on working this territory."

"None of us can stay. We scorched the earth."

"That's a shame, too, because there wasn't anybody who loved the Salvation Coast harder than he did. He believed in this place in a way us natives never could. None of us would have ever dared think a miracle could come here."

"I think you'll find that the word 'miracle' will be about as welcome as a skunk at a garden party from now on," Sabbitha warned him. "I can't believe you're so naive that you don't see that. We'd be better off losing it from our vocabulary. Or at least keeping it to ourselves."

"I can do that. The real miracles are always the private ones anyway. Like this one."

Sabbitha didn't answer, and Grady went back to concentrating on making it through the wreckage safely with her in his arms. She opened the truck door with her free hand and he set her gently on the seat. She smoothed the tatters of her dress, then raised her hand to brush her hair from her face. But her hair was gone.

"Say, where's that pretty band I fixed for you?"

"I mislaid it," she said. "In the river."

"In the river?"

"I threw it in some creek."

"Why, Miss Hunter, that was my finest piece of work!" Grady's eyes narrowed. "What creek was it?"

"Hairband Creek."

"I'm not acquainted with that one, and I know most all the rivers and streams around here."

"I don't know what it's called. I don't know the names of anything around here. It was the first damned creek I saw the night I walked out on the congregation."

"You should keep track of things like that, you know. You shouldn't throw away a snakeskin hairband just anywhere. Someone is bound to find it and put it on. There might still be a miracle or two left in it."

"No. I used them all up."

"You never know."

"I do." Sabbitha was categorical.

"If you say so. Now, let's get some food into you — if you can call what I have left food."

Grady went around to the back of the truck, to where the remains of his provisions were stored. Some breakfast cereal. Snacking cakes. Half a summer sausage. A few drops of whisky. All of it thirst-inducing. He'd always heard that shipwrecked people die of thirst before they die of hunger.

He brought everything up to the cab in an open cardboard box. Sabbitha didn't seem worried about thirst. She fell upon the food.

With a petrified Hostess Twinkie in one hand and a bitten-off salami in the other, she looked around at her latest shelter.

"I've seen entirely too much of the insides of pick-up trucks lately," she declared with her mouth full.

"Maybe you have. But do you know any other way of getting

out of town? There are no buses, no taxis, no trains and no planes. As a runaway Messiah, your position is a little delicate."

"It is?"

"You know very well it is," Grady said impatiently. "You know your followers. If they see you, they'll kill you. They'll shoot you for desertion. That's what I call delicate."

"They wouldn't do that! They can't shoot me, I'm the general."

"Not any more, you're not. Generals don't go AWOL."

He drove carefully down the main street. The stores looked as though they'd suffered through a race riot. Rainbow steered around a barricade of burning picnic tables as a man loomed out from behind it to shake a fist at them. A rock clanged off the front fender and Rainbow cursed.

"Why are they doing that?" Sabbitha asked.

Grady glanced at her in disbelief.

"Don't tell me you've forgotten already! This world has to end so the new one can begin. Just because you deserted doesn't mean they have to stop believing in all that. A lot of people lose and go on believing."

He glanced in the side-view mirror, on the lookout for assailants from behind. A smoky, reddish-orange smudge hung in the sky. It was the Midway congregation hall, going up in flames. The site of so much crime and redemption. The followers were burning down their temple before anyone else could.

They picked up speed at the edge of town. Grady Rainbow swung the wheel southward and checked the gauge. He calculated they had enough gas to get them back to Doctortown. And if they began to run low, he had the tools and the will to steal what they needed to finish the journey.

They drove through a landscape black and impenetrable with pine and tangled in the arms of scrub. A quarter-moon hung over it, and the first chill of autumn was in the air. A terrible place for any living man to be out wandering in, Rainbow thought. At one point his headlights picked out a truck parked askew by the side of the road, one tire in the ditch. He slowed and rolled by it in neutral. It wasn't Gazarra's make or model. Rainbow put it into gear and accelerated.

Sabbitha broke off watching the black wall of trees.

"It doesn't look like it's changed," she said.

"What?"

"The world, Mr. Rainbow. It was supposed to have changed."

"Those are just trees — what do you want from them? Believe me, the world has changed. It has for you and it has for me, and it certainly has for the followers, wherever they may be. No one's been untouched, no matter how small their role."

"We're just individuals. The world, the whole thing, was supposed to change."

"I'm sorry, Miss Hunter, but I see things on a smaller scale. That's the way I am. The world's in the details. And on that scale, it did change. You may judge that it wasn't a change for the better — that's up to you. But you weren't failures, you and Gazarra, no matter what you think."

"What optimism! All I feel is a sense of relief."

"Like the end of a bad love affair."

"I've heard love being used as a metaphor a lot lately," Sabbitha said. "I don't like it any more."

"Sorry. I wouldn't presume to speak for you, but that's the best way to understand what happened to poor Gazarra. Look at it this way: you love a woman and you tell the whole damned world about it. Then she dumps you. You can't walk down the street and pretend it never happened. You've got no choice — you've got to hit the road. That's why Gazarra quit on us. He was in love with an

idea. But the idea dumped him. Loving an idea," Grady speculated, "must be harder than loving a woman."

"Is it that hard to love a woman?"

"Oh, no, it's too damned easy! Besides, a woman'll give you a
break sometimes. An idea won't."

Grady laughed, and she naturally followed suit. His laughter
was balm on Sabbitha's frayed soul. Their silence in the dark cab was
companionable — even intimate, Rainbow hoped. She was a half-
dead refugee in rags, but she was still a woman, and she needed
flirting with. Flirting would bring her back to life as surely as his
Hostess Twinkies and summer sausage would. The tires hummed
evenly on the road, cool, clean air washed in through the vents, there
were fistfuls of late fireflies in the damp hollows of the woods. He
and Sabbitha were driving out of madness on the wheels of their
laughter and a faithful, battered pick-up truck. It seemed to be the
perfect American happy ending.

"I suppose you'll be going back to your home town," Grady
said wistfully. "Where did you say it was again?"

"I never said. My home town is on the list of scorched places
now. It always was, as a matter of fact. Otherwise I wouldn't have
left it."

"Home towns are like that for most people. Personally, I never
had that problem. I stepped right into my father's shoes."

"And they fit?"

"I guess so. I never noticed any blisters."

"Then you're lucky," Sabbitha told him. "One of the fortunate
few."

The miles spun by on the empty Coastal Highway. There wasn't
another car, truck or bus on the road. It was as if they were in a
quarantined zone. But once they reached the border of the ragged
realm established by Sabbitha's followers, the reception would be
anything but warm. There'd be the usual avenging spiritual and

civil authorities who step in after the outbreak has cooled. Grady Rainbow could always cite his family's long and glorious history in Doctortown, and challenge anyone to prove that he'd actually been a rule-breaker and not just the observer he was. But there was no hiding Sabbitha Hunter.

"You know what I couldn't get used to back there in Midway?" Rainbow confessed after a while. "It was worse than the killings: the way all those strangers would get together and . . . mate. Fornicate, like they say in church. I mean, here's a couple of folks who've never seen each other before, never met, and they proceed to get naked and do the holy of holies together without even knowing each other's names. I mean, that's something. How could they do that?"

"It *was* an accomplishment," Sabbitha agreed.

"I don't think my body would obey me if I asked it to do that."

"It was for a cause you didn't share."

"I guess you're right." He hesitated. "So did that make it easier to . . . you know, lie down with the Crab Man, for instance?"

"It was a romance. A love affair of the headiest kind. You said so yourself."

Grady Rainbow looked unconvinced. She was avoiding the question, but he couldn't blame her. Anyone would avoid a question like that one, and most people wouldn't have even asked it.

"Is that jealousy I hear gnawing away at your faithful heart?" she inquired.

"It does pain me."

"It fascinates you, too."

"I suppose it does. But not for the reasons you think. I don't have a thing about pornography; I don't want to stand on the outside of more attractive people's lives and look in. No, I always wanted to know what it was like for you. And why you were doing it."

Sabbitha smiled. "You are one patient, liberal-minded suitor. Most men would have given up in horror a long time ago."

"I have faith. I'm a believer after all." He put his hand over his heart. "Don't ask me why. An overblown idea of myself, maybe. I always considered myself different from the crowd who loved you."

"You are, Grady. You're here, for starters. And right now, that's a lot."

Up ahead, a single yellow caution light flashed at a crossroads. Under the light, a hobo with hair like weeds appeared momentarily. A believer on the run, or an old-fashioned tramp? Rainbow didn't stop. He had one refugee on board, and one was enough.

On the bench seat next to him, Sabbitha began to scratch at herself with studious application. The parasites were completing another life cycle. Their egg cases were opening under the Messiah's skin, and the young were eating their way to the surface where they would copulate with one another, without concern for romance, or joined bloodlines, or even their partners' first names.

They reached Alma a few hours later. Grady Rainbow drove through the town to reconnoiter, even though it was pitch-black night. He knew his people, and he wasn't surprised at what he and Sabbitha discovered. The little congregation hall where Sabbitha Hunter had performed her first miracle was a blackened hollow in the ground, the chimney bricks scattered around the once-green lawn. The embers heaved and glowed through the thin ground fog.

"Burned it and shot the fire." Rainbow wasn't laughing this time. "I wonder if the non-believers torched it."

"Or the believers," Sabbitha speculated, "trying to make off like they never were who they were."

"On the Coast," Grady told Sabbitha, pulling away from the

scene, "once someone's been something in public, they can change their minds all they want, they'll always be that thing as far as everyone else is concerned. The stain doesn't go away. People can make off all they want, but they'll always be who they were."

"I like that," Sabbitha said. "It's like a tattoo — permanent. For once you have to stand by what you did, instead of pretending you never were at that party."

"I'm glad you appreciate that, but it'll make your life harder. Now let's go see what else they did."

Grady got back on the Coastal Highway. He pushed the truck as hard as it would go until they came in sight of his property on the edge of Doctortown. At least the buildings were still intact. He could tell that much by their familiar dark shapes against the night.

As soon as his tires hit the gravel parking lot in front of the WE BUY SNAKES! sign, a shotgun blast burrowed into the passenger side of the truck, just behind the cab.

Rainbow bailed out of the pick-up as it rolled to a stop, and Sabbitha crouched on the floor. He threw his hands in the air and began shouting his name. Next thing they knew, someone was running across the parking lot in their direction, a rifle in his hands.

"Sorry there, Mr. Rainbow, sir! I thought you was one of them, coming back for second helpings."

Sabbitha peered out the window. She recognized the apprentice who had changed colors when she touched his cheek. He looked at her, then looked away. He was still afraid of being bewitched.

"I didn't know who they were," he told Mr. Rainbow, "whether they was believers or regular folks or something in between. A couple carloads of them showed up this very night, and I could tell they had harmful intent. Me and the tanning-shed help, we opened up on them from a few places, and they packed up and left. I think we got us one, too, judging from the screams."

"I appreciate it, son."

"Man's got to defend his livelihood. Only thing is, I wish I knew which side they were on."

"By now," Sabbitha told him, "it doesn't matter any more."

The apprentice eyed her and said nothing. It was another one of her riddles, and he didn't like riddles.

As he sat over the whisky that slowly calmed his nerves, with Sabbitha keeping him company shot for shot in the oily air redolent of snake, Grady Rainbow told her, "At first light tomorrow, I'm going to take a ride downtown and correct a few popular misconceptions. Then I've got to figure out what I'm going to do about you. Sad to say, but it probably isn't safe for you to linger here."

"I'll lie low," she promised him.

"That probably won't be sufficient. I'm afraid we're going to have to get you far, far away from here."

"Hard words to say, Grady."

"Yes. I suppose the party's really over. At last."

This may well be Sabbitha Hunter's last night in my life, he realized. Maybe I ought to try something. You know, *something.* He gave her a long, sad-eyed, moony look and caught her scratching at her belt-line, then further down. He decided to give it a pass. To his great regret.

Regret if I don't, he calculated, and remorse if I do. What a damned shitty deal this life is!

It was unfair. That life is unfair occurs to every person who's been drinking. Here he was, missing his rendezvous between the sheets with the Messiah. Probably the only damned Messiah he'd ever meet, too. And all because he was too careful, and not flexible-minded enough, to accept catching whatever little inconvenient bugs she might be carrying. If only he'd had the chance, he would have shown her how a woman of her caliber ought to be treated. He wouldn't have carted her around from town to town like a freak in a sideshow.

Rainbow emptied another ounce of whisky down his throat, and served Sabbitha one at the same time. He marveled that a woman could sit up through the raw hours of the night and drink with him like a man, adding the thrill of her womanliness, scratching or no scratching. Now here was a change in the world he personally approved of: when women would be more like men.

He listened to that formulation clanging around in his brain with the alcohol and thought, No, that's not it. I know what I mean, but I can't quite get it right. Whisky and bad nerves have seen to that.

"Did I hear you say the party's over, Grady?" Sabbitha asked him; some of the Messiah's old imperiousness had crept back into her voice. "You're wrong there. It's not."

"Oh, I suppose there's a few stragglers left back in Midway, beating their heads against a wall. If you want to call that a party. I wouldn't."

"That particular outbreak may be over, I'll grant you that. But the Messiah — the Messiah lives on."

"Yeah? And where does she live? In the realm of possibilities, like the old peddler once told me? And where does that leave you? I don't think I want you having to go through that stuff all over again."

"I know that, Grady," Sabbitha smiled. "But she does live on. The need lives on. If you don't have her — or him, I'm willing to entertain that notion — then who's going to look after the world? Who's going to supply the yearning and the heat? The poetry, if you'd rather call it that way. You can take the Messiah out of your life, and a lot of people have. But it'll be a poorer place to live, I can guarantee that much."

He looked away from her and stared at his glass, and its empty, baleful eye. That was the damnable thing about loving a woman like Sabbitha Hunter: you could lose her at any time.

"I know you don't like it, Grady, but you can't do anything about it. The Messiah is part of the human race. As long as you have one, you have the other. People can curse what happened in Midway till their dying breath, and who knows, maybe they'd be right to. But you can't turn your back on the Messiah — she brings us every longing that makes us who we are, human and inhuman alike. Personally, I wouldn't want to have to swim against that tide."

"So what does that mean? Do we have to wait some more? I don't think I have the patience for it."

"No," Sabbitha laughed, "no more waiting. At least our little adventure taught us that much. I just have to have some place to hide for a while, Grady. But I don't want to be exiled to some desert island, that's not my style. No, somewhere in plain sight will do just fine."

Her voice went dreamy, and Grady knew that some mischief was about to befall the world and him with it. Some great celestial hijinks were glittering in her eye, the kind that a woman who can be anything she wants to will spring on you. She reached into the inside pocket of her tattered jacket and handed him a stiff sheet of paper. Very official and formal looking, but somewhat the worse for wear, his tired, bloodshot eyes told him. He read it once. He had to read it again. It was the deed to a house. Her big white house, back in Ebenezer.

He shook his head. "So that's where you're from. I didn't know that place could produce a woman like you."

"Take this and do something with it," she told him. "You'll think of a way. You're a man of the world, you know how things work."

Then the Messiah did something that she'd done many nights in Grady Rainbow's best dreams. She opened her arms to him. She smelled of bourbon and fat, garlicky summer sausage. She smelled of masonry dust and sodden, charred timbers. She smelled like someone who hasn't been around running water for a time.

Why not here?

Why not now?

Why not us?

"The Lord have mercy on us if you ever come back!" Rainbow blasphemed joyously.

He held her so tight her ribs ached. She needed it.